THE LONG REACH OF NIGHT

THE LONG REACH OF NIGHT

ADRIAN COLE

WILDSIDE PRESS

THE LONG REACH OF NIGHT

Published by Wildside Press LLC.
www.wildsidebooks.com

"The Exile of Earthendale" first appeared in *Hexa* magazine (Belgium) NO 6, 1980 and was first published in English in *Fantasy Tales*, Volume 8, no 15 (Winter) 1985.

"Thief of Thieves" is a revised version of the story published in *Weirdbook* magazine no 14 (U.S.A.) 1979.

The remaining stories are all published here for the first time, although some of them were originally placed with magazines and the small press in the late 1970s and early 1980s, but sadly, these markets folded before the stories came into print.

Amongst these lamented magazines were Charles Melvin's *Escape*, Bruce Hallenbeck's *Night Gaunt* and *Dragonbane* from Triskell Press, to name but three.

"The Burning Ice, the Freezing Fire" began life as "Daughter of Demons," then became "Daughter of Hate," before its final revision for this volume under its new title.

DEDICATION

I would just like to say a special thanks to those who have encouraged me to keep going with the saga of the Voidal and his dubious companions at a time when the Dark Gods were definitely gaining the upper hand.

Mike Chinn,
whose letter out of the blue, asking for any unpublished Voidal material, led to the entire saga getting into print after 25 years! Cheers Mike, here's to Old Miseryguts.

Pete Colebourne,
For saying the right thing at the right time

Sean Williams and **Phil Harbottle,**
for their generosity in
pointing me to **John Betancourt** at Wildside.

Darrell Schweitzer
for encouragement along the tortuous, dark road

And to **John** himself, for bringing the saga into the light.

CONTENTS

EXORDIUM

Having come thus far in the rendering into prose of the dark genesis of the enigmatic entity known variously as the Voidal, the Fatecaster, the dark man and the wanderer in the void, not to mention sundry other things probably best not recorded, I feel an ironic compulsion, a craving almost, to progress the saga. I say ironic for, in starting this history, I have tempted the worst of all possible fates, the full fury of the gods who have incarcerated me here. In the past, my indulgence in freedom of expression led, ultimately, to my present dilemma, this walling up.

In my lonely isolation, every whisper, each breath of air beyond these walls would be like a shout to me and I have listened, oh, how I have listened, for a sign that I am observed, scrutinised, weighed. Yet, curiously, there has been no such sign.

One might suppose that I, in my solitude and ennui, would long for such an intrusion, but I have very mixed feelings on the matter. An artist is nothing without an audience, but if a succulent young calf recited the most moving poetry imaginable to an audience of ravenous wolves, I doubt that their attention would be focussed on the quality of its couplets or the flow of its metre. Such torment!

Even so, the silence that has followed my first grim volume has been even more intense than that which preceded it, prompting me to continue. The Gods undertake nothing without purpose, as this black history testifies, and it occurs to me that their silence may well be the unspoken approval of my indulgence in this narration. I cannot believe they are unaware of my labours, but of course, I have to confess this may simply be my own arrogance, the remnants of self-importance. It may be, horrible thought, that I am no longer of consequence to them. Could they have forgotten that I exist?

Ah, but, I am torturing myself needlessly! I must remain on my guard, for only one who has taken complete leave of his senses would trust the powers beyond these walls. However, having come this far in the telling, I am compelled to move on. I owe it to the countless scribes and gossipers, poets and balladeers who have contributed to the convoluted tapestry.

Read then, again, of he who was cursed with the burden of the Oblivion Hand, and of crimes, punishments and of penalties. For of one thing we can all be certain, for every act there is always a price. Always.

> **—SALECCO,** The Persistent, The Optimistic, sometimes called the Dreamer and whose daydreams are dark, whose dreams are darker, and whose nightmares are better not shared at all.

PART ONE

THE PREPOSTEROUS LIBRARY

I have spoken of my own predilection for the written word, for marvelous histories, no matter how dangerous. But I am nothing to the fabled Effelgung and his worlds-spanning Library. It would be easy to believe that every thought of every mind is recorded there. But of course, such things are not always readily available to those allowed to browse. They are very much in his keeping.

And like the gods, he does not bestow his favours lightly, nor without certain requirements. Elfloq, like a bee about the honeycomb, discovered this simple truth. Oh, yes indeed.

——**Salecco**, the admirer of Great Libraries, of which he is most wary.

* * * *

Elfloq the familiar, glided silently through the shimmer of astral mist, glancing behind him from time to time, even more alert than usual for one who lived on the edge of his nerves. The astral realm, that endless expanse that flowed like silk between the many dimensions of the omniverse and normally as safe a place as any for a small being such as he was, shivered with whispers, hints that dangers were abroad. These were strange times, Elfloq mused.

He was, he felt sure, being followed.

This was not in itself unusual. Indeed, wherever he went among the many dimensions, he never felt safe from prying eyes or cocked ears, not to mention talons. But was even this haven breached? It seemed so.

He swooped down on membranous wings to a shadow that jutted from the mist. Confirming that the outcrop was of rock and not the head of some sleeping monster or calcified demon, he alighted, taking cover in a fold of the crag that afforded him a view of the astral murk about him. Moments later his keen ears picked up the sound of wing beats: soft and hardly stirring the air, but no doubting it.

A creature, no bigger than his own diminutive size, circled his precarious hiding place. As the mists shifted, fickle as clouds, Elfloq grunted in recognition. And to some extent, relief. This was no fire imp, demon or other tormentor. It was, like himself, a familiar. Moreover, one that he knew.

He ducked down out of sight and let the creature curve in flight about the rock and alight on its pinnacle. It scratched itself, feigning nonchalance, its puckered face squinting out into the mists as if its real goal was out there.

"Ho, Owlworm!" called Elfloq from the shadows.

The familiar hopped up as if pricked, favouring the rock with a scowl that did nothing to improve its ugliness. Then, gargoyle-like, it sat again on the rock. "I know you," it said.

Elfloq poked his head up and grimaced. "You should do. You've been following me for long enough."

"Nonsense. You flatter yourself, Elfloq. I have urgent business. Why should I be following you? I have a master to serve."

Elfloq masked his emotions. A master? Fortunate indeed. A familiar without a master would not survive long. None knew it better than he, whose own master, the shadow-hung Voidal, was elusive as a rumour. He had not found him for a long time, not even so much as a clue to his whereabouts. If he didn't find him soon – well, he did not want to dwell on the consequences.

"You survived the debacle on Moonwater, then?" Elfloq said, referring to the demise of both their former masters along with several other misguided sorcerers in the all too recent incident. Both had fled like scalded cats, seeking comfort in the vicissitudes of the many dimensions. It was an occupational hazard for familiars.

"I did, though precious few of us were so fortunate. None of our former masters lived. They overreached themselves, toying with sorcerous powers that they could not control. Always the same. Too much power. Not one sorcerer survived Moonwater. I might have known you'd find your feet, though."

Elfloq's frog-like features widened in a grin. "Even so, Owlworm."

"Your former master, Quarramagus, is no more. Extinguished like the other power mongers. But I presume you must have found another one to serve."

Elfloq feigned diffidence. "Oh yes. I am on a mission for him even as we speak. Quarramagus, was a mage of great power, but it was nothing compared to the power of the one I serve now."

"Indeed? And who is this extraordinary demi-god?" snorted Owlworm.

"I'd rather not say. Even his name sends out ripples of unease."

Owlworm's face wrinkled into a smile. "Really? Then I won't pry."

"And who have you taken up with?"

"Me? Oh, I haven't done too badly. Could have been worse."

Elfloq knew that Owlworm was bursting to boast about his new master. Just as he was dying to know whom Elfloq served. Nothing burned as brightly as a familiar's curiosity. Owlworm's would be no less a force than Elfloq's own.

"You had talents, as I recall," said Elfloq. "I would not have expected you to serve anyone less than a sorcerer of the highest order. Don't be modest, Owlworm. Confess it, you have won to the service of someone who moves in the highest of circles."

A smug grin enlarged Owlworm's face. "Oh, yes. Yes indeed."

Elfloq choked back his disgust. "Surely you can tell an old companion."

"Well, since you must force it from me. I serve the exalted Effelgung."

This did take Elfloq by surprise. Who had not heard of Effelgung, the great and worthy Librarian, caretaker of what was universally agreed to be the largest and most complex library in the omniverse?

"Effelgung," repeated Elfloq. "The keeper of books and records? The clerk of the files and histories?"

Owlworm glared indignantly. "Effelgung is the Keeper of Absolutes, Lord of the Sacred Texts, Supreme Protector of Knowledge. He is not a *clerk*."

"Pardon me," said Elfloq with a bow. "I did not mean to insult the divine status of the Librarian, the Warden of, of – "

"Forbidden Documents. No, I should think not."

In truth, Elfloq was mentally rubbing his clawed hands together in excitement. Effelgung and his legendary library were notoriously impregnable. Only beings of great power and influence got anywhere near them. Elfloq knew that a visit to Effelgung's hoard of written treasures would have afforded him unsurpassable knowledge. But he had never dreamt of breaching the hallowed halls of such a place. Until now.

"And you are *his* familiar?" he said to Owlworm, filling his voice with respect and admiration.

Owlworm preened himself, chest swelling. "Yes, I have that honour."

"It's no less than you deserve."

"And you, Elfloq. Will you not tell me now who it is you serve?"

Elfloq bent his head in mock humility. "Owlworm, you embarrass me. You, who serve the mighty Effelgung, ask me whom I serve. Why, he is nothing! A mere fry in an ocean of leviathans! Don't humiliate me by asking. I am too impressed. Let me enjoy more news of your triumph."

Owlworm was easily flattered and clearly more interested in his own success than hearing Elfloq's no doubt exaggerated account of his own doings. "I'm returning to him now."

"Then I won't pry," said Elfloq. But how do I win his confidence? He knows me too well. He would trust me less readily than he would a serpent.

"Perhaps," said Owlworm, scratching behind his tufted ear and appearing mentally to chew over some weighty problem, "perhaps you could visit the Exalted Halls of Reference. Just for a short time, mind. Effelgung is a jealous lord."

That's it! Thought Elfloq. *He can't resist showing off! Now that he's won himself a position of real merit, he can't keep it to himself.* "My dear Owlworm, your generosity knows no bounds."

"True, true. But I know you, Elfloq. Unless I show you my fortune, you won't really believe me."

"Nonsense! Of course – "

"No, no. I'll prove my success. You shall visit the Exalted Halls. Just for a very short time. Secretly and with your assurance that you will keep it to yourself."

"But of course. Discretion is my watchword, Owlworm, you know that," Elfloq smiled.

The two familiars spread their wings and lifted, light as gossamer, up into the astral. Owlworm led the way, and behind him Elfloq could scarcely control his excitement. Effelgung's library! There, surely, he would uncover invaluable knowledge about his master.

* * * *

Owlworm's squamous body teetered on the edge of the huge beam as he peered through the festoons of cobwebs at the place beneath. It was a hall of monstrous proportions, one of the many that housed Effelgung's magnificent Library. High up above the floor of the vast hall, the two familiars hopped along the beams under Owlworm's fretful guidance.

"Effelgung will be working somewhere in the heart of this wondrous edifice," he told Elfloq. "The gods themselves send him directives. He is always burdened with work. We won't be noticed."

In which case, mused Elfloq, we should be able to avoid undesirable consequences.

"Best if we stay up in the rafters," said Owlworm. "Random wandering down below would lead to certain disaster. What do you know of this place?"

"Only what the legends say," replied Elfloq with a shrug. "Most of it nonsense, I imagine. To keep the inquisitive away."

"Oh, no!" sniffed Owlworm. "No, no. The Library is fraught with danger. When we were on Moonwater together, serving the mages there, we were less likely to get caught up in their meshes of sorcery than we would be here."

"But this place is a monument to the written word. Why, every wall is built not with bricks, but with books, grimoires, tomes – "

"That is so, of course," nodded Owlworm, and indeed, in the hall below, the colossal collection of books could clearly be seen, rising from the shadows at floor level to the soaring heights of the rafters. In this gigantic hall alone there must be books enough to fill the libraries of a world. And scrolls, pamphlets, letters, papers. Elfloq felt he would go dizzy just looking at them.

"How many such halls are there?" he said.

"Dozens," grunted his batrachian companion. "But there are other halls, other rooms, their purposes varied and complex. Effelgung's Library is not merely a repository of manuscripts."

"Is it not?"

"No. There are doors here, doors that lead to the strangest of rooms. Gateways to elsewhere. There are certain grimoires here, Elfloq, that no one dare open. For they themselves open a way to realms that you and I have scarcely dreamed of. This Library is one of the omniverse's great crossroads."

"Well, well," murmured Elfloq, trying not to sound too interested.

They crossed the maze of thick, black beams, each as wide around as a room, and came through a narrow opening to another, smaller hall. One wall was lined with shelves upon which could be seen row upon row of dusty jars.

"Biographies," said Owlworm. "Of demons, goblins, imps. Preserved in ash and bone. Open a jar at your peril. The shades of the deceased appear, shaped from the mouldering contents, and speak their tales. Only a sorcerer dare lift these lids, for those within forever seek a way back to life."

"Then let them rest," mumbled Elfloq as they passed across a beam to an exit.

"Ah," said Owlworm. "A Chamber of Enlightenment." He pointed down to the several immense tables below. On each of them was a book the size of a catafalque and a candle as thick around as Elfloq's waist.

"May we look more closely?" he said.

Owlworm was about to demur, but Elfloq ignored him and dropped down as deftly as a spider on a thread of web, landing beside one of the great works. He lifted the cover, disturbing a small storm of motes, but Owlworm was beside him, gibbering nervously.

"Don't open it! You don't know where it will lead you!"

Elfloq regarded his companion with a mischievous grin. "Lead me?"

"It's a gate, you idiot! Open the book at the wrong page and you'll find yourself wandering into it and the gods alone know where it'll be. Either that or something will emerge from the page, something too terrible to name."

Elfloq patted the closed cover and more dust swirled. "Well, well. I am impressed, Owlworm. This really is an extraordinary place. And what's through that door?" He pointed to a thick, wooden door banded with black hoops that looked as though it would have withstood an army.

"Through there? That will be one of my master's Curse Chambers. Not a room to visit for your health. Some of its secrets would blast a god, believe me."

"A bagful of its contents would be invaluable," said Elfloq. "Are you sure we can't just peep?" He put a claw on the door and felt it vibrating like flesh.

"No! Come away." Owlworm made to fly upwards again, but there was a movement in another doorway.

"Is that you, Owlworm?" said a deep voice, and the air trembled.

Owlworm screwed up his features and tried to make himself as small and inconspicuous as possible. "Master, I – "

The figure that emerged from the doorway was huge, a vast, rounded shape, wrapped in a thick white gown, the hem of which was embroidered exquisitely in golden letters. Under each arm, the figure carried a book that would have taken two lesser men to handle. Effelgung, for it was no lesser a being than the exalted Librarian himself, turned his immense head and observed Elfloq, whose claw still rested on the forbidden door of the Curse Chamber.

"Oh, I wouldn't tamper with *that* door," he said solemnly, his voice like a bell, tolling the doom of a world.

Elfloq withdrew his arm as if it had been scorched. "Profuse apologies, most omnipotent Warden – "

"You must be Elfloq," said Effelgung. His eyes were twin suns, their gleam alive with what seemed amusement, possibly irritation at the intrusion. The rest of his face was an explosion of white beard, an avalanche that reached to his hugely curving waist.

"You *know* me, sire – "

"Of course. I sent Owlworm to fetch you."

Elfloq gaped, but Owlworm had already taken to the air. "I take it you'll have no further need of me for the time being, master?" he said with feigned nonchalance.

Effelgung made a dismissive movement with his arm, as though the tome he carried was no more than a pamphlet.

"Fetch me?" Elfloq was murmuring.

"Yes, little familiar. Come this way." The huge Librarian swung round and left the chamber, and Elfloq found himself trotting along in his wake, like a gull following a ship in full sail. So he *had* been pursued by the wily Owlworm. Duped and brought here for a reason. How naïve of him to think otherwise! Even so, to be here, in this treasure house of secrets! There must be a way to capitalise on this.

Effelgung led them through a number of small rooms, each stuffed with books, to a round chamber that seemed to have nothing but tapestries on its walls. These were extraordinary, rich in colour and detail, the work of undoubted master artists. Elfloq could not help but marvel at them. One in particular took his eye, depicting as it did the disastrous fall of the sorcerers on Moonwater. He was trying to discover if he, himself, was somewhere among its elaborate workings, when Effelgung called for his attention.

"Sit!" said the Librarian, indicating a tall chair that appeared to have been carved from a singularly large emerald.

Elfloq perched on its edge, waiting.

"You want to know why I sent for you," Effelgung went on, setting down the two huge books on the table before him. He sat behind it in an even larger emerald chair, his robes billowing out around him like clouds.

"I am honoured, highmost Keeper – "

"Good, good. Now then, whom do you serve?"

"I would only be too glad to make myself available to your own worthy self – "

"Never mind the flattery, Elfloq. That's not what I asked. Your master, correct me if I'm wrong, is the Voidal, is he not? The so-called 'wanderer in the void' who has so upset the Dark Gods."

"Well, since you put it that way, sire – "

"I do. A tenuous alliance, I'll warrant. A man who has been cursed with immortality, doomed to wander for an eternity, missing his identity, his soul. Not the most auspicious of partners, I should have thought. Yet you cling to him."

"He has power, my lord."

"Hardly his own to utilise. He's a pawn!"

"It is his sad burden," Elfloq nodded.

"And you, I gather, serve him whenever you can. Hungry for a share of such awesome power, eh? I know, I know. My ears, Elfloq, are very long. As you can see, I acquire all manner of knowledge. My network is omniversal. Well, such devout servants as yourself are invaluable. I find myself in need of such loyalty myself."

"Owlworm has done well."

"Him? He's helpful, but limited. No, I need someone with true guile, with the skills of a master thief, the inquisitive mind of a Divine Asker, the determination of a demon. In short, little familiar, I need you."

Elfloq almost toppled from the chair. "Me, almighty one? A simple familiar, little better than Owlworm – "

"Nonsense. You have the cunning of a god. And the scruples of an alley cat. And obviously you are extraordinarily courageous. You must be to consort with so cursed a being as the Voidal."

Elfloq would have quavered, but he realised that Effelgung was actually praising him. "Well, that's kind of you, sire."

"I need you to perform a simple task for me, Elfloq." The Librarian leaned forward over the table, and for a moment Elfloq thought he was about to be engulfed. "I will, of course, pay you handsomely. What do you say to that?"

"I am sure, master, that the payment will fit the deed."

Effelgung smiled, his profuse beard quivering. "What do you desire most?"

Elfloq suspected that the Librarian knew this already, but he did not say so. "To be reunited with my master, of course. No self-respecting familiar could want less."

"Quite so. But it's not easy for you to find him, is it? Given that the Dark Gods persistently fling him out into the shadows beyond all knowing. I, on the other hand, am privy to all sorts of knowledge. Windows, gateways, spy-holes."

"You know where I can find him?"

"I could send you to him, when he next emerges from the darkness."

Elfloq would have felt a surge of joy at this, but he was too well versed in the ways of the omniverse. There was always a price, always a favour to return.

"I don't ask much," said Effelgung, leaning back.

"What do you wish, sire?"

"A book."

"A book," Elfloq repeated.

"Just a book. One that was stolen from me."

"It is valuable?"

"*All* my books are valuable."

"You want me to steal it back."

"I do, Elfloq. A task suited to your skills."

"I hope, lord, it is not similar in size to those two volumes before you."

"No, indeed. It is a very small volume."

"And its name?"

Effelgung drew in a vast breath. "I cannot reveal it! Too dangerous. If others knew that the book was abroad, no longer in its correct place on my shelves, what chaos might ensue!"

"Uh, so how I am to know this book? By its cover?"

"No! Too grave a secret."

"By its smell, then? Or does it emit a sound, a tune, perhaps?" Elfloq was beginning to wonder what he had got himself into.

"None of these things. To find the book, you must find the thief."

"I assume, master, that you know who this thief is?"

"I do. He is the Laughing Facemaker. The offspring of a human father and a demon mother, a wicked hybrid with diabolical powers. Transmogrification, shape-shifting and so on."

Elfloq would have asked more, but Effelgung rose dramatically, swept his robes around him and walked to another door. He rattled its bolts and stared down at the familiar. "Behind this door, Elfloq, lies the answer to many riddles."

Elfloq could only watch as the huge Librarian pulled back the bolts and then took from his robes a large key. He inserted it in the one fat padlock and clicked it open. The door seemed reluctant to move, even when Effelgung applied his not insubstantial weight to it. But inch by dusty inch, it did move, until at last a gaping dark hole, cavernous and intimidating, seemed to take the place of the entire wall.

Effelgung motioned Elfloq within, but the familiar hovered on the threshold, as though about to step into an infernal abyss.

"Oh," said the Librarian, his bulk quivering with what might have been mirth. "Silly of me. We need light." He made a snapping sound with his fingers, and in the air above him a dancing circle of light appeared. Like a firefly, it wove its way into the chamber beyond.

Elfloq crept forward, aware of the massive shape of his host behind him. The room beyond was not large, circular with a conical ceiling, more beams draped in web. There was a single table, and as the fire-glow brightened things, Elfloq could see heaped ashes beside it, as though a particularly large volume had been burned. On the table was another fat volume, lying open.

Effelgung closed the thick door with a bang that reverberated around the bare walls. Elfloq felt as though he had been shut in a tomb. The air was still, utterly lifeless.

"It was here that the crime was committed," said the Librarian.

"Those ashes – "

"Are Owlworm's predecessor."

Elfloq felt himself shrinking into an even smaller ball of terror. "His, his –?"

"He was far too interfering for his own good. He came in here against my express wishes and took from the shelves up there a single, slim volume. *The* volume."

Elfloq saw a curved shelf on which a few small books rested, a perfect set, though it was true, there was a slender gap in their midst.

"He went further," said Effelgung, cheeks puffed out in annoyance. "He opened the said nameless work. And so – disaster. The Laughing Facemaker was out."

"Out?"

"Out! Out from his prison, the book. And my faithless servant was fried alive for his troubles."

"And the culprit?"

Effelgung hovered over the opened book on the table like a mountain about to fall upon it. "He opened *this* dreadful opus."

"And what opus would that be, master?" said Elfloq, trying to see what was written on the vast pages, though it was impossible as his eyes were only just on a level with the tabletop itself.

"It is a monstrous construction. A dire creation by an adept whom I will not name."

Elfloq sighed. Effelgung was proving singularly reluctant to name names. There seemed little advantage in cloaking so much in mystery.

"It is *The Skullworks*," said the Librarian, as though to contradict himself. "And our villain has entered it insouciantly."

"Ah," said Elfloq, thinking aloud. "It is a gateway out of here."

"No, no. It is a world of its own, true. But like others of its kind, it is still contained by the Library. It is the repository, however, of many forbidden secrets."

"Would they be too terrible to name?"

"Absolutely! Armed with them, the Laughing Facemaker could return here and yet break out of this miraculous building."

"And you want me to find him."

Effelgung nodded. "It will take someone discreet, Elfloq. Someone who would be least expected. If I went into *The Skullworks* after him, or if I sent a dozen ferocious warriors, the Laughing Facemaker would simply elude us all. You, on the other hand, could hop in there and hardly be noticed." The Librarian slipped from a sleeve a thin volume. "This is the book from which he emerged."

Elfloq grimaced at it. In doing so he noticed that it did not match those on the shelf. "The others all have scarlet binding, sire, while that one – "

"Is bound in the skin of a shark-hound, a particularly vicious creature. Yes, I thought it best to disguise this work. He would recognise the original at once."

"But, but – forgive me, illustrious one, but didn't you say the book was stolen – "

"It is incomplete, now that he has escaped from within it." Effelgung handed the book to the baffled familiar. "Take it. Guard it with your life!"

Elfloq shrank back. "But what must I do?"

"You must persuade the Laughing Facemaker to open it and read what is written within."

Elfloq nodded slowly, taking the book. His own squamous flesh crawled at the feel of the shark-hound binding. He was about to flip it open, but the shadow of the Librarian fell over him like a thundercloud.

"No! *Do not read it yourself!* Do you want to end up like Owlworm's predecessor?"

Elfloq dropped the book with a frantic squeak of denial.

"The Laughing Facemaker will not be expecting a visitor like you. He may be on his guard, however, where books and the written word are concerned. But if he reads what is written in that book, we will have him. It will draw him back into it as surely as water sinks into a drain. Then you can bring it back to me. Well, pick it up, pick it up!"

Elfloq obeyed, though he held the book as if it were infested with plague.

"I'll get Owlworm to find you a shirt. You'll need to keep the book concealed about your person."

Elfloq groaned. A book of secrets that he dare not open, a world of the gods knew what horrors to visit, and a dangerous madman on the loose that he must trick. All this for a chance to meet again his own elusive master. Whether it was worth it or not, he was in this up to the hilt. Effelgung was evidently not a man to be denied.

* * * *

Effelgung, although generally reluctant to name names or to divulge secrets of any kind, nevertheless provided Elfloq with a general working knowledge of the world of The Skullworks. It was, said the Librarian, a world within a world, the enormous head of a former magician, who had learned far too much for his own good. He had offended the gods to the extent that they beheaded him, distributed his body throughout the Nine Hells of Snarlwake, a particularly obnoxious underworld, and locked his skull away in its own private hell. Within this hell, the Skullworks, numerous imps and vagabonds toiled at mining the lost memories and knowledge of the extinct magician, preserving and cataloguing them. Periodically Effelgung used magic of his own to retrieve them.

The Librarian opened the huge tome to a page that illustrated in vivid detail a massive skull, the size of a city, perched atop a precipitous cliff face. Behind it a bloated moon gave it a pallid halo and shadows flitted across the great curved dome of bone that was its brow. Elfloq, kneeling on a tall chair, studied the picture, which seemed to be as large as he was, listening to the voice of Effelgung as it plied him with yet more details. The voice seemed to drift away and the picture magnified itself.

Elfloq heard other sounds, but they came from *within* the picture. He clutched at the little book under the thin shirt he now wore and turned to ask Effelgung a question.

The Librarian was not behind him. Neither was the Library. It was a bare plain, stretching to a wall of night, pocked with mires and slippery rocks. Elfloq swung this way and that, only to see the same dreary scene. He looked down: the chair was gone. He knelt upon a rock. Something flew by overhead, cloaked in shadow. Ahead of him, the cliffs under the Skullworks reared up menacingly. He had arrived.

* * * *

Elfloq had had no alternative but to obey Effelgung's instructions. He had flown up into the queasy night outside the great skull, then under the shadows of one of the cavernous eye sockets. It seemed to be as large as the moon beyond the Skullworks. Shivering with unease, the familiar had flown within. It had been like entering the ultimate black pit, utterly dark and shapeless.

He had emerged as if from a dream, opening bleary eyes on a bizarre scene. Here now, perched on a rock ledge, the familiar drank in the view. Below him was one of the innumerable bone caverns of the Skullworks. Cathedral-like in dimensions, it was filled with throngs of small beings, most of them no bigger than Elfloq himself. They crawled like ants over the floor and curved bone walls, studying them intently. "Gleaners," Effelgung had said. "Picking up every morsel of knowledge they can find. There are ancient vibrations in the bone. Each tremor has meaning."

Elfloq could think of nothing more mind numbing than a life dedicated to such as this, but these creatures probably knew nothing else. Rising, he carefully worked his way along the ledge towards an opening, a natural crack in the bone. Seeing there was light beyond, he wriggled through, to find himself in another large chamber, a duplicate of the one he had left and with a similar host of gleaners.

Several times he traversed chambers such as these, sometimes thinking he was merely travelling in circles, but eventually he found himself in a corridor, like a dried artery up into another realm of the Skullworks. Spurred on by light ahead, he hopped up the slope to a tiny open doorway. The room beyond looked more hopeful.

Effelgung had spoken about this place. "Resting Hall," he had called it. It was not unlike the heart of an inn, with two long bars at either side of it and dozens of booths and tables. Brands burned smokelessly along the walls, and individual tables were lit by candles, though mysteriously these never seemed to burn down, as if reconstituting themselves as they melted. There were a few gleaners here, scattered about the long hall, all sitting in silence, mulling their thoughts and sipping at tankards.

"Don't be afraid to go in," Effelgung had advised. "If you are to find out anything about the whereabouts of the intruder, it will be in one of the Resting Halls. Don't be afraid to quiz people. They all do it. In fact it's all they do."

Elfloq took hold of his nerve and entered, moving slowly and as unobtrusively as possible to the long bar to his left. Behind it a tall figure pushed a tankard forward and Elfloq took it, nodding his thanks.

"Found anything interesting?" said the man mechanically.

Elfloq imagined the man was staring through the shirt at the little volume. "Uh, no. A modest selection. Very minor spells. Not worth cataloguing."

"It's been a while since any of our regulars came up with anything worth gossiping about. It's worrying. Makes the gleaners restless."

Elfloq exchanged a few more pleasantries before extricating himself and wandering over to a table that was not too conspicuous. Where to begin? Experience had taught him that in these situations it were best to keep eyes and ears open, mouth firmly shut. He listened to a conversation on his right, where three imp-like beings were talking animatedly about something they had found, but it could only have been of interest to them. Other groups came and went, but Elfloq heard nothing more about an intruder or anyone that might have been the Laughing Facemaker.

Two gargoyle-like beings sat down at his table, grinning at him in such a way that he wondered if their minds were all they should have been, but they hailed him in friendly tones.

"I am Ratripper," beamed one.

"And I am Skewerpole," said the other.

"Elfloq, at your service."

"New here?"

"First session," said Elfloq, keeping to Effelgung's instructions. The Librarian had told him that no one would question his right to be there or pry into his personal details. Everyone in the Skullworks had other things to look for. Individual privacy was, ironically, shown great respect.

"Ah," said Ratripper. "Don't be too put off. Some of us take a long time to stumble on anything worth finding. A lot of the really good stuff has already been tapped."

"True, true," nodded Skewerpole, scratching his face as if it were alive. "I heard that someone found a blasting spell earlier. Down in the Vein of Echoes. Didn't know what they had hold of until it blew their arm off! Hah!"

"No!" said Ratripper in mock horror. "They have been repaired?"

"Yes, but some idiot used totally the wrong fusion cantrip and the poor devil who was injured ended up with an arm as large as he was. Spent an age dragging it around complaining before one of the overseers put him out of his misery."

"And the blasting spell?" said Ratripper.

"Nothing major. Probably deliberately hidden to cause a bit of a stir. Things are very dull in the Vein of Echoes." Skewerpole scratched even more furiously.

"I would like to be able to regale you with interesting tales," said Elfloq, "but alas, my time here has been very tedious. Where would one look for something fresh? Who else is new here?"

Ratripper gazed about the hall. "None of this lot."

Skewerpole was staring at Elfloq. "Something fresh," he murmured. "New people are the last people you'd expect to get news from."

"You don't find new people interesting?"

"We don't talk about our time before this," said Skewerpole, his features screwed up as though a particularly nasty smell assailed his nostrils.

Elfloq swigged at the ale. "Pardon me, I'm still learning the rules." He had forgotten Effelgung's warning. But not trying to find out about a person's history went right against the grain of Elfloq's essential being.

Others came to the table, and they were almost indistinguishable from Ratripper and Skewerpole, who disappeared without ceremony. Elfloq learned nothing. The Laughing Facemaker could have been any one of them. It would have been a perfect disguise.

How do I draw him out? Elfloq wondered. *I have only myself as bait.* He blanched at the thought. Better to try all the other tactics first. Except that there didn't seem to be any. *I can't even use the book. He'll see it as a threat.* He stared into his tankard. Many more drinks and he'd slump into unconsciousness. Maybe that wasn't such a bad thing.

"Stayin' awake for the party?"

Elfloq blinked. He must have nodded off, seemingly for longer than he would have liked. He looked up. Another squat being, not unlike Ratripper, was grinning at him in that demented way which seemed to characterise the inhabitants of this mad place. The Resting Hall was fuller now, bodies packing in, jostling, voices raised in a babble.

"Party?" Elfloq muttered.

"Yeah. Some taleteller is doing the rounds. The place is packed out already. I'd lay off the booze, fellow, or you'll miss out. Our host does this from time to time. Gets in someone to liven things up. He'll be here soon."

"Who is he?" said Elfloq, sobering quickly.

"Dunno," said the other. "Who cares? Long as he spins a good yarn or two. Most of it'll be propaganda. To keep everyone's spirits up. You know, promises that we're all on the verge of finding something really important. Big secrets. But if he's any good, it'll be fun."

Like many of the others in the by now seething hall, Elfloq got up on to the table, his hunched companion joining him. Over by the bar, a space had been cleared. An air of anticipation hung over the space, a readiness. Slowly, rippling out like waves from it, silence spread, until the entire hall, stuffed though it was with living bodies, fell very still. Light dimmed theatrically. The captive audience gaped, the embodiment of eagerness.

Then, like a breath of mist, the taleteller appeared. A uniform gasp went up, then silence fell again. A disembodied voice called from somewhere. "Give welcome, please, to the Laughing Facemaker."

Elfloq tried not to gape as the gleaners cheered. The man who now drifted to and fro across the makeshift stage was dressed in a long, grey robe, his white face partly hidden under a cowl. He lifted his hands dramatically, assuming the stance of a sorcerer or mage, and indeed, his audience was enrapt, held under his spell.

"Citizens of the Skullworks!" he called, voice as piercing as a dagger. "This is your story. I tell of hard labour, determination in the face of frustration, a difficult, exhausting path. Ah, but what treasures lie at the end of it for he who searches, who gives his heart to the hunt!"

Elfloq ducked down an inch or two, for he could have sworn that the eyes of the performer were focused very much in his direction.

The Laughing Facemaker launched into a stirring tale of gleaners who, for ages untold, worked in the mines of the Skullworks, pulling from the bone shards of magic, lost lore, gems of sorcery. It was, as Elfloq had been warned, a tale designed to stir up gleaners' pride, an assertion of their importance. In itself it was well enough spoken, though Elfloq saw through its pomp easily. But what amazed him was the way in which the actor changed roles. One moment he was the high sorcerer, towering over his audience, long fingers like wands directing stars of magic, the next he was half the size, bent over and knotted into the frame of a gleaner. His cowl fell away to reveal a gleaner's face, features compressed, skin wrinkled. Several characters marched, hopped and hobbled to and fro across the stage. And each face changed as though sculpted from wax, the details extraordinary.

Elfloq had to shake himself to avoid being drawn into the magic. Around him he could see and sense that the gleaners were bedazzled by it. Elfloq had seen religion discharge a similar function on many occasions. He wondered, however, what the Laughing Facemaker expected to get out of this. But at the end of the extravagant performance, he found out.

The Laughing Facemaker, having described the glorious fate bestowed upon those gleaners who had discharged their duties effectively and efficiently (that is, they were released from serfdom and transported to a better life beyond the Skullworks) took the rousing cheers and applause with a smile that split his face from ear to ear. His laughter sparkled, infectious. *Oh yes, mused,* Elfloq, *he is well named.*

"How may we pay you for such wondrous fare?" various gleaners were saying.

"'Tis nothing," laughed the actor modestly. "All I ask is a chance to swap tales with you as you relax and drink."

Yes, of course, thought Elfloq. *They'll tell him anything he wants to know. If there is a way out of this world, that's how he'll get to know of it.*

The familiar blended in with the crowd, sipping his ale carefully, keeping one watchful eye on the Laughing Facemaker. For a long time the actor was partially submerged under worshipping gleaners, but gradually their numbers thinned. They all had various places in the Skullworks where they slept, on ledges, in tiny chambers or in disused corridors. It was a loose but entirely satisfactory arrangement, the environment being perfectly safe. Still talking animatedly about what they had seen, they left the hall in groups, some singing, all convinced that life was rich and fulfilling.

Elfloq was slumped back in his seat, feigning sleep, though he waited his chance. It came as the Laughing Facemaker himself sat at a nearby table, a platter of steaming broth and meat before him. As he tucked in, the last of the gleaners bowed to him and departed. Behind the bar, a shadowy figure stacked tankards quietly.

"An interesting tale," Elfloq ventured.

The Laughing Facemaker turned his flashing smile upon the familiar. "You don't have the look of someone who was impressed by it," he said. He waved a fork in an imperious gesture that indicated Elfloq should join him.

The familiar did so, but without displaying enthusiasm. He dropped tiredly into a seat and set his tankard down. "Not at all," said Elfloq. "I compliment you on your delivery. You stirred the host."

"But you will not go to your rest happy."

Elfloq sighed. "In this place? Forgive me, master, but I cannot pretend to be happy in the empty head of a dead sorcerer who no one remembers any more."

"It sounds to me," said the actor, wiping gravy from his chin, "as though you would like to breach the walls and go elsewhere."

"No point in denying that," Elfloq smiled, sipping his ale. He had one eye on the shadow behind the bar, but it was too preoccupied in its duty to be listening in.

"What would you give to get out, eh?"

"Whatever I could."

The Laughing Facemaker observed him keenly. "What do you have?"

Elfloq puffed out his cheeks. "Not very much. Information. Gossip. I glean more of that than old spells and other junk."

The Facemaker's laughter rang out. "Well, my tale didn't reach you at all!"

"Your pardon, master, I did not mean to insult you – "

"Not at all. I prefer honesty. So, you have learned a few truths. Well, learn another, but guard it with your life."

"Master?"

"I, too, seek a way out of this hellhole." He tapped the bridge of his nose with his forefinger. "Keep it to yourself, mind."

"Of course. But you mean that you do not come and go as you please? You do not simply enter the Skullworks and leave it at will?"

The actor shook his head. "No. I seem to have got myself trapped here. I was hoping that by winning the adoration of the gleaners, I might find a way out. Of course, if and when I do, I would be glad to consider taking someone with me."

"Someone, perhaps, who would make a good servant?" said Elfloq with a sly wink.

Again the Facemaker laughed and this time the shadow behind the bar did look across, but only to smile tolerantly.

"So, how do you advise me?" the actor said, face suddenly more serious.

"Well, things are not necessarily what they seem here. For instance, master, certain facts have been deliberately obfuscated."

"And you have uncovered a few?"

"Umm. Take, for example, the written word."

For once the Facemaker scowled, and his face was not pretty to look upon. It was as though Elfloq had pushed a spike of pain into his gut. "Oh?"

"It's nothing, master. Just that, well, we've always been given to understand that there are no written records here in the Skullworks. Everything that is found is passed on to the authorities by word of mouth. And they, we are told, simply remember it. There are no pamphlets, manuscripts, tablets of stone even."

"There is a danger in such things."

"Oh, I have no reason to doubt it, master."

"Hold to that. But what is your point?"

"It is whispered that such things do exist here."

The Laughing Facemaker regarded his food as if it suddenly congealed into something unpleasant. He pushed it aside. "By whom?"

"This is important?"

The actor glared at him and Elfloq hid his terror with difficulty.

"I see it is," he said. "Books are evidently banned for a reason. I would rather not know the details – "

"You said they do exist here."

"Yes, only earlier I was talking to two gleaners."

The Laughing Facemaker leaned forward, and in his eyes, Elfloq saw the hunger of the demon, the true power behind the man. "Do go on," rumbled a voice stoked in the fires of hell.

"*They* said, and I merely pass on their babblings, master, no more than that, *they* said that they had a book. One they had unearthed in a part of the Skullworks that has long been overlooked."

"What about this *book*?" The actor spoke the word as if it were a curse.

"They hinted that it might have been a means to – "

"To? To?"

"Escape. Oh, I laughed, of course, master. Stupid thought. But I did wonder why the book should have been hidden away so remotely. Evidently no one was meant to find it. But it was, I gather, pure chance that it turned up."

"Their names?"

"The gleaners. Oh, Ratpiddle, or something. And Scruple."

"You are certain?"

"I can see this is of great weight to you, master – "

The actor's eyes – demon's eyes – blazed. "Oh, yes. Think hard! Their names."

"Ratripper! Yes, that was it. And, and – Skewerpole. I'm sure."

The Laughing Facemaker sat back, expression changing back to one of mirth. He swigged his ale, wiped his mouth and chuckled. "I didn't mean to startle you. What is your own name, by the way?"

"Elfloq, master. Lately of service to the mage, Quarramagus of Moonwater."

"Lately?"

"He overreached himself. Particles of him are now spread far and wide throughout the omniverse."

Again the laugh. "So you have no master?"

"Uh, no."

"Well, perhaps your luck will change, Elfloq. We'll talk again. Get some rest." The actor rose abruptly and left with a dismissive wave.

Elfloq emitted a gusty breath of relief. The small book inside his shirt burned like a beacon. This was going to be very tricky. The mere mention of the word 'book' was like issuing a personal curse to the Laughing Facemaker. How to get him to open one?

* * * *

Elfloq did retire from the Resting Hall, and having found a convenient, out-of-the-way ledge, slept off the last effects of the ale. Of course, there were no "days" in the Skullworks, but after a period of sleep that passed for a night, the gleaners went back to work. For the time being, Elfloq decided there was no other course for him to take either, so found a chamber where he could join an industrious gang who were glad to have an extra pair of hands.

The work dragged on, and at the point when Elfloq thought he would petrify with boredom, a sudden commotion broke out at the far end of the chamber. Everyone ceased what they were doing and pressed forward.

"What is it?" said Elfloq.

"A disaster, in one of the side tunnels," someone whispered, the message flitting round the company like a startled bat.

The gleaners were reluctant to look into the matter, so Elfloq found it easy enough to slip through them to the end of the tunnel. Two gleaners slumped there, eyes wide in horror.

"Problems?" Elfloq said.

"Yes, yes. Ratripper and Skewerpole."

"Oh? I know them. Where -?"

One of the gleaners pointed. "We heard two loud bangs."

"Like a very bad spell," said the other.

"I ought to investigate," said Elfloq. No one demurred, so he shuffled uneasily up the tunnel. It was low, a dried artery, curving gently upward to a bend. Elfloq came to this and peered round. The smell hit him first. It was acrid, sulphurous. Yes, probably a spell.

Then he saw the two heaps of ashes. They had a familiar look. It took him no more than a moment to realise why. He had seen such a heap of ashes in the chamber of Effelgung. Owlworm's predecessor. Who had been blasted by the Laughing Facemaker.

Elfloq turned and crept back down the tunnel.

"Well?" said the gleaners who had gathered there in a little gaggle. Elfloq shook his head. "They have dug up their last treasure. I suggest you wall this tunnel up. Who knows what other gruesome magics it conceals."

"Yes, yes, wall it up!" said the gleaners and the cry became a chant, echoing back down the corridors.

* * * *

When he next visited the Resting Hall, Elfloq selected a quiet corner where he could observe without too many people being able to observe him. As it was, it proved a dull period, and apart from one or two large groups of gleaners, Elfloq's peace was not disturbed.

When the place was almost empty again, a strange figure appeared, almost out of thin air, and sat itself down opposite Elfloq. Short and squat, with features that would have turned an imp to stone, it scowled at Elfloq.

"It's me," it said, thick lips drawing back in a shark's smile.

Elfloq pretended to be amused. "Really, master?"

"Forgive the guise. But I find it easier to move about the Skullworks this way." The actor's voice was as transformed as his remarkable face.

"You were right about the dangers of books," Elfloq said, taking a long pull at his ale. He had had plenty of time to consider his next tactics with the Facemaker.

"Oh?"

"Ratsplitter and Skewerpole." Elfloq replenished his tankard from a large jug. It was going to be necessary for him to appear more than a little drunk if his ploy was going to work. "Blown to ash."

"Is that so?"

"Umm." Elfloq drank again. "Ash. That little red book they were talking about – "

The eyes of the actor opened, their stare hot as a brazier. "Red book?"

Elfloq did his best to describe one of the books in the set he had seen in Effulgung's chamber.

"So that meddling Librarian was trying to trap me," murmured the actor.

"Um?" said Elfloq from behind the tankard. His eyes appeared to glaze. "Librarian? They didn't shay that. They shed Efful – Efful – "

"Effelgung? What of him?"

"I think they worked for him."

"I should have guessed it. And what of this red book?"

"Poof!" said Elfloq, flinging out an arm to indicate an explosion. "Musht've been blown to asheswishergleanersh."

"You are sure?"

"Tunnelsh been warred up. Walled up."

The grotesque figure sat back. "Good. That's very good. Let's have no more talk about books."

"No," agreed Elfloq, again pretending to take a long swig. He set down the tankard, looked about him in the ludicrously secretive manner of the drunk and winked at his companion. "Min' you," he said, leaning on the table so that his chin was no more than an inch above it, "you can't jus' dishmish these shings."

Elfloq had to grit his teeth in firm resolve as the dreadful gaze of the Facemaker blazed down on him. "I said, let's forget the book."

"Sure, sure," said Elfloq, nodding stupidly. "But you can't stop gossip. I tol' you, I pick up a lot. An' I hear shings. Gleaners talk about booksh. I don'mind forgetting it all. 'F'you shay sho." He rambled on, ignoring the fierce stare. "*Killing Spells, Agnarphand's Complete Cycle, Disruptive Acts* by the wizard Shuddersnake, a' so on, an' so on. *Demonic Doors*, etshetera, etshetera." He rattled off the spurious titles as convincingly as he could. " Who cares? Turn 'em all to ash, eh? Like good ol' Ratspiddle."

The Facemaker leaned forward, his voice very low, but as menacing as death itself. "Where did you hear these books named? Here? In the Skullworks?"

"Psht! So what? Gleaners ramble on. Probably make it all up."

"The books you name sound real enough. But they don't belong here. Who spoke the names? Gleaners from outside?"

"No, no. No gleaners are from outside."

"You are from outside. From Moonwater."

"Oh, yes, yes. A few like me, rudderless, with no masters. We get toshed in here. But they all gossip. They all know about the books. Authorities can't suppress them," Elfloq giggled, though inside, his heart was pumping madly.

"You said *Demonic Doors*, did you not?"

"I heard that name," Elfloq nodded.

"Is it here?"

"Well," said Elfloq, leaning forward and making a great show of gathering his wits together. "I heard someone say that it is."

"But such a huge volume would be very hard to hide," said the Facemaker suspiciously.

"Huge?" said Elfloq. Ah, this was a trap, a test. He shook his head. "No, no, this one isn't huge. Must be an abridged version."

The Facemaker nodded very slowly. "Not necessarily. But it's serpent skin is said to be poison to the touch of anyone but a demon."

"No, not poison. It's shark skin. No, a shark-hound. Whatever that is. Hasn't poisoned the gleaners."

Again the Facemaker nodded. "And does it have an embossed symbol on its cover? A golden dragon?"

Elfloq screwed up his face. "No. Cover's blank. So they say."

"Then it may very well be here. You haven't seen it yourself?"

"Me? No," Elfloq snorted, slumping back. "Don't want nothing to do with books, master. Like you said, dangerous! Damn 'em all."

"Yes, damn them all. But it is possible, Elfloq, that if I am to – if you and I were to escape the Skullworks, such a book as the *Demonic Doors* might actually help us."

Elfloq leaned forward blearily. "Izzat so?"

"Possibly. Who has this book?"

"Don't know."

The Facemaker seemed to control his temper with difficulty. "You could find out, though?"

"You wan' me to?"

"Perhaps you could obtain it?"

"Steal it?"

"Buy it?"

"*Buy* it?"

"What do gleaners want? Not their freedom."

"Big spells! High sorcery."

"That's it! You could swap them their little book for something far more valuable."

"But," said Elfloq, dumbly scratching his head, "I haven't got anything. Even that red book is supposed to be destroyed."

"I'm sure I could find something," said the Facemaker.

"Takes gleaners a long time to find things – "

"I'll conjure up something. You stay here."

Elfloq waved airily and sank back into his seat as the Laughing Facemaker slid from his chair and left the hall as swiftly as an escaping spider. Elfloq grunted, pushing the tankard away. Gods, but this was not easy. One slip and he was demon's meat, that was for sure.

* * * *

Elfloq would have slept, but his nerves would not let him. Instead he used the time to rid his head of the last of the effects of the ale and spoke to a number of gleaners, trying to discuss with them the dubious matter of books. *Better to look the part*, he told himself. *For all I know, the Facemaker doesn't trust me and is disguised as one of them, watching me.*

None of the gleaners claimed to know anything about books. But Elfloq returned to his table and waited.

When the Facemaker returned, he had taken on another of his extraordinary disguises. But Elfloq guessed that the short, muscular being with the grizzled face and hands like hammers that sat opposite him was indeed the actor. The Facemaker took from under his arm a thin slab of marble and dropped it noisily on the table.

Elfloq saw the runes carved neatly across the face of the polished stone. "What is it?" he said under his breath. "I don't recognise these runes."

The Facemaker's absurdly wide face broke into a smile. "That's because they are gibberish. I just made it up. Tell the gleaners what you like. It can be a dragon spell, or a withering curse. Use your wits."

"In that case," said Elfloq, picking up the slab and tucking it under his arm, "I can tell you that it is the lost Thunder Song of the War Trolls. Immensely valuable. It should fetch a good price."

"Oh? Say, *Demonic Doors?*"

"At the very least." Elfloq stood up. "Very well. I go to do business at once. The next work shift is about to start. Once it's over, meet me outside the Chamber of the Right Eye. I should have what we need by then."

* * * *

Effelgung had told Elfloq that he must lure the Laughing Facemaker into the chamber behind the right eye of the skull and by the light of the moon, get him to read from the book. This would then absorb him and Elfloq would simply have to pick it up and fly out of the Skullworks, directly towards the moon. Effelgung would do the rest. What could be simpler?

Elfloq had spent a restless work period. He had broken up the slab with the false "Song" engraving into scores of pieces and scattered them with difficulty. Sooner or later someone would find a piece or two and wonder how *marble* had got here. But with any luck Elfloq would be well gone by then.

He had then joined a small band of gleaners, ferreting for lost lore. His mind conjured up a thousand ways in which things could go wrong, but at long last the moment had come for him to go to the appointed chamber. Once the remaining gleaners had drifted away, he made his cautious way to the corridors that led to the Chambers of the Eyes. They were supposed to be off limits, but there were no guards, as the gleaners never thought to disobey the orders of the authorities.

Elfloq loitered in the shadows beyond the tall threshold to the Chamber of the Right Eye. Beyond it, bathed in moonlight, he could see the massive, curved ceiling of the chamber, the immense open Eye looking out over the vast emptiness beyond the Skullworks. Then, from almost beside him, a shape seemed to flow into being from the very bone itself.

It was the Laughing Facemaker, his features vivid in the rays of moonlight, his eyes gleaming with eagerness. "Well?"

Elfloq patted his chest, the book under his thin shirt. "Too easy," he grinned. "The gleaner who had the book was desperate for promotion. He was about to render it up in order to claim his prize, but the Thunder Song of the War Trolls was too good an offer to miss!" Elfloq chuckled and motioned the Facemaker to follow him into the Chamber of the Right Eye.

He slipped over the threshold before the tall figure could stay him. Inside, moving to the great circular opening itself, Elfloq stood, awash with moonlight. He took from his shirt the book bound in shark-hound skin. "And this was my prize."

The Laughing Facemaker came closer, fascinated by the treasure. "You have done well, Elfloq. And now, entirely appropriately, I will have the last laugh." He reached out for the book.

Elfloq controlled his trembling hand with great difficulty, passing the slim volume to the actor. The latter took it and held it for a moment. He looked at Elfloq as if he would read the familiar's face, and thus his scheming mind. He looked at the book. He looked again at Elfloq.

Then, mercifully, he opened the book. Light from the huge moon illuminated the pages. The Facemaker turned them, eyes roving across every inch.

Elfloq waited for him to dissipate, or flare into flame, or do something to indicate that he was about to dissolve into the book. Nothing happened. Elfloq tried to speak, but could not move.

The Facemaker turned the pages ever more rapidly, his face becoming a sudden mask of anger. "What is this?" he snarled. "WHAT IS THIS?" He held the book up for Elfloq to see.

The pages were blank. Every one of them.

"I, uh, I — "

"Is this the Librarian's doing? By the Nine Hells of Zarubac, *I'll chew on your liver for this!*"

Rather than wait to see whether the Facemaker meant this, Elfloq leapt upwards, spread his wings and executed a deft turn in mid-air. He almost tumbled through the eye socket, but before he could plummet, righted himself and swept upwards, clawing for the skies. He heard a terrible shriek of fury behind him, but did not look back.

Up towards the bright moon he flew. It filled the night sky, vivid yellow, like the eye of a god. Behind him he heard the whoosh of wings and could not resist a glance over his shoulder. Horror of horrors, the Facemaker had opened his cloak, spreading it like two wide bat wings and was flying in pursuit. But his *face*! It was contorted in demonic anger, literally. Row upon row of fangs gleamed, dripping with saliva. The eyes blazed with feral fury. The demon really meant to rip Elfloq apart for his trickery.

The moon seemed somehow to swell, its light blazing more like a sun's, and Elfloq felt himself blinded by it. It roared, coming at him like a fireball. He screamed, but everything was lost in the sound of an explosion.

* * * *

Elfloq tumbled forward, hitting something that was not as hard as a wooden floor, nor as soft as a carpet. It gave a crunching sound as he rolled, then he dropped down what seemed to be a step. When he felt himself fetch up against a solid surface and stop, tangled in a heap of wings, arms and legs, he opened his eyes. He had bumped into a wall. He stared upon the most bizarre of sights.

He was back in Effelgung's chamber. Before him, spread over the floor like a big fat carpet, was yet another book, opened to reveal huge sigils and designs. Beyond it was a table on which lay another open book, and beyond that stood the enormous Librarian. Before Elfloq could speak, a shape blurred up out of the book upon the table, its terrible face shaping itself into the maddened mask of the Facemaker. As the demon materialised in full, its eyes fell on the sprawled familiar, and two claws reached out.

The demon leapt forward with a snarl of triumph, landing on the carpet-like book. As it did so, Effelgung took the covers of the book on the table, *The Skullworks*, and slammed them shut with a loud *whoomp!*

At this, the Laughing Facemaker swung round. Elfloq tried to press himself back into the wall behind him, but it was all too solid and resisted him.

"Welcome back," said Effelgung, leaning on the closed *Skullworks*. And on his face there was a broad smile to rival anything of the demon's.

Even as he spoke, the sigils on the pages of the huge book writhed and formed themselves into tendrils that rose up the legs of the Laughing Facemaker. The demon screamed, tearing at the invaders with his substantial claws, but already he was being pulled down, down, ever down.

Elfloq watched incredulously as the demon was drawn into the pages of the very book itself. The last thing to go was the face. No longer laughing, but contorted horrifically into the ultimate snarl of indignation. As it faded, the huge book began to shrink. It became no bigger than the volume Elfloq had carried to the world *of The Skullworks*. Its covers closed and Effelgung bent down and picked it up with one chubby paw. It was red, matching the set of books on the shelf behind him.

As the Librarian slipped it back on to that shelf, into the gap from whence it had been taken, Elfloq read the golden print on its spine. *The Laughing Facemaker*.

He struggled to his feet, glaring at the Librarian's smug grin.

"I was nearly killed!" Elfloq spluttered. "That - that book was full of blank pages! I tricked him into reading it! I did what you said! But it was *blank*!"

"My dear Elfloq," said Effelgung, going to the door of the chamber and unlocking it. "I never doubted your skills. If anyone could trick the demon into opening the book, it was you."

"Then why -?"

"Was it blank? Well, what I did have reservations about was your *loyalty*. If you had trapped the Facemaker, how could I be sure that you would return to me? The book *was* a key. For all I knew, you could have taken off anywhere in the omniverse. The Laughing Facemaker would have made you quite a slave.

"I decided that the best way to trap him was to have him lose his temper. That way they lose all concentration, all guile, you know. I guessed that his anger would focus into one thing, that being your good self. But, no harm done. The timing was excellent. I had every confidence in you."

Elfloq's mouth hung open, and all that emerged was a squeak of frustration.

"Now, come along with me. Success is not without reward. I must find that volume of Salecco the Banished."

Elfloq managed to pull himself together and he hopped after the huge form. "Salecco?" he mumbled.

"Yes. He writes about your master, the Voidal. And about you. Quite lucidly, too. Which is how I knew your nature."

Again Elfloq felt flabbergasted.

Effelgung chuckled. "Don't worry. No one else gets to read Salecco's work. I don't let even the gods near it. But if you are to be reunited with the Voidal, I'll need to see where he is."

"You mean, my master's history is chronicled? *All* of it?"

"No, no. Not yet. But enough to indicate where you need to go from here."

"I should like to read this Salecco the Banished."

"Really? I should have thought you'd have had enough of books for now."

Elfloq held up a hand in submission. "Yes, sire. Just as you say. Enough books for now." *Or indeed*, he thought, *for a long time*.

PART TWO

THE MARCH OF THE DAMNED

Man has, since the first dawn of his existence, been obsessed with both creative and destructive drives. As time has rolled forward, Man's ingenuity in devising weapons, the machinery of destruction, has known no bounds. It is probably true that Man has spent more time and energy at this exercise than any other has, and entire worlds have been blown asunder and scattered as bloody testimony to this.

The gods, of course, are no different. Except that they are far more inventive and grotesquely imaginative than any Man could be. Their weapons disintegrate entire universes, though one has to allow that this is partly what defines a god. Power is potential annihilation, and what is a god if not a manifestation of power?

Which leads me to this next series of tales.

—**SALECCO**, who has never in all his long
existence caused the death of a single organism.

* * * *

Elfloq the familiar, flying erratically but not aimlessly through the astral realms (for nothing that Elfloq ever did could be termed aimless) had noticed a certain exaggerated furtiveness surrounding the movements of a number of minor elementals hereabouts. Indeed, had the little creatures not been flitting about on waspish wings, Elfloq would have said to himself that they were scurrying, even skulking. Curiosity warped the batrachian face of the familiar into a thoughtful smile. Something was afoot in this gloomy dimension of the omniverse, and his psychic nose for incident suggested that there was more than a degree of importance attached to the skullduggery. That, coupled with the information he had lately gleaned from the remarkable library of Effelgung.

To divert and challenge one of the tiny elementals would, Elfloq knew from experience, have been a waste of energy. They were tight lipped and loyal. Therefore he decided on a course of action more in keeping with his character: he adopted a manner surpassing in stealth that of the elementals and followed one of them.

This creature was obviously the bearer of tidings which both excited and disturbed it. It sped through the astral murk and shortly made a dive downwards, preparatory to plunging out into the dimension where its master would be waiting. Elfloq was the essence of discretion (otherwise he would long since have perished on one of his numerous escapades). As the elemental materialised in its master's dimension, Elfloq did so also, being sure to keep himself a reasonable distance away.

He found himself in an enormous hall, the exact dimensions of which were impossible to determine. Those shadowed perimeters pulsed with powerful sorcery. Elfloq was quick to utilise a tall column of smoked marble, hiding behind it, peering into the light ahead to see where the elemental had gone. Several other tiny shapes popped and fizzed into being and flitted on towards the light like moths. Twin candles rose up, giant trunks of tallow, and the flames that wriggled atop them threw a huge pool of light upon the polished floor of the hall. Between these candles sat, or rather sprawled, a vast, living bulk.

By the eerie light, Elfloq discerned that it was man, though one in whom normal proportions had run amok. The girth of the being weighed him down in such folds of fat that the likelihood of him rising to his feet (which were not visible) seemed remote. There was no neck, but a truly huge head and two watery eyes, glazed over as though they looked far off into dimensions not even guessed at by ordinary mortals. Elfloq suspected that this was a god, though one who had certainly fallen upon hard times. Even so, the familiar was doubly cautious: he had met crippled gods before and their powers were assuredly not to be despised.

"One at a time!" roared the gross god as a gathering of elementals began babbling to him whatever tidings they had brought. They darted back in a uniform cloud, then reorganised themselves, a spokesman stepping forward. Elfloq grimaced, for he could not hear. Stealthily he edged his way around the pillar and secreted himself behind a row of what appeared to be statues. He moved nearer, up the line to within mere feet of where the whispered dialogue was in progress. The statues, he now realised, were all of forbidding warriors in fantastical war gear - war gear that spoke not of one but of many of the dimensions and worlds of the omniverse. Indeed, there were statues here that were forged in the guise of gods, real and legendary. Their shadows prodded at him, moved by the wavering light.

"You are sure?" the reclining god was saying, tremors of woe and apparent disaster in his voice.

"Yes, Omniscience," replied an elfin voice.

Elfloq forgot the armoured replicas of gods and listened intently.

"On the Uttermoor they have gathered themselves, as jackals to the meat, as maggots to the carcass, as flies to the feast."

Elfloq's pointed ears quivered. The Uttermoor? Few ever spoke of the place. Fit only for the dregs of the omniverse, the thrice damned, it was located in a dimension dreamed by a madman, or a diseased god. Deep below other dimensions, it ran like a warren of drains, rife with evil life, divested of intelligence, fit only for a ghastly struggle in primordial slime. Its denizens had contact with nobody else, and the place had long since been abandoned to its decay, even by the gods. Like a deep well beyond all the many hells, it had been left to suffocate itself slowly into non-existence.

"How have they gathered themselves?" retorted the god. "How could such a sink of ordure organize itself, even into a rabble?"

"There is one, master, who has raised himself from the depths of the Uttermoor to mould what little mind there is there into, not a rabble, but an army. An army containing countless followers, master. That endless ocean of excrement hides a legion as innumerable as the stars! They worship their master as the only true god, and call him Ugnarg, the Supreme Iconoclast. He was once a great necromancer, damned to the Uttermoor for his heresies."

The god snorted impatiently. "Well, there have been numerous other would-be sunderers of the gods. Doubtless many of those have also been hurled into that very same Uttermoor by my colleagues of yore."

Of yore? mused Elfloq. Then this god had indeed known better days.

'Tell me simply, has this Ugnarg the means to perpetrate his intended assault on other dimensions and their gods?"

"It is as you feared, Omniscience," replied the elemental. "Ugnarg has had his minions scouring the omniverse for an age. And over the millennia they have found the severed and scattered pieces of the Slaughterer, the Man-Weapon. Even now they are reassembling it on the Uttermoor."

The effect of these words upon the god were as direct and incisive as a bolt of lightning. His mass shuddered like the threat of a lava flow. The great mouth sagged unhappily. *"How much have they restored?"* it gasped.

"All save the war helm."

The god emitted a wail and rolled back onto the hidden couch, rocking the walls of the hall so that the elementals were tossed as though by a wind. "There were a thousand fragments of that infernal machine, each cast into as many lost regions of the omniverse! How could this Ugnarg have located them all?"

"Time is nothing to the immortal Ugnarg, or so his followers say, Divinity. And he undoubtedly retains a degree of power," came the hesitant reply.

The words seemed to sting the god. "Time? Yes, it bears no meaning for me either. How long ago was it that I created that accursed thing and earned for myself the wrath and punishment of my fellows? A thousand eons? Ten times that?"

"Long enough, master, for Ugnarg the Supreme Iconoclast to gather together the pieces that were riven by those same gods. Soon the Slaughterer will walk again."

The god shook his massive head despondently. "No one can wrest power for himself alone. Those who try must surely bear the stigma of the gods forever after! I rose above my station, thinking myself greater than the sum of the others. I, Zargovyl, once arms master of the gods, the greatest creator of weapons the omniverse has ever known! All came to me and bowed to my skills. Until the day I made the Slaughterer and sought to rule them all with it. Pride, arrogance, ambition! Not weapons, but weaknesses! They brought me to this, smashed my talent, ripping to pieces the Man-Weapon. Since then I have lingered here in this dismal fortress, with only the relics of my past glories to remind me of the days that once were." He looked lovingly on the rows of monstrous warriors.

There was no reply from the elementals. They knew all this, of course, and had suffered similar outbursts on occasions too numerous to name. Zargovyl tortured himself frequently with sorrowful reminiscences, but such was the nature of his punishment.

"One day I may atone," Zargovyl mumbled. "One day. Yet now you bring me this disastrous news! This upstart, Ugnarg, has almost reassembled the Slaughterer! The gods will surely bring him down for such insolence - but if he unleashes that horror on so much as a single remote moon in any of the dimensions, I will be blamed anew! Gods of the Abyss, is there no way that I can thwart the lunatic, bound as I am to this hovel?"

Already the elementals were retreating in a cloud of alarm as the huge colossus rose up unsteadily. Zargovyl snatched at a long rod of black metal and swung it about him in frustration. With shuddering steps that made the hall groan with protest, he stamped down the aisle of the warrior-statues, swiping at each of them with the rod. Green light sizzled in balls, cascading sparks that flared across the stone. Statue after statue tottered then crashed on the hard floor as Zargovyl cursed them all roundly and imaginatively.

Elfloq was forced to quit his hiding place as chaos broke out around him. A heavy weapon clattered inches from his small form, forcing him involuntarily into the light. Zargovyl saw him at once and directed the rod at him. Elfloq made to dive back to the safety of the astral, but a green nimbus of light wove about him in a circular web and he found himself buzzing like a firefly in a jar.

Zargovyl's temper momentarily abated as he paused before Elfloq's trapped form, wheezing and sweating like a huge fish out of water. Those twin eyes, vast as moons, loomed above the familiar, whose wings hummed in an effort to keep him hovering in the air.

"Greetings, Omniscience," ventured Elfloq, with a winning smile (or so he took it, though in fact this was not as winsome as he imagined).

"Who dares send a spy into my very halls? To whom do you belong? Speak! A word out of place, mind - a suspicious *twitch* - and I will dissolve your every atom."

"No enemy, Exalted One," cut in Elfloq at once. "No harm shall befall you at my hands. Indeed, Illustrious Lord, how could it?"

Zargovyl grunted and put aside the rod. The green nimbus was gone and Elfloq fell in an untidy sprawl at the huge feet. He scuttled back from them and looked up at the god. "Your dilemma, Omniscience. You seek a way to overcome it."

Zargovyl grunted once more and sat down where he was with a thump, though he still towered over the familiar. "What is that to you, paltry familiar? How can the affairs of gods concern a particle of dust such as yourself?"

"Perhaps I bring you your destiny," said Elfloq, not without cheek.

Zargovyl scowled, his grotesque face multiplying its lines and puckers tenfold. "Oh, and will you thwart my enemies so readily?" He stared unhappily into the distance, pondering.

"Perhaps my master can be of use."

"Really? And who is your confounded master? Some ambitious backworld sorcerer? An ice-world shaman? I need the aid of *gods*, not men."

"My master frequently traffics with gods."

"Indeed?" snorted Zargovyl indifferently.

"I presume, Most Wise One, that you know of the Voidal."

At the name, Zargovyl's bulk appeared to quiver, sending ripples along the landscape of fat. "The Voidal? Who has not heard of him? Accursed by the Dark Gods, drifting for eternity. I have my own problems without considering his! But - do you call *him* master? It is decreed that no man shall call him friend."

Elfloq shrugged. "I am not his slave, it is true. Nor am I, as you can see, a man. But the Dark Gods appear to have relented somewhat. I have been of some use to him."

"And you think the Voidal can help me? How ridiculous!"

"If you'll pardon my impertinence, Worthiness, not so. The Voidal can be a valuable, ah, *weapon*, in the right hands. And you understand weapons."

"Since you know my dilemma, I trust you have devised some scheme, involving your dubious master, by which you can absolve me?" said the god with neither enthusiasm nor belief.

"But of course, Superlative One. Invoke the Voidal - "

Zargovyl's expression silenced Elfloq at once. "*Invoke the* -! And incur a penalty far worse than that which I now am paying? Do you think me that addled?"

"But if you were to put the Voidal to good use - send him out against this vermin from the Uttermoor - he will triumph for you and win you the favour of the gods who punish you. For such a victory they would surely pardon you and certainly waive any fee for calling up the Voidal."

Zargovyl puffed out his cheeks, considering deeply. He went over the familiar's words a number of times, muttering them to himself, weighing them, to see where the flaw must lie. Yet there did not seem to be one. In truth, the gods would assuredly be pleased if Zargovyl could nip the plans of the demagogue Ugnarg in the bud and destroy the Slaughterer before it could again break loose. "Tell me, honey-tongued familiar, what is your master to gain from this venture? That is, if he survives it, for this is no spawn of the slime he must fight, but the Slaughterer, the greatest of my creations." Zargovyl's eyes rolled upwards as he said this last. "And...and greatest of my follies," he added for the benefit of any invisible eavesdroppers.

"Ah," said Elfloq, with another contorted grin. "I see you are a man - that is to say, a god - who understands the noble principles of exchange."

"Well, if you *can* bring about the destruction of Ugnarg and bring me the remains of the Man-Weapon, then you may ask of me what you will," avowed Zargovyl, a trifle hastily, but his desperation now exceeded his caution.

Elfloq, standing and waxing a more confident air, nodded. "As you know, my master has been dispossessed of a number of items, to whit, his complete memory, his identity, his...soul..."

Zargovyl spluttered, anticipating what would come next. "Think not to ask me for *that*! I have it not, nor access to it. The Dark Gods guard such a secret with terrible jealousy."

"I ask only that you give to my master the secret of how to reach it. He already knows that it is in the keeping of Thunderhammer, smith of the gods." Elfloq himself shuddered as he recalled what he had learned from the Songster, Grabulic, who had shared harrowing events with the Voidal at the Keep of Necral and later in Ludang. Grabulic had told Elfloq that his master's soul was chained by the smith of the gods.

Zargovyl was nodding. "Aye, on his mountain, Firecrag."

Elfloq masked a smile of triumph. *Firecrag*! "How is my master to come there?"

The god was uneasy, lost in thought for a moment more, but then he nodded again. "I can divulge the way there, but that is all. Bring me what you promise, and I will teach your master the rituals and gate-passes that will bring him to secret Firecrag. But I'll help no more beyond that."

"It is enough," replied Elfloq, hardly able to keep the glee from his voice.

"And now?" prompted the god, anxious to be on with the uncertain business he had set in motion.

"You must have been shorn of many powers, Effulgent One, but not, I trust, the power to summon men and set them down where you will in the omniverse?"

"That is so."

"Then summon the Voidal. You must set him down on the Uttermoor. I will meet him there and we will undertake all that I have promised. It is within my gift."

"You possess far more confidence than I," sighed Zargovyl, but he was mollified to have a degree of hope.

* * * *

Out of the endless dark where only his dreams floated with him, the dark man bobbed up to awareness. The void slipped away like retreating night, replaced by translucent cloud. He stood on soft, spongy ground beside a pool slick with green scum. In the clinging mists he could discern shapes, stunted and twisted like the crippled hands of old men; they were smeared with moss, blotched with lichen. In his head, the whispering voice had gone, the voice that had woken him and which would have brought him here. For what purpose? The Dark Gods never used him without purpose, that much he did remember.

Above him there was a thrumming of wings and from the weeping mists dropped a figure, crouched in the dismal light, folding membranous wings to its sides. It advanced on the dark man cautiously.

"Elfloq!" called the Voidal, smiling in spite of himself. "So you have contrived yet another meeting between us. I can only assume it is you who are responsible."

Elfloq eyed the man, twice as tall as himself, with a mixture of fear and respect, for he would always be wary of those colossal powers within him, though he was happy to serve them. "Yes, master. You are here through my intervention." At once he plunged into an explanation (omitting his exploits in Effelgung's Library) and the Voidal nodded, with another wry grin. He stood motionlessly, his right hand hidden inside his nightweb cloak.

"So you have indeed contrived my coming to this foul and dreary domain," the dark man said as the familiar finished his breathless explanation. "And you have promised victory to Zargovyl. You are presumptuous, as ever. I do no more than the work of the Dark Gods. I may have won back certain things from them, but not my free will."

Hastily Elfloq confirmed that Zargovyl had promised to point the way to Firecrag and Thunderhammer, keeper of the Voidal's very soul. At this, the dark man's eyes widened, their green fires fanned by unaccustomed hope.

"He promised that? Does he really have the audacity to divulge to me such a secret? He would ignore the decree of the Dark Gods?" But his expression turned to one of scepticism and he stared about at the stunted trees. "Where is this place?"

"This is the Withered Wood, the Wood of All Worlds, at the heart of the Uttermoor. It is its only link with other dimensions. None who come to or leave the Uttermoor may do so by any other route (save the astral). The Wood was created by Lernitac, a fallen mage who was once cast here by demons he had foolishly sought to control. He formed the Wood that ruptures all worlds so that he could escape the Uttermoor and travel wherever he willed in pursuit of the demons that had bound him. It is through this Wood that Ugnarg and his forces must come on their evil crusade into other dimensions. With the, uh, Man-Weapon before them."

The Voidal grunted. "We waste time here. Let us find this Supreme Iconoclast before he readies his armies." He strode forward, Elfloq hovering behind him. They passed through the strange groves of trees that listened like ghosts and went out on to the desolation of the Uttermoor. They threaded through the many bogs and pools of slime that gleamed like ripe sores on the terrain. Knuckles of rock pressed through the cankered surface of the moor, and as the mist drifted aside like a torn shroud, they could see the endless tors, rising up out of the miasma like bastions. The appalling stench of decay was heavy on the air and the mires steamed and hissed with the escaping gases of putrescence. The Uttermoor was like an immense carcass, rank with dissolution. Yet the Voidal's face was expressionless as he travelled across that forbidding, soulless landscape.

Beyond a huge nest of boulders he could make out a dim light. Elfloq flitted across to investigate and came back quickly. "A solitary inhabitant of the moor. Dozing and doubtless dreaming of healthier places. Few can be worse. If the damned of this dimension did not so fear the Withered Wood, they could flee. But they believe there are frightful denizens guarding it. Only Ugnarg, it seems, has the will to override their terrors."

The Voidal glanced briefly back at the Wood then made his way as swiftly as was possible across the treacherous marsh to the boulders. He slipped between them silently and saw the being, snoring, a thin club beside it. The dark man went to the dreamer, picked up the club and tossed it out into the bog. The splash woke the stunted underman, who was no taller than the diminutive familiar. He drew back in terror at sight of the dark man standing over him.

"What do you want with lowly Scurm?" he wailed. "I am loyal to the Supreme Iconoclast! I serve obediently! I was not asleep! I have not neglected my duties! None of the Feasters have shown themselves in the Wood!"

Elfloq dropped beside him, silencing him with a hiss. "Be still!"

"Ugnarg is your master?" said the Voidal. "Where is he? Show me the way. I have come to fight alongside him." He extended his left hand and helped the pitiful creature to its feet. It seemed a poor excuse for humanity, its hair caked in slime, its eyes haunted by misery. There was no fight in it, only blind submission.

"The Supreme Iconoclast? I will take you. Scurm is your servant." The shrivelled being led them through the bogs, Elfloq at once taking to the air. Scurm eyed him with even more fear than he did the Voidal.

The journey over that ghastly terrain was tortuous and long, for the party had to weave and thread around many frightful sinks of filth. They at last came to the top of a weathered tor, where Scurm stopped. He turned his sorrowful eyes upon them. "Ugnarg is beyond, preparing his weapons and army. I must go back to my post."

"Our thanks," said the Voidal. "We will see that you are rewarded."

"No need!" gasped Scurm. "I should not have left my post, I think. No word of that, I beg you. That is reward enough."

"Very well."

Scurm turned and trudged off despondently through the gloom. Clouds of gas billowed low over the tor and wrapped him from sight. The Voidal and Elfloq stood at the stone peak of the tor, staring out over the sweep of the blighted valley beyond. They could make out countless scores of beings from this unpleasant realm, all cheering gutturally and making a din fit to rouse the gods. With infinite care, the Voidal picked his way down through the rotting boulders, mindful of their sharp edges. The undermen were as grotesque as their dimension. Bleached corpse-white, they were splotched with muck, daubed with mud contours that served as war sigils. They had dredged themselves up from the slime where they dwelt like reptiles, and the residue of bestiality that clung to them spoke of near mindlessness and depravity. They carried crude weapons, no more than pieces of rock or twisted shrub roots split into points. Eventually the Voidal was able to see into the heart of the amassed multitude of the damned, where a circle had been cleared. Two figures occupied this circle, which was marked by small menhirs, and the undermen kept outside these.

A great silence dropped over them as one of the figures at the heart of the circle raised its arms. This was the messiah, Ugnarg. He was larger in body than most, his thick hide a mass of sores and scars: his head squatted on his shoulders like a bloated bubble, huge and anthropoidal. If he had once been a dignified necromancer, he was now in the guide of a beast. He pointed with a muscled arm at the thing standing over him. "See!" he shouted, his voice ringing back from the far rocks so that the Voidal could hear him clearly. "See! Your Supreme master has been provided with the means of bursting the walls of our prison! We shall thrust our way out of the Uttermoor and spread retribution and havoc amongst all other worlds! Even the gods will fall to us. The Slaughterer is whole again! Great and terrible will be its vengeance!"

The Voidal stared in fascination at the diabolic weapon, once made by Zargovyl. It stood ten feet high, roughly in the shape of a man. It was cast in black armour, each part of it like a section of the man it represented. Once, these segments had been torn asunder and flung wide across the omniverse, but the hellish smiths of Ugnarg had rebuilt the machine. It looked invincible, its star-forged plates forbidding as the void. On the shoulders sat its helm, the face a mask of pure madness, hammered into a bestial, ferocious scream of war. Horns rose out of it, curled and pointed, thrust up scathingly at the heavens, pointing to all the omniverse which it coveted and longed to rend. Motionless, it stood like a devil at the gates of eternal pain, eager to unleash chaos.

A tremendous cheer swelled up from the ranks of the undermen and broke like a wave over the strutting form of Ugnarg. He pointed to one of the tors that overlooked the valley. "See, thrice damned brothers! See how you shall be avenged for the horrors perpetrated upon you!"

As if in answer to Ugnarg's cry, the sorcerous monster came to life and walked. It raised a stiff arm, directing it at the distant outcrop of rock, high up against the murky sky. Scores of undermen fled from before the Man-Weapon. Suddenly a liquid bolt of white energy roared outward like fire from the hand of the Slaughterer and flashed away in a continuous stream. It slapped against the rock of the far tor in an eye-searing explosion. The tor began to melt, spilling streams of hissing lava down its slopes into the bogs. When the Slaughterer dropped its arm, only half the height of the tor remained, glazed in vapour. A cry of astonishment went up from the ranks.

"This is nothing!" laughed Ugnarg. "A simple demonstration. The Man-Weapon was designed to split worlds in twain!"

Elfloq had alighted beside the watching Voidal. "Can such a boast be valid?"

"Perhaps. Remember, Zargovyl built it. And he, you told me, is a god."

"Then do we oppose this horror alone, or is my calculation accurate?"

"Your calculation?"

"That the Dark Gods would be glad to annihilate this filth and would again make you their instrument of destruction." He nodded meaningfully at the Voidal's covered right hand.

The Voidal's face clouded. He had no wish to know the answer, but knew that he must, even though the very thought of the Oblivion Hand made his flesh crawl. Reluctantly he pulled his right arm free of the cloak, murmuring in disgust. *The hand was not there.*

Elfloq gasped with ill-suppressed glee. "Gone! Just as I supposed! Our coming here was not our own doing."

The Voidal's face darkened with fury. "This amuses you?" he snarled. "Do you still think you can use me, as they do? While the Dark Gods control my every step, binding me to their accursed puppeteering, *you* think to toy with my destiny!"

"No, no!" squawked Elfloq, flitting back from the awesome figure. "I think only of your own cause, master, not theirs. Consider this - they may use you here, but Zargovyl will reward you - "

"*If* he is permitted!"

"Surely he will be! The Dark Gods have allowed you once-forbidden knowledge before now."

The Voidal nodded slowly. "I put no trust in them. They serve only themselves. You and I are their fools. There is always a price." His fury was abating, but sadness had crept into his voice as cold steals upon the land at winter. What memories they had allowed him were as biting as frost: Ludang and its horrors were etched clearly in is mind.

"How should we act?" asked the familiar.

The dark man snorted derisively. Those memories had rekindled his anger. "Act? I have a mind to stand and watch, no more. I am sick of being used. Let events unravel themselves."

"But how -?"

"We wait. No doubt the tide of circumstances will suck us in and cast us upon the shores of consequence."

Elfloq grimaced. His master was not usually given to such verbosity. But its bitter irony was not lost on the familiar.

The Voidal scowled at emptiness. He had come here to false hopes, thinking to act for himself at the backs of the Dark Gods, but it was not so. The Oblivion Hand had gone out to do its grisly work. He felt the resolve to strive for his own destiny weakening, and fought to control his anger and frustration.

Above the tors a great orb had risen, like the sightless eye of a titan. By the light of this glistening moon the valley was cast into brilliant light. The frightful features of the undermen came into sharp focus. They chanted litanies to the moon and Ugnarg shook his clubbed fist at it. "Let the Moon of Dreams be your god no more!" he told his minions. "False god, I will cast it down!" But before he could make good his promise, a shadow fell across the valley, cast by that vast moon.

All eyes looked up at the tor between moon and Ugnarg. The granite stacks that rose on its crest had shaped themselves into a formation resembling a huge fist, and from that fist extended a long finger - its tip rested at the very feet of Ugnarg in accusation. As the moon crossed the heavens, the tip of the shadow finger swung with it to lie at the feet of the Slaughterer.

In fury, Ugnarg directed the weapon to blast the stone fist apart. It obeyed at once and the tor disintegrated, melting its crest in a sizzle of molten rock. But the memory of the shadow, the pointing finger, could not be erased. Ugnarg screamed at his hordes, exhorting them to go forth to victories, yelling at them, blasting away their doubts as the machine had blasted the tor.

"To the Great Abyss with all gods! I will blind your Moon of false Dreams forever!" With this, Ugnarg directed his Man-Weapon to act again. It pointed both arms at the Moon of Dreams. Scarlet fires, rivers of livid hate, streamed forth into the vaults of heaven and for moments after their meteoric passing there followed an expectant silence. Then the Moon of Dreams quivered, its pink iris enflamed, churned to crimson blood. A roar as of an avalanche of worlds shook the Uttermoor to its granite roots. Fissures split the Moon of Dreams into a thousand-year-old face, spreading until they became black chasms. In a dazzling explosion, vast segments of moon flew outwards in a welter of colossal disintegration. Darkness followed, blotting the sizzling remains of the shattered heavenly giant from view.

"See how we eradicate what opposes us!" Ugnarg screamed. "Come, we are ready! Let us away to the Withered Wood. We shall swarm through its portals and begin our crusade. Raise the sleeping damned! Gather them like the lice of the world. Death to all gods! The reign of Ugnarg begins!"

This was echoed by shrieks of joy and excitement. With the Man-Weapon, the undermen now believed they could go out and reap a thousand empires.

Elfloq's jaw had dropped in stunned amazement at the obliteration of the moon. He finally shook himself out of the shock and pointed to the endless lake of marshes that threaded the valleys of the Uttermoor. "Look!"

Up from the depths were bursting thousands of undermen, beings who had wallowed there, exploding now like boils. There was no knowing the bounds of the Uttermoor and of the incalculable expanses of reeking mire. From them, whole worlds of imprisoned undermen would emerge to follow Ugnarg.

"How is this legion to be checked?" gasped the familiar.

"You surprise me," said the Voidal. "Did you not take this into consideration before starting this reckless escapade? What now of your *calculation*?"

Elfloq grimaced. "Well...I, uh, I could hardly have been expected to envisage such a swarm. And to see a moon obliterated!"

"Perhaps this will teach you something about the follies of meddling in the affairs of others. I wonder. But the numbers here do not matter. It is Ugnarg's sorcery that controls them. Some evil magic warps their minds to his. Destroy him and the Slaughterer and the undermen will subside once more into their filth."

Elfloq's crooked smile returned. "It seems to me that the Dark Gods have already cast Ugnarg's fate, and that of the Man-Weapon."

"And what of ours?" growled the dark man.

Elfloq had no immediate answer. Before he could think of one, a hoarse shout behind him made him spin in fear. A group of undermen, dripping with the muck from which they had lately arisen, had found them out and were calling to Ugnarg. The Voidal rose up, reaching idly for his sword haft, but he and Elfloq were exposed on the shoulder of the tor.

Ugnarg saw them and would waste no time questioning them. He barked a command to his automaton and the hand of the Man-Weapon swung round, singling out the Voidal. Elfloq took to the skies and slipped on to the astral at once, a cowardly move, but one that unquestionably preserved his existence. The Voidal, meanwhile, had no time to avoid the shuddering deluge of white fire that flowed to his breast. It struck and he felt the universe shatter into a million blazing embers, each member a part of him. After that there was nothing.

Ugnarg laughed aloud. But he thought he heard an echoing laugh where the dark man had been standing. A laugh of joy, or of relief?

* * * *

Elfloq hovered about on the astral for a considerable time, or so it seemed to him. Guilt racked him, but terror overcame even that at first. He had deserted his master, which was unpardonable. Somehow he must atone, and quickly, or the consequences would be dire. Therefore he slipped back on to the Uttermoor, though at a sensible distance from the scene of his and his master's discovery. The armies of Ugnarg were swarming up the tor, thicker than flies. It was impossible to see the tail of this buzzing mass as the undermen seethed up from the mires. But of the Voidal there was no sign.

In desperation, Elfloq flew high over the armies, aiming for the Withered Wood. Far below he could see the van of the armies, where the twin figures of Ugnarg and the Slaughterer marched resolutely onward. They were joined by still more dwellers from the moors, some less man than reptile. Elfloq went on ahead through the vapour clouds to the Wood. He dropped down into its highest branches, though these were hardly taller than a man's head. Like some dejected spirit, the familiar stared out through the rolling mists at the oncoming swarm of undermen.

A movement below caught his eye. He stared in amazement at what he saw. Like a crab scuttling for the safety of a rock pool, a hand made its way slowly over the grey stones into the sanctuary of the Wood. Elfloq shivered as the thing passed below him, black as space. He flew out into the mist, still unsure what to do.

Vague light shifted about him and he caught odd sounds, the peals of a distant explosion, rippling echoes. In the mist, something began to coalesce, something with ghostly substance that darkened like a stain. In a moment the mist obscured it. Elfloq prepared for a second flight, for there was gathering power at work: the Feasters in the Wood were supposedly legendary, but it would be foolhardy to trust in that.

A voice called to him from the mist. He stared, flying cautiously towards a jumble of rocks. One of them moved and he let out a squeak of fright. But it was a man.

"Familiar!" called the voice.

Elfloq dropped like stone, alighting gingerly. "Master!"

"It seems that my immortality has not deserted me, as I had hoped."

Elfloq scowled. "Hoped, master? You...you mean you *invited* the Man-Weapon's attack?"

The Voidal shrugged. "All *I* seek is peace. I have no desire for eternity. Unless it be the eternity of death. To be dissipated, my essence vaporised, would be enough for me."

"But what of your soul? If we triumph - "

"*We?*" snorted the dark man. "This conflict is not ours, its conclusion nothing to us! We are merely the means to its end. Don't talk of *our* triumph, witless familiar."

"We stand to profit."

"Perhaps. I remain sceptical."

Elfloq was nonplussed. The dark man's despondency was a serious obstacle to his own ambitions. The utterly dismal nature of this realm undoubtedly contributed. "Yet you have not been without victories in the past. You have reclaimed something of your memory - "

The Voidal's green eyes shone with ill-suppressed anger. "Yes, and what of that? The anguish that has brought. I have learned something of myself, but perhaps I would be better not knowing." Ludang and the events there haunted him now, the fate he had been forced to meet out to the woman he had loved.

"But, master, the path to your soul itself may lie open! One day you will surely be restored to what you were."

The Voidal stared at him for a long, chilling moment. "Your persistence is like a sea, Elfloq."

Elfloq looked away from the power in his master's gaze. "I have chosen you as my master. My status can be no more than a reflection of yours."

To his relief, the Voidal laughed. "Ambition alone moves you, not compassion."

Elfloq was relieved to see genuine amusement on the dark man's face. "It is true, master. If I can aid you to unlock the vaults of your stolen power, why then, could we not spite the Dark Gods themselves?"

The Voidal frowned. "How much do you know of what was taken from me? You have learned something?"

"Why, only that the Dark Gods would not so restrict you unless they *feared* you, master. And if they fear you, it is because they fear you may best them."

Again the Voidal laughed. "Gods of the Abyss, you are becoming a philosopher! Yet I confess I take a grudging comfort from your blabbering."

Elfloq pointed out at the marshes. "Ugnarg and his armies are coming. They will overrun the Wood and stream out to conquest."

"Let them come," said the Voidal. "It is not for us to stop them." He said no more but walked pensively into the mist. Elfloq sensed his mood, but there was a lightening of it. The familiar would have to tend these embers of hope. But for the moment he was anxious to learn what transpired out on the grim moors. He flew to watch from a height.

Ugnarg and the Man-Weapon were almost at the periphery of the Withered Wood. The Supreme Iconoclast turned to his army and his voice rose in a great shout that carried far back, repeated by others. "Hear me! Beyond lies the way to other realms, the Wood you so fear. Let there be an end to your terrors. I have dispatched the Feasters elsewhere, and if there remains any guardian within to devour us, I will destroy it and open the gates. Now the time has come for the Slaughterer to realize its full power. Watch and see us united!" So saying, he walked to the Man-Weapon and made it bend before him. He opened a section of the monster's steel guts and climbed in. The steel clanged shut.

The leading undermen cried out, some murmuring superstitiously that the Slaughterer had devoured their leader. But in a moment the Man-Weapon stood up and from its helm issued the now magnified voice of Ugnarg. "It is done! The Slaughterer and I are one. We go forth to clear the way of all who stand against the new regnum."

This met with cried of jubilation that rang back down the valley for miles. Elfloq flew back into the Wood. There were no signs of the Voidal. Had he truly abandoned the omniverse to this pestilence? The familiar decided to watch further proceedings from the gnarled branches of a tree. He had the uncanny feeling that he did not watch alone. At the first sign of trouble, he could slip back on to the astral. His insatiable curiosity rooted him and he watched as Ugnarg lumbered into the Withered Wood, smashing aside the trees to force the Man-Weapon into the centre of the little grove. Here there was a stagnant pool, ringed with green muck and unpleasant growths, rotting logs. Its surface was still, silent.

The Man-Weapon stood at its edge haughtily, both arms pointing down at the pool as though about to boil it. "Here lies the way!" cried Ugnarg to the few undermen who had ventured this far with him. "Watch as I pass through it to the first ripe world beyond."

He stepped out into the pool. The muck slopped at the steel feet of the Man-Weapon as it began to wade out into the stinking waters. It was waist deep when it reached the centre, standing motionlessly, readying to sink down through the watery gate. The undermen watched in awe, expecting turmoil, but a booming laugh echoed from the helm. "The way is clear! There is not a world we cannot reach. Follow, and we will topple the very gods!"

At this, several of the undermen whooped and rushed into the pool to join their master. As they did so, a darkness foamed around the Wood. The murky waters gurgled, rippling rhythmically, ominously.

Above, on his perch, Elfloq saw the weird movements of the pool clearly. There were mildewed branches and thin logs at its edge. One of these logs began to stir, then bend in its middle, thickening and crooking itself. The Man-Weapon, instead of sinking down into the scummy gate, rose up slowly. In a moment it was free of the slime, standing on what appeared to be the bed of the pool, which was *rising*. But it was not, Elfloq then realised, the floor of the pool at all.

It was the palm of a huge hand.

From the pool's edge, thick fingers rose up, their growth wider than any of the trunks around it. The undermen caught in their grasp squirmed as they were pulped like insects. Then the Man-Weapon was enclosed as the curling black fingers drew up like the legs of a monstrous spider.

Ugnarg understood what was happening as the rest of the undermen fled screaming into the Wood, beyond which their massed legions waited. At once twin gouts of white fire shot down from the hands of the Man-Weapon, searing the flesh of that god-like hand. Yet only the dripping slime burned. The grip of the hand tightened so that the Man-Weapon disappeared from view. The hand became a fist, and it *squeezed*. It glowed white-hot as the furnace within its grasp increased, like the heart of a star.

* * * *

The dark man dreamed.

He saw a monstrous shadow, hewn from the black of nightmare. This frightful juggernaut stamped through the vaults of the stars, pointing at suns, bursting them like fruit with its malevolent intent, dragging into its halo of incandescent destruction a million worlds, tugging the fabric of the many dimensions into a knotted rug of turmoil and cataclysm.

In his dream, the dark man reached out for the awesome figure as if it were a toy, snatching into the vortex of the hand the livid chaos of the destroyer, gripping every last vestige of its malign desecration.

Hand and destructor clashed, and in the shuddering pandemonium, whole universes burst out in to eternity, tides of evanescent energy washed the omniverse, their ripples felt at the edge of existence.

At the very brink of time, gods lifted their heads, as if they, too, shared something of this mad dream.

* * * *

Elfloq shielded his eyes but could not look away. The fist went on squeezing remorselessly. Molten matter dribbled through those crushing fingers, hissing as it slithered down in greasy globules into the pool. The cascade of white matter became a gush. It poured, filling the grove with thick steam clouds. The pool boiled, heaving with bubbles. Beyond the Wood the dark pressed in eagerly. Slowly the white heat of the fist subsided so that it darkened and charred. A few trickles of molten matter fell into the dregs of the pool.

The fist unclenched at last. In its open palm was nothing more than a ball of steel, blackened and burnt out. It rolled on to the bank of the pool, caught in the mud there. The hand subsided, swallowed by the black loam at the pool's bottom. With its going, the gate had been sealed.

With the passing of Ugnarg, the binding spells upon the Feasters were broken. Now they shrieked avidly as they tore back from their interdimensional prisons, howling like a storm about the trees, forming into solid denizens. Elfloq could only watch in revulsion as their glowing, transparent bodies wriggled gigantically, slithering through the Wood. Their nodding, shapeless heads split wide to form mouths like portals on lunacy. As one, their demonic company rushed out upon Ugnarg's disorganised rabble, volcanic with glee. A nauseating conflict ensued, for the hordes of the damned were mindless now, easy meat for the dreadful Feasters. These horrors gorged themselves until they burst, their bellies splitting to vomit floods of horribly altered undermen. These, being damned, were chained to a permanent existence here on the Uttermoor and death was no release to what was deathless. Like serpents, they writhed back into the marshes. The stinking remains of the Feasters also sank into the mire, beyond vision, but not memory. They would rise again when called upon.

Elfloq finally turned from the repulsive, though compelling, spectacle. He recognised the figure at the edge of the pool. Too tall for an underman, it came out of the shadows and stood by the side of the empty pool, shrouded in the last vestiges of steam. Elfloq flew down beside the dark man.

"The conquest of the gods was, predictably, not to be," said the Voidal. He glanced down at the ball of melted metal. It was already cold.

Elfloq bent down and poked it experimentally. Satisfied that it could do no more harm, he tried to lift it, but it was too heavy. "You will have to carry it, master."

"No," the Voidal grinned. "Cast it into the muck. It is nothing now."

"But, should we not take it back to Zargovyl, as proof that the Slaughterer is no more?"

The Voidal held out his arms. "And would you show him these?"

Elfloq leapt back, even though he had guessed what he would see. The hand had been restored.

"Can Zargovyl free me of this?" asked the Voidal bitterly.

But Elfloq gamely tugged at the cold metal orb and succeeded in lifting it. "I will take this, master. It may yet buy you a passage to Firecrag and Thunderhammer. You must not forsake your cause. If you win these other things, you may yet rid yourself of that hand for all time."

The Voidal studied his right hand briefly, then pushed it back under his cloak. "Very well," he said resignedly. "Go to Zargovyl. I will accept whatever he will pay for his trophy. No doubt you will bargain hard, familiar."

Elfloq's wily smile had returned. "In that you *can* trust, master."

The Voidal watched him struggle with his burden, which already seemed lighter, and fly up into the darkness. Elfloq went out on to the astral, buoyed by the knowledge that he had unquestionably forged another link in his relationship with the Fatecaster.

PART THREE

A QUESTION OF DEBTS

And so the familiar comes to meet an old acquaintance. One infinitely better versed in the ways of deceit and deception than himself. But Elfloq grows wise as he flies his crafty path. At least one truth is very clear.
What you see is, in all likelihood, probably not what you get.
　　　　—**Salecco,** who would never presume to compete with the cosmic deceivers

* * * *

In the great hall of Zargovyl, the once mighty armourer of the gods, all was silent, as if its once industrous master had abandoned the shadow-hung place. Spiders and roaches had set up their own kingdoms here, indifferent to the whims of the gods, fallen or otherwise.

When Elfloq the familiar slipped from the astral realm to alight here for the second time, he wondered if Zargovyl had, after all, been negated, or possibly removed to some other dismal place to serve out his exile. Fallen gods were prone to such treatment. These thoughts prompted muttered oaths and curses from the little familiar, who had laboured hard to get here, burdened as he was with the metal relic he had brought. Exasperated, he let it fall to the dusty floor: its clang reverberated back from vast distances and bounced from innumerable columns as though in challenge.

"Zargovyl!" Elfloq called, a shade apprehensively, for one never took overt liberties with gods, even discredited ones. He peered into the gloom. The huge warrior statues gazed down at him, balefully he thought. "I have brought it! What about the debt you owe my master?" he added softly to the silence.

At the end of a row of black statues there came a breath of movement, soft as butterfly wings. A fat candle seemed to ignite itself, its dim halo valiantly attempting to illuminate the hall. Elfloq began lugging his trophy along the hall, grunting with exertion and grumbling about the laziness of gods.

He came to the foot of a low dais, the top of which remained in shadow. "Are you there, arms master? I have brought you a gift."

There was certainly something upon the dais, staring down at Elfloq, for he could see its outline, and indeed, its eyes. They gleamed - far too narrow and piercing to be those of Zargovyl. Softly their owner moved into the circle of candlelight and looked down, a cold smile upon its thin lips. The scarlet robe, the long, jet-black hair, the unforgettable features - all these were known to Elfloq, etched forever on his inner eye.

"Darquementi!"

The Divine Asker, Inquisitor of the Dark Gods, inclined his head gently, as if to a person of some importance. Or so Elfloq imagined.

The familiar spluttered. "I did not realise you had business with the arms master."

"Erstwhile arms master."

"Or else I would not have shown such discourtesy, such effrontery as to intrude. I will leave at once - "

"No need for you to scuttle off in such embarrassed haste, Elfloq. My business is with Zargovyl, certainly, but I also have business with yourself."

"I?" gasped the familiar. "Great lord, you surely jest!" He attempted a scornful laugh, but his throat betrayed him and he managed no more than a spluttering cough.

Darquementi raised a long hand for silence and Elfloq controlled his cough with some difficulty. The Divine Asker stepped into darkness and lit yet another candle. In its pallid glow could now be seen the reclining vastness that was Zargovyl. His great face mooned at Elfloq, a vast painting of anxiety. The former arms master breathed out a gale of a sigh, as if he had been holding his breath for a considerable time.

"Well?" prompted Darquementi sardonically. "No words to say to each other? No excited greetings?"

Zargovyl looked as if he was about to speak, but his gross chins sagged as his head dropped and he regarded his monumental paunch.

Elfloq stood in front of the metal trophy he had laboured to bring here, but its coldness offered no support, reminding him of its somewhat damning presence. It was pointless trying to hide it from someone who was generally referred to as 'all-seeing.'

"Shy, Elfloq?" said the Asker. "Unlike you, who once burst into my private apartments in Cloudway and demanded knowledge."

"Why must you toy with us!" Zargovyl suddenly groaned. "You know everything."

Because, thought Elfloq, the Askers like to see us *squirm*.

Darquementi nodded. "Apologies. My purpose. I act, as ever, for the Dark Gods. I am their questioner, their inquisitor. And sometimes, their messenger. Of course, it is not usual for them to send one of *my* exalted rank upon some common errand. You will, therefore, deduce that my coming here is a matter of some weight."

Elfloq trembled at these words. *Weight*. Then his sins had found him out. Punishment would be - but he forced himself not to think of such horrors.

Darquementi pointed to the partially obscured relic, which had some-how positioned itself behind Elfloq. "What have you brought with you from the insalubrious region of the Uttermoor?"

Elfloq stood aside guiltily. "This bauble?"

"Your pardon. I thought it to be the remains of the Man-Weapon, the much vaunted Slaughterer," said the Asker coolly.

Zargovyl emitted a gasp, almost lurching to his feet.

Elfloq nodded. "Not my doing, of course. Merely the work of my mast - uh, the Voidal."

"Your master, yes," replied Darquementi. "No need for subterfuge here. So the dark man has destroyed Ugnarg's mad plan of conquest and has made an end of that compromising weapon."

"It is an immeasurable relief," said Zargovyl with real depth of feel-ing, "that the cursed thing has been rendered harmless."

"Ah - you are pleased that your creation has been destroyed," ob-served Darquementi.

Zargovyl nodded violently. "I went to some lengths to eliminate it - "

"Oh, but I am aware of that. As are *my* masters. They are well pleased that the destroyer of universes is no more."

Elfloq brightened at this. Perhaps the Asker was here on more re-warding terms after all.

"Ugnarg's rabble have subsided, fused for the most part back into the filth from which they emerged," said Darquementi with an airy wave of his hand. "There will be no more rebellion on the Uttermoor."

"Well," breathed Elfloq jauntily, "it's good to know that the Dark Gods are pleased. And my part in the affair was so small as not to be worth a moment's consideration. Thus I will, of course, remove my inconsequential self from your presence and waste no more of your valuable time - "

Again Darquementi's hand rose, but this time in an imperious gesture. "You will leave only when you are dismissed."

Elfloq stood rigidly.

"Are you forgetting certain matters?"

Zargovyl and Elfloq exchanged glances, neither of them anxious to speak what was in his mind, though sure that the Asker could read it anyway.

"I speak," said Darquementi, "of certain debts."

Debts. The word hung over the hall like the immense fist of disaster, puissant as an avalanche.

"Debts," repeated the Asker. "The omniverse has its rules. Bargains struck by men and gods alike should be honoured. Ill to those who do not live by this fundamental law. Tell me, Zargovyl, are you not aware of the price one must pay for invoking the Voidal? You did charge the Fatecaster with the destruction of your creation, or did I merely dream that?"

Zargovyl sighed. "Yes, yes. But to be fair, it was done in the name of the Dark Gods."

"But the Voidal is the tool of the Dark Gods!" the Asker laughed. "He acts on no one else's behalf. You invoked him - do you deny it?"

For a brief while it seemed that Zargovyl might do so, but he shook his head.

"Good," said Darquementi. "There are many ways to pay for such a service. My masters always like to charge a fitting fee." He mused for a moment.

Zargovyl's hue was now a ghastly gray that had nothing to do with the poor light.

"While Ugnarg had possession of the Slaughterer," went on the Asker, "did he not cause a degree of destruction on the Uttermoor?"

Elfloq shrugged. "A few tors, lord. A variety of wind-blasted stones. He merely expedited their erosion."

"And what of the heavens there? What of the Moon of Dreams that the undermen worshipped? A minor adjustment to its orbit, perhaps?"

Elfloq gave considerable attention to his feet. "I had overlooked that."

Zargovyl was nodding. "It was obliterated."

"It winked out like an eye," agreed Darquementi. "Plunging the Uttermoor into deeper darkness. Yet it does not seem wise to leave such a place in darkness, wouldn't you say? There may be, after all, another uprising one day, however unlikely. Best then to have the Uttermoor watched. A new Moon of Dreams would seem an appropriate answer. Better the undermen worship a new moon than a new messiah."

"Indeed," nodded Zargovyl, though he was perspiring profusely.

"Quite so," agreed Elfloq, wondering what the Asker had in mind, fearing that it would not be altogether pleasant. It wasn't.

"Since, Zargovyl, you agree that a new moon is required, perhaps you would be willing to submit one of your eyes for that purpose?"

Zargovyl's breath caught in his throat. Both of his eyes bulged in horror.

Darquementi studied them. "Or, better still, to be sure of a constant vigil, both of your eyes?"

A faint whimper escaped Zargovyl's compressed lips. Elfloq felt himself shuddering as he attempted to compute the nature of the punishment that must surely fall upon him.

Darquementi allowed both of his victims to contemplate the awful suggestion he had made, silently enjoying their turmoil. At length he spoke. "There are, however, certain mitigating circumstances involved in this affair. The Dark Gods have no doubt that you saw the evil potential of the Slaughterer and that you were at some pains to end the ambitions of its lunatic master."

"I was!" avowed Zargovyl, sensing reprieve. "Drastic pains!"

"The Dark Gods were aware, millennia ago, that Ugnarg was gathering the scattered segments of the Slaughterer they had once dispersed. But they allowed him to continue, thus giving him an endless time of hope. Greater the pain and frustration when that hope was smashed. Ugnarg will not rebel again. His spirit lives on, but it is now utterly broken. To some extent, Zargovyl, you are absolved."

The former weapons master began to blurt his thanks.

"To *some* extent," repeated Darquementi. He turned to the quaking Elfloq. "And it was you, was it not, who suggested to Zargovyl that he should summon the Voidal?"

"I may have *mentioned* the possibility - "

"I wonder if you should pay for your indirect invocation."

Elfloq's shivering worsened. It would mean something beyond death, long and agonizing.

"You claim to serve the Dark Gods?" Darquementi challenged him.

"Always!" avowed Elfloq.

"Since your brain cannot control your tongue, better to still it altogether than let it betray you. You claim to serve the Dark Gods - very well, you shall do so. Now, tell me, what do you and your master most desire?"

This abrupt change of questioning surprised Elfloq, who could only stammer. He dared not admit to the wants of the Voidal, who longed to be free of the yoke of the Dark Gods.

"Would it be the path to Firecrag, Thunderhammer's domain?" suggested the Asker, with a horrifying innocence. "Is this not what you sought from Zargovyl? A secret way to the smith, beyond the eyes and ears of my masters, there to purloin a certain article?"

Elfloq nodded unhappily. It was evidently useless to deny anything.

"You shall go there and your master also. But not secretly. And there you both shall serve the Dark Gods, rather than yourselves."

Elfloq was certainly relieved by this news, but still his face was clouded.

"You seem disappointed."

"No, no, not I, lord. But my master will curse me when I tell him of this errand. He will likely cast me adrift." *But of course, it was precisely what the Asker wanted*, Elfloq told himself.

"Oh, but why should you tell him? He need not know of our meeting. Use your silver tongue, Elfloq. You are fabled for your cunning."

Elfloq frowned suspiciously. There was deceit of some kind at work here. Darquementi would sow disharmony between him and his master. Yes, that was what they wanted. To slide a wedge between familiar and Voidal. Elfloq tried to feign indifference. "And what are we to do on Firecrag?"

"There is insurrection, or will be. You must put it down as you did that of Ugnarg. The Dark Gods wish to work against it *discreetly*. But there will be difficulties."

Elfloq managed a smile. "We will take our chances."

"Success is not guaranteed you by our masters. There are gods involved, and significant powers. Much balances on the fulcrum of Firecrag."

"And if we are successful?"

Darquementi laughed harshly. "You seek a reward?"

"The, uh, pleasure of the Dark Gods will suffice," muttered Elfloq.

"Ah, at last you have said something sensible. Memorize those words, little familiar. You would do well to adopt them as a motto."

The Asker turned to Zargovyl. "Well, arms master that was, you still have a debt to pay, though nothing so expensive as your eyes. How are your old skills? Have you forgotten how to forge the stars into weapons, how to make infernal engines from suns?"

For the first time during the whole exchange, Zargovyl brightened. "I have not been permitted to make weapons for eons, nor have I done so."

"But you could?"

"I have no other skill."

"Excellent! You shall work again. There is a weapon you must create. For the Voidal. And you, familiar shall deliver it to him, on Firecrag."

"But, but, if he refuses it - "

"Of course he will refuse it! But that will not be an option for him."

Which, mused Elfloq, will neither please him nor enhance me in his standing. Yes, they mean to sever us if they can.

"And what must we do there?"

"Discharge your debts. I will tell you how."

And for a long time the Divine Asker spoke, the familiar growing dizzier as his theme expanded.

PART FOUR

ON MURDERERS' MOUNTAIN

Man has a very clear concern about death. Regardless of whether it is believed to be a door into another life, heavenly or hellish, it is something to be avoided at all costs. For Man, the survival instinct means staying alive, no matter what. Consequently for Man, there is no such thing as a fate worse than death, in spite of what has been written on such matters. The lowest form of Man, however thinly his brains have been brewed, will conform to this ferocious, even killing desire, to remain alive. (There are of course, exceptions, suicides being the obvious example, but madness of a sort drives these unfortunates and madness stands outside the normal order of things.)

For the gods, death means little more than a night's sleep. What the gods fear is immortality. Oh yes, immortality is a wonderful thing if it does not embrace eternal pain, suffering, humiliation, and so on. But endless suffering? Well, that is a fate worse than death.

Believe me, I speak whereof I know.

        —**SALECCO**, the Deathless and not the most content of (former) gods.

* * * *

Firecrag, the domain of Thunderhammer, smith of the gods, rises up in the form of a huge mesa topped by a vast plateau, like a colossal banqueting table spread at the feet of those the smith serves. The yellow and scarlet skies into which this huge mountain rises are occasionally smeared with belching clouds fanned by the ironworks of the smith: embers often chase each other in packs, winking out in remote distance. Sound rolls and throbs like thunder when the smith works, reverberating out into infinity. Over the edge of his plateau, Thunderhammer can look down into an unfathomable deep, the roots of the plateau lost in swirls of vapour, mists and steam that seep through the very walls of the rock from its core, where lie the furnaces and anvils of the smith. Looking outwards into heavens that seem filled with perpetual dawn, the smith might catch a wispy glimpse of other, smaller plateaus, though he little cares who or what lives there. Nor does he know much about the terrain at the floor of his mountain.

Thunderhammer's domain is also called Murderers' Mountain. This is due to its peculiar nature: that being its apparent bizarre sculptures. These decorate the entire sides of the mountain walls, from rim to mist-lost base, on all approaches, as though they are the work of countless generations of sculptors and patient artisans. Innumerable thousands of forms, piled one on top of the other in struggling disarray, appear to clamber ever upward in frozen postures of agonized determination. For the most part they are men and women, though other anthropomorphic shapes may be found if one looks closely.

These seemingly petrified beings are *not* cut from the stone, however. Nor are they in fact absolutely motionless. They were once fully alive and have been set here in near-immobility by powerful gods, ensorcelled so that their infinitely slow movements are undetectable to the eyes of both men and gods alike. Each begins at the bottom, in near darkness; he claws his way upwards, feeling every push and kick, bite and scratch, every grab and nudge as he goes. He is hopeful that one day he may reach the plateau lip, crawl over and stand upon the tree-hung level where the smith works, his mobility restored. Those that do achieve this goal will perceive a confused terrain: laval rocks jut at the edges of lakes of boiling gray mud, interspersed with growths unique to this realm, their blooms red-hued and garish.

In the centre of the biggest lake stands a low hummock of solid ash, and on this there is a huge stone face: in its hideously laughing mouth may be glimpsed the shifting darkness of another dimension, riddled with scarlet stars. It is the ultimate aim of the stone men to cross the lake to this orifice, for should they plummet through it, they will be free of Thunderhammer's realm and the endless suffering they have known there, free to find a new beginning.

Each one of the frozen people has once been a murderer, and has done some foul deed for gain, for money, for spite, for jealousy, for many other reasons, all earning themselves a particularly despicable reputation.

Some have committed regicide, or have acted in the supposed name of the gods, such as the infamous Ipsol, the Skulk of Illhallows, notorious for his regular knifing of monarchs. There are many others there, such as Quaghukk or Yortannig, both crude killers, or the more sophisticated assassins such as Cyraveen the Sly and Rutep of Dermidian, said between them to have ended the lives of at least a thousand victims. Harroca Otil is there, too, he who had brought about the legendary demise of the Chameleon King and Godmaker, Iguannevin. So too is the terrible Gorlowb, slayer of babes. Their status has become one and the same. All now fight and grapple with agonizing slowness, unable to kill each other, but capable of giving and receiving advanced pain. Those below curse those above, those above clawing upwards, ever upwards to where distant hope stands and spits down upon them.

Around them swoop the various aerial terrors of the Grabberlings, who defecate upon the murderers and scrabble at them, sometimes tearing pieces from them, squawking with malice. There is worse, for sometimes Thunderhammer immerses a great steel working in one of his mudlakes and the gray filth slops over the edges of the plateau and deluges the climbers. Those at the top naturally suffer the worst in such cases. Thunderhammer for the most part ignores the climbers, occasionally looking them over to see that all is as it should be. He sings in his work, and the pinnacles above Firecrag echo back his songs, even above the thunder.

* * * *

For once there were no echoing booms of song to shake the far towers of Firecrag. Thunderhammer's tools clanked and sparked off the metal he worked for the gods, but he himself was uncharacteristically silent, lost in very deep thought. He was disturbed by something, which was in itself most rare. Nothing usually interfered with his life and work - gods did visit him with their commissions (and some of them were less than savory) but they meant no harm to him and he could not recall ever having been cheated by them as he would doubtless have been cheated had his dealings been with men.

However, lately he had been conducting something of an affair with a particularly fiery creature, namely Cellotristi, Warrior Goddess of Ironwrath. At first the smith had been a trifle suspicious about the seemingly motiveless visits to Firecrag of this shimmering queen of fire, but she had a seductive way of convincing him that it was him that she sought, not his skills as a smith. (He was, indeed, a most eligible lover.) Their relationship, though unavoidably tempestuous, had been fulfilling, but it had become slowly obvious to the smith, who was no dullard, that his lover did indeed seek a boon. Indeed, a significantly unique suit of armour which would be impervious to many of the weapons and bolts of the other gods of her pantheon. To have given her such a suit would have unquestionably have aroused the ire of the gods, for Cellotristi equally unquestionably planned to wreak havoc of some kind, this being in her turbulent and bellicose nature. Therefore, albeit reluctantly, Thunderhammer refused her the gift.

He was then treated to a real understanding of a thwarted lover's anger. At once the affair was at an end. However, there were going to be numerous repercussions, Cellotristi promised. Thunderhammer knew only too well that she did not make such withering promises lightly. Disaster would certainly befall him.

Indeed, Cellotristi returned to him on her frightful winged warsteed, the Deathmare, and screamed a terrible threat, namely that she would choose her moment to awaken fully the climbers of Firecrag, so that the entire host would overrun the plateau, destroying all before plunging through the orifice on the ash island to freedom. It would take the gods a dozen eternities to find and bind them all again. Unless, of course, Thunderhammer relented and would make the suit for the Warrior Goddess.

He refused.

She left, but Thunderhammer lived in fear of her threat, for she was extremely powerful. No doubt she had seduced other gods to give her additional powers, such as old Anneroob, who had long lusted after her. The smith needed ways to protect his charges, but so far had discovered none. He could not appeal to the gods, for this was his realm and his to tend. Its problems were his. He had been chosen to oversee Firecrag for good reason. He must be resolute. Yet he was sad to think that all Cellotristi's love had been lies. A way to thwart her would come to him.

It did, but in the most unlikely of manners.

* * * *

Elfloq peered over his shoulder for the hundredth time. Yes, that milky ovoid was still following him, trailing silky threads, like strands of tacky web. Zargovyl's mysterious weapon had a life of its own, and the familiar was only too glad not to have to carry it. It was half the size of his head, opaque and absolutely silent. He could not begin to guess at its full potential. All he had been told to do was guide it to Thunderhammer's domain, though he had not been told the way. *How do they expect me to get there without instructions!* His mind grumbled.

He turned to scout the astral ahead and blinked in amazement. The ovoid stopped as he did. Elfloq was looking at scarlet and orange skies, not the gray mist of the astral. He had made the inadvertent transition into another dimension, though this was no accident. Darquementi, servant of the Dark Gods, had seen to it that he had come to Thunderhammer's domain. The familiar could see Firecrag below him, and could smell its fires and fumes. He could hear the occasional thunderbolt as a huge hammer struck at hot steel. The smith was at work.

The Divine Asker had told Elfloq that he and his master would be sent here to do the work of the Dark Gods and not their own. Well, the familiar had thought hard about that. He was supposed to guide this silent weapon to the Voidal, but he had conceived of a better idea, though to put it into operation would necessitate terrible risks.

Down in a spiral Elfloq flew, followed by the orb, which was never more than a few feet from him. He alighted on some black rocks and squinted into the mouth of an extremely tall cave. Thunderhammer worked there, silently shaping a long sword that glowed white with heat. Elfloq watched the smith beating the weapon, filling the skies with sound. Thunderhammer's skin was livid scarlet, like his skies, veins standing out like embossed tattoos as he worked. His body was coated with a gleaming sheen of perspiration; all he wore was a breechcloth. Elfloq had been told that the smith often sang jubilantly, but he did not do so now. Instead his craggy features were made even more so by concentration and apparent anxiety.

"Greetings!" called Elfloq as the din momentarily died. It was not until he had repeated himself several times and Thunderhammer had put down the sword that the huge smith noticed Elfloq. "Greetings," piped the familiar again. "How goes the work?"

"On Pellurine's sword? It will soon be ready for its blooding. Has Pellurine sent you for that purpose? How timely. Come down, then, and I'll quench it in you. You'll give it an added magical quality, I'll warrant."

Elfloq flapped back with a grimace of disgust. "I'm not from any Pellurine! I am no one's piglet to be spitted!"

"Oh? Then why the interest in the sword?" said Thunderhammer, puzzled.

"Only out of politeness, noble smith. I merely inquire after your health, your prosperity - "

Thunderhammer's unexpected laughter shook the cavern and Elfloq felt rock loosen underfoot, so took to the air. "Noble smith? An uncommon compliment. Few trouble to call me that, though I would hope I am deserving of it. At least by the gods, for whom I have wrought well. But you - what are you? And whatever is that hovering *thing*, hovering behind you like an embarrassed infant?"

"Since you are interested in it," said Elfloq with a less than pretty grin, "I will tell you its function." He allowed the hovering orb to come into the light. "It is a weapon. A most potent weapon."

"And to whom does it belong?"

"Why, myself, of course! Can you not see how faithfully it follows me, as you have remarked? It is like a loving hound."

"Indeed, I can see that. You must be a terrible mage to command such power. No doubt you have taken the guise of so puny a creature for good reason."

"I hear mockery in your voice," sniffed Elfloq. "But you are in no position to mock weapons of power. Not when such a weapon would be a great boon to you."

Thunderhammer scowled. "Do you read minds also, great mage?"

"Perhaps."

Thunderhammer laughed again. "You have the body of a familiar, but the manners of an imp! To whom do you belong?"

Elfloq scratched an ear. Obviously it was going to be useless to continue pretending he was his own master. The smith was all brawn and muscle, but certainly not without intelligence. "To one who would help you."

"Evidently he knows of my quarrel with Cellotristi?"

"Great fires of the Bloodworld, who does not!" Elfloq laughed. "Why, the omniverse rings with the tale. Such conflicting temperaments, such volcanic characters!"

"Really? And who is my benefactor?"

"One that you know of. But tell me, what do you think of this weapon? Is it not a marvel? Its properties are staggering. It will blunt any power, halt any charge of energy, absorb any spell or blasting cantrip. Even catch a bursting star. Made, I swear by the Abyss, by Zargovyl himself, he who was once banished by the Dark Gods. Yes, the very same Zargovyl who was the arms master of the gods!"

Thunderhammer's interest widened. "Zargovyl? He gave me lessons once, long ago. A master indeed, though as I recall, a somewhat corrupt one. And he has fashioned this thing - for me?"

Elfloq nodded, but drew back, the orb with him. "Ah, but not for nothing, as you'll appreciate."

The smith smiled, amused by Elfloq's cheek. "I see. And what must I do to earn this weapon? Forge a magical suit of armour, just as I was to do for Cellotristi? Or make some destructive object to enable Zargovyl to break out from his banishment? Now that I think of it, I have heard nothing of a termination of his sentence."

"But you will. He is no longer banished. He serves faithfully once more."

"Really? Has the old fiend repented? Remarkable. So, what of the price you speak of?"

Elfloq felt himself tauten, knowing that Thunderhammer's temper, if unleashed, would be worse than any tempest. "High, high, but well worth it. Uh...you are the warden of certain *items* are you not? Deep in the arteries of Firecrag, perhaps, or buried beneath the climbing murderers, or below the gray lakes, you keep certain imprisoned souls, locked away for eternity. Is this not so? I have heard this. True? Hmm?"

Thunderhammer's brow had darkened. "For the gods, yes. It is a special task set me. I honour that task faithfully."

"Quite, quite. But for this magnificent and unique weapon, would you not consider the release of one of those souls?"

"Which one?"

"That of a certain enigmatic man - a man who wanders the omniverse with no memory, no identity. The Voidal."

A unique silence fell upon Firecrag, as though all that lived there had stopped at the sound of the dark name. Thunderhammer picked up the still glowing sword and spat upon it. It hissed spitefully. "You ask me for the soul of the Voidal?"

"For such a weapon as this - is it not a fine bargain?"

Thunderhammer's shoulders shook, though not with rage. He was laughing. "You are either a fool or greatly ignorant, little familiar! You wish me to take that weapon and give you a *better* one! It would be like you giving me a rotten length of wood in exchange for the blackest sword ever forged."

Elfloq gasped in spite of himself. "Is the Voidal such a terrible power?"

"Your ignorance is evident. You are foolish to suggest such a bargain. Forget the soul of the Voidal. Put it, and the dark man, from your head for as long as you exist. And pray that you never meet."

"Then you reject Zargovyl's weapon? Even though it would be more than a match for Cellotristi?"

"Oh, no, I'll take the weapon," Thunderhammer chuckled. "Give it to me and begone, before I cast you in steel and set you outside my door as a wind chime."

Elfloq darted well out of reach and the orb followed him. "Give it to you for naught? No, I will not do so! There is another who would own it."

Thunderhammer's laughter was as mocking as a slap across the head. He turned and gave a whistle that was like steam escaping the vent of a volcano. "To me, slaves! To me at once! Work to be done."

Immediately the cavern discharged a muttering company of fire imps. These were no bigger than Elfloq, though far skinnier, their scales crimson, their eyes like hot chips of rock from Firecrag's lava. They saw Elfloq and pointed wicked claws at him.

"Relieve him of that orb," said Thunderhammer. "And if he proves to be a nuisance, pluck off his wings!"

Delighted to have something destructive to do, the imps took to the air like hornets. Elfloq shrieked and beat his membranous wings frantically, swerving up and away, the orb still close behind, matching his speed. He had not anticipated such treatment from one of the smith's reputation.

There were few places that Elfloq could flee to - the astral would be of little use as the imps could slip on to it with equal facility. Elfloq would have to hide. He flew up above Firecrag and looked for somewhere. He saw other misty pinnacles and made for one of them without wasting further time.

It rose up like the pointed spire of a cathedral, and although its sides were sheer, many cracks had been weathered in it and the rock looked to be crumbling. Elfloq would find a bolthole and secrete himself. He flew around the rock pillar and descended into mist, for a moment losing the imp pursuit. He spotted a ledge and made for it, alighting and pressing himself close to the eroded walls, out of sight. A rush of wings testified to the passing overhead of the imps. They appeared to have missed him. He settled back into the crevice thankfully and pondered what actions to follow. Darquementi had instructed him to take the weapon to Firecrag and had said that the Voidal would be there. His only hope now was that the dark man would appear, so that he would not have to return to Thunderhammer's mountain.

A shriek above him ended his temporary pondering. The imps had found him. Before he could flee again, a bevy of them winged down to the ledge and faced him across a gap of no more than a few yards. Elfloq wriggled out of concealment, but they had hemmed him in so that he could not take to the skies again. They clashed talon on talon, giggling horribly.

"Ho, dung-worm! Come out from your hole. We'll pull out your scales and feed them to you," cackled their leader, hopping from one foot to the other in manic glee.

"Keep your distance, droppings! If I unleash the weapon, you'll all be smoke."

"Threats, eh?" laughed another. "We'll rip your wings off and see you climb down to the very bottom of this spire. Then we'll have your legs off and watch you wriggle away like a worm!"

Elfloq had no weapons and his hands were not sharply clawed, but he knew he must fight. He spat and made a grab for one of the imps. They only laughed the more, for they thrived on tormenting and giving pain. Their nails shone in the bloody sunlight like razors and their eyes bulged hotly with eagerness. Three of them made a rush for Elfloq and at once he found himself driven back, his arms cut and slashed, his batrachian face buffeted by their blows. Two imps were overhead, preventing him from astral flight.

"Rip his eyes out!" chittered one of them. They soon had the familiar on his back and their wicked claws dug into his flesh. One sat triumphantly on his chest.

"Your wings will make pretty decorations for our caves," said this one, reaching out. Elfloq knew absolute terror, for without his wings he would never leave this place. He swore and cursed, but the imps only howled with mirth at his defenselessness. He felt his membranes straining against their grip.

Abruptly there came an awful shriek. The imps leapt off Elfloq to see what had happened. One of their number stood on the brink of the precipitous drop, clutching at its throat. Its neck clicked, broken, and the body span out into space. From it flopped a bloated spider, dropping on to the ledge: the imps drew back from it. They saw that it was not a spider, but a black-gloved hand, dismembered but shockingly alive.

Elfloq got to his knees, massaging his bruises. He grinned at the hand, knowing it for the Oblivion Hand, grim burden of the Voidal. It rose up as if wielded by an invisible being and smashed its way through the wings of an imp, ripping cartilage and membrane. It turned on the others, blessed with impossible life, and punched at their heads, pulping two before the others could fly up in alarm like fowl. The attack was so ferocious, so fantastically fast, that Elfloq found himself standing alone in a matter of seconds.

"Flee, you scum!" he shouted, but they watched him from higher up.

The hand had fallen to the rock. It waited, crouched like some blood-mad predator awaiting the first flicker of movement of its prey. One rash imp flew down at it and tried to grasp it with a prehensile foot, but the hand was too fast. It caught the ankle and pulled. Muscles tore and the leg of the imp was almost wrenched clean out of its socket. The hand flung the imp far outwards and it crashed down into the rocks and was mercifully lost to sight. It was the signal the others needed to fly up and away as fast as their wings could beat.

Elfloq stared at the black hand. "Gods of the darkest places, I never thought to be relieved to see you," he told it, as though it was a living being. But as it scuttled towards him, he drew back, all the old dread returning. Behind him, in the crevice, the orb floated nearer to the ground. The hand darted past Elfloq like a rodent and snatched at the trailing filaments of the orb. Before the familiar could speak again, the hand dragged the weapon to the brink of the precipice and carried it over.

Elfloq cried out in dismay and ran to look, but the hand had not plummeted down into obscurity. Instead it was deftly climbing downwards like the arachnid it resembled, still clutching the tendrils of the weapon. Elfloq took to his wings, checking to see that the imps had indeed fled - they had - and followed the hand. He wondered as he did so if the Dark Gods were aware of his attempt to bribe Thunderhammer, instead of carrying out his instructions.

Far down into misty darkness the Oblivion Hand climbed, until in the end it was almost lost to sight. It reached the very foot of the rock tower and wound its way through a treacherous cleft into more gloom. The sides of this chasm were so sheer and shadowed that it was like entering a cave, but Elfloq had no alternative than to follow. He had to go on foot for the cleft was too narrow to allow him flight and he kept stumbling on the broken scree.

When the hand stopped in the murky twilight, the familiar saw a drunken figure reeling out of the shadows ahead. It swayed before him, an arm flung across its eyes as if it had just woken from a deep sleep or drugged trance.

"Voidal!" called Elfloq, voice redolent with relief.

The dark man squinted at him, and after long moments grunted. "Elfloq? Am I still dreaming? What is happening? We were on the Uttermoor, talking of Zargovyl - "

"That's all past. Master, we are at the very foot of Firecrag! I have brought us here. Zargovyl spoke of the way: he was as good as his word and told me," Elfloq lied. "He was glad to do so, for he was greatly pleased to see the husk of the Slaughterer, which I took to him."

The Voidal absorbed the gabbled words with difficulty. Gradually their importance registered with him and he stiffened, looking up. "Firecrag! The lair of Thunderhammer?"

"Aye, master. We are not far from its bottom."

The hand began wriggling across the dark stone to the Voidal's feet. He raised a boot reflexively as if to crush a rat, but the hand avoided his falling heel with ease. "What is this?" the dark man hissed.

"A weapon, master," explained Elfloq hurriedly. "Zargovyl insisted on giving us a weapon. Uh…yourself, that is. Your work on the Uttermoor pleased him well."

The hand released the filaments of the orb and it rose up, moving quickly in the shadows. The Voidal flung out his right arm to protect himself from its sudden lunge. At once the orb attached itself to the stump of wrist where the severed hand should have been. The Voidal gasped and beat at the orb with his free hand, but it was immovable, like a feasting parasite. It began to hum and then glow a dull scarlet, like a hideous eye.

"I have no need of this hellish thing!" the Voidal cried, drawing his sword from its ebon scabbard. He meant to split the scarlet eye and slice it from him, but Elfloq stayed him, in spite of his revulsion.

"No, master, don't destroy it! We will need its power in this place. Zargovyl rightly warned of the dangers. Only that weapon can win you what you seek here."

The Voidal glared down at the hand, reluctantly sliding his sword back into its scabbard. "Damn the gods! First I carry their repulsive hand, and now it is replaced by this vileness. What does it do? What is its function?"

"I have not seen it operate, master, but was told that it can counteract any sorcery or energy hurled at you. Should you seek to wrest from Thunderhammer the hiding place of your soul, you will stir up his ire and certainly bring an attack upon yourself, for he has already set his imps upon me. They sought to render me flightless, aye, and to blind me."

"Then this Thunderhammer is a poor host," said the Voidal, thinly smiling at the familiar's expression of outrage.

"But if he attacks you, you can deride him."

"I will find him and demand of him what I seek. But will he give up to me such a valued prize?"

Elfloq permitted himself a knowing smile. "Oh, I think he will, master."

"Why? Have you learned something?"

Elfloq picked at a tooth with a degree of feigned nonchalance. "Well, I have not been idle - "

"It would amaze me if you had been."

"Certain gossip has reached my ears. It would appear that Thunderhammer finds himself in a somewhat unenviable, even compromising, position."

"Namely?"

"He has earned the disfavour of a certain Warrior Goddess, one Cellotristi of Ironwrath. She intends to revisit Firecrag and unleash some particularly unpleasant curse upon the smith."

"Why should this involve me?"

"Well, the weapon you now bear is less aggressive than defensive. It could easily absorb any sorcery flung out by this spiteful goddess. Thunderhammer would be grateful, doubtless sympathetic to a bargain of sorts, and your soul may yet be unlocked from its clandestine vault."

The Voidal snorted. "I should have guessed that you would have mapped out a course for me to steer, however stormy. Tell me, where did you hear of this affair of Thunderhammer's?"

"Where? Why, the very astral throbs to the scandal! Thunderhammer's lustiness is well known. It is hardly unusual that he took to his bed such a vixen as Cellotristi. You should hear the tales - "

"Another time! And Zargovyl - why should he help us? Yes, I know he was glad of the destruction of the Man-Weapon, but if he showed us the path here, that was enough and his part in the bargain should have been over. I know the gods. They give nothing away freely. There is always a price. Why should this weapon be given in addition to what you bargained for?"

Elfloq managed to avoid looking into the suspicious green eyes. "Well, of course, Zargovyl was once greater than Thunderhammer, even taught him some of his skills. I expect he has a softness in his heart for the smith and would not see him destroyed by this trollop of a goddess. And Zargovyl waxes generous now that his exile has been lifted. It's quite understandable."

"The smith destroyed? Cellotristi is that powerful?"

"So it seems. But, with the weapon, Thunderhammer will assuredly triumph."

The Voidal shook his head. "Something in what you say is contrary to the ways of the gods. I'll find it out. If the smith were destroyed, either physically or merely discredited in the eyes of the gods he serves, why then, they would have to find a new smith. Who better than the old arms master, Zargovyl, whom you tell me has earned the favour of the gods again? If he stands to gain such a position as that now held by Thunderhammer, then he would not hesitate to *expedite* his downfall, not hinder it! Elfloq, there is treachery in this."

Elfloq groaned. "But...but..." he mumbled, trying to twist the argument back in his own favour. He dare not let the Voidal know that the Dark Gods had engineered their passage here, rather than him.

"Zargovyl seeks Thunderhammer's position," said the Voidal. "So this weapon means treachery. I will not use it."

"But how will you bargain with Thunderhammer?"

The Voidal was staring out into the darkness. He was silent for a long while and that silence made Elfloq shiver. "The Oblivion Hand," muttered the dark man at last. "Where is it?"

Elfloq peered about him. "It has scuttled off once more."

The Voidal glared at the weapon that pulsed vividly at his wrist. "This has replaced my right hand, the hand of the Dark Gods. Zargovyl has no power over *them*. He could not order the hand to leave me with any sorcerous command, nor will it to bring this foul weapon and *graft* it on to me. This cannot be the tool of Zargovyl. It must be that of the Dark Gods! What is their part in this?"

"Master, I swear - "

"Elfloq, you lie in your teeth whenever it suits you! You *say* you serve me, but you serve yourself first." The Voidal looked hard at the familiar then, as if trying to rend any barriers of deceit that might be there. "Or does your first allegiance belong to the Dark Gods? Do you deceive me in their name?" There was a terrible, though suppressed, fury behind the Voidal's words and in his eyes a power that could not be met.

Elfloq cringed back. He had known no terror to equal that of the Voidal's hate.

The Voidal abruptly softened his angry tone. "Tell me, Elfloq," he said softly, "do you betray me? Are you part of this curse that dogs me?"

"No! Never. I chose you freely. That was never the will of the Dark Gods. Of course, they know of my service to you, but why have they not smitten me because of it?"

"Am I to believe you?"

"I serve you first, though they blast me to ash for having said it."

The Voidal was surprised by this. It was not like Elfloq to compromise himself with the gods and seemed to be more than careless bravado. "Perhaps they use you, as they use me. You have won certain things for me, but usually through pain."

"I mean only for you to prosper, master."

The Voidal gave a resigned sigh. "Very well. But do not seek to deceive me in this business. I ask you again, why am I here? Does Zargovyl direct my moves, or is this another of the wretched tasks set me by the Dark Gods? Tell me all you know, honestly, and I will not damn you for it. If you do seek to serve me above *all* others, be honest with me, no matter how dire your tidings."

Elfloq tried to swallow the lump of unease in his throat, coughed, then nodded. The die was cast. His bluff was called, and he knew it. Quickly, so that he had to be slowed down more than once, he told the dark man the truth of the matter, that Darquementi had masterminded the entire visit to Firecrag. Elfloq expected to be chastised when he had finished, but the Voidal was lost in thought.

"So this weapon is to *aid* Thunderhammer," he mused. "And it is Cellotristi who is to be brought down. How powerful is she? What do you know of her?"

"A truly ambitious goddess," said Elfloq. "One who seeks far more power than she has and that which she has is already colossal, I am told. She once fought the Toad God, Batrogga, drained him and made of him an imbecile. Darquementi told me that you and I were not guaranteed success against her."

"Is that so? She is that powerful? Then they must fear her. And if I were to side with her, it would certainly mean the overthrow of Thunderhammer!"

"Indeed!" Elfloq enthused, not anxious to miss an opportunity to repay the smith for unleashing his fire imps.

"Thunderhammer would know this, I think. Then I have something to bargain with him. Should he return my soul to me, I'll aid him. Otherwise I will let Cellotristi ruin him. *Drain* him, eh? What do you say to that, Elfloq? Are you with me, or does the idea frighten you? It should do. The Dark Gods will curse us both more loudly if I thwart their intentions. Whatever they may be, for I am not sure. They are ever devious. Which of these two bickering lovers do they truly support? At any rate, it seems I am given a choice, an unprecedented thing. A choice! There is something a little pleasing in that." But his mind remained unsettled, for he knew this might yet be a testing. The Dark Gods could simply be trying his obedience, to see if he would still defy them.

Elfloq was shaking his head. "I am with you, master, I promise you. Already I have tried to bargain for you." But he clammed up, deciding on discretion.

"Oh, and is there some further fragment of this tale still unknown to me? Speak up, little familiar. No secrets. Bargained already? How? With whom?"

Reluctantly Elfloq spoke of his abortive attempt to bribe Thunderhammer and win the secret of the Voidal's soul from him.

The Voidal laughed. "Is this true?"

"It is why he set those infernal imps on me - "

"Then you do serve me, having thus gone against Darquementi's instructions. Your next meeting with him will be a prickly one."

Elfloq squirmed. "If we do meet."

"Who knows? But I am pleased at your efforts, even if you hid them from me. Doubtless you thought it would spare me further pain, eh? Aye, well we may not be in so bad a position. It seems to me that the Dark

Gods are gambling. As you say, we are not guaranteed success. So they must fear this Cellotristi, unless they are deceiving us both.

"Perhaps, in the interests of safety," said Elfloq, "we should assume that they are."

The Voidal grinned. "Quite so. Come, let us begin by scaling Firecrag. I will offer Thunderhammer his salvation. And for once, *I* will do the bartering."

And for once, it suited Elfloq.

* * * *

As Elfloq could still not take to the air, they found it difficult to pick their way through the narrow ravines in the cloying mist, stumbling and cursing in the almost dark. They wound their way through a zigzag of intersecting rifts, some hardly wide enough to let them pass, but Elfloq insisted he knew the general direction in which Firecrag's base lay. Eventually they came out into a much wider canyon and though the mist swirled around it like a dust storm, they heard a thousand murmuring voices, very low, as if a vast conclave had gathered and was plotting some unwholesome deed.

"What are they saying?" the Voidal asked.

"The words are indistinct," said Elfloq. "But it will be the murderers. Their black thoughts and blacker curses echo round the mountain."

The dark man strode through the mist and, moving to his left, found himself looking down over another enormous precipice that seemed to drop into a mythical, invisible hell. "I see forms in the rock, Elfloq. It seems that we stand upon the top of Firecrag, not at its base."

But Elfloq called to him and he crossed broken rock to a rising cliff face. "That is a secondary tier downward," explained Elfloq. "The way to the plateau is up here." In front of him, as if emerging from the living rock of the earth, were the first visible men in stone, heads gazing upwards motionlessly, other men on their shoulders, and so on, up into the drizzling mist. All around this first base of the mountain went this unique sculpture and it was from this that the murmurs and groans were drifting.

The Voidal looked appalled. "How many other layers are there down below us? Firecrag has the dimensions of a world! Still, we must climb it."

Elfloq nodded agreement, himself now taking to the damp air. The dark man began the ascent. He felt eyes upon him and heard muffled cries as though from a great distance. Up the enormous mound of near-petrified humanity he began to clamber.

Someone has torn free! whispered a voice, sharp as winter wind.

What is the secret?

Tell us!

How, how!

Help us! Wailed other voices in his ears, tearing at him as he ascended the often precariously steep climb. Presently there were hundreds of voices whispering at him, demanding to know how they, too, might escape their stone prison. The Voidal closed his mind to the babble, concentrating on hauling himself up over backs, feet gaining purchase on shoulders.

At last he came above the mist into orange light. Elfloq was nearby, hovering over the huge drop. "You are making excellent progress, master," he called.

"I'd fare better if my ears were deaf to their cries. Do you hear them?"

"I do. They are souls in a frozen hell."

The Voidal rested, looking outwards. Beneath him, all was again obscured in mist. He knew that the climb went on for an unguessable distance yet. It was difficult without both hands, but he knew Zargovyl's weird weapon would be immovable.

Elfloq was gazing down into the mist, which itself seemed to vibrate with pain.

"What is it?" the dark man asked him.

"We are followed," said the familiar, but would add no more.

The Voidal began his climb anew. After he had gone a short distance, he heard a shrill cry in the sky, and looking up thought the imps had come to attack Elfloq again, but it was the Grabberlings. They were clawing and snapping at the transfixed murderers, their talons raking the stone, chipping at it frantically. Elfloq flew up to chase them off, for they were small, and they swooped away from him. One dived for the Voidal, though, and instinctively he raised his arm to fend it off. Its hooked claws closed on the orb, but as they did so, the Grabberling burst in a shower of feathers and gore. The others screamed with one voice and flew rapidly away, keeping their distance.

After that there were no more hazards, just the interminable climb. The whispering voices of the murderers remained a fixed sound, grown now into an ocean of misery, for word of the Voidal had spread around the entire mountain. They cried for release, offering fantastic treasures as reward, but the Voidal moved on upward, shutting out their despair.

How long he toiled up he could not guess, the daylight in these reaches seemingly permanent, the only night that of the deep trenches far below. Finally he reached the plateau and climbed over the last of the stone men, who himself seemed to be striving the last inches to freedom from immobility and a dash to the lake. Elfloq dropped from the sky, alighting beside the Voidal.

"Will you rest before confronting the smith?" he asked.

"No, I must act quickly. I have my doubts about everything that happens here. I have said I will threaten Thunderhammer with betrayal, but I am still not certain what the Dark Gods wish. I suspect their every breath."

They stood for a while, watching through the swaying plants the gray mud of the lakes as they bubbled far out over the plateau. They could hear the ring and clang of Thunderhammer's tools in the distance and from time to time a peal of his thunderous efforts rocked them. Something rushed by them: a man freed from the stone. He threw himself into the lake, screaming at its sizzling embrace, but he swam furiously for the far-off ash island and the promised gate to elsewhere.

"I feel their bitterness, their resentment," said the Voidal. "It scorches as that lake scorches the swimmer. To harness such a force and to unleash it, would be a frightening act."

Elfloq made to reply, but gave a sudden yowl, lurching forward. The Voidal swung round to meet an attack from behind, sword drawn, but he saw no one. Elfloq was clawing frantically at his back, as if overrun with ants.

"Master!" he shrieked, almost hysterically. "Something digs into me! Some vermin! Free me, free me!"

The Voidal twisted him round and was about to spit this assailant with the sword, but his face clouded as he saw what it was. "By the Abyss, it is the hand! Elfloq, *it is the Oblivion Hand!*"

Elfloq's huge eyes bulged in horror. "The…hand? Gods and devils, is this to be my doom? Is this Darquementi's revenge? I am to be pulped by this abomination?" he howled, still trying desperately to reach it, but his folded wings were in the way. The hand, however, did not appear to be bent on dismembering him, for it had become motionless, like a great tic that had settled comfortably on its host.

The Voidal touched it with the tip of the sword, but there was no reaction. "I do not understand," he said. "The hand has affixed itself to your back, though it is dormant."

"It will suck me dry - "

"You *feel* it doing this?"

"No, but it will, I know it will! It can only mean to harm me. Get it off! Get it off!"

"Perhaps not. Perhaps it is your lot to carry it until I have finished with Zargovyl's toy. I suspect this is an example of the Dark Gods' humour, for who would know better than them how much this a burden would grieve you?" The Voidal laughed softly. "Well, then, Elfloq. You have cast your lot with me, and doubtless they heard you. Now you truly share my burden. Is it not heavy?"

Elfloq moved stiffly, wooden-legged, his face puckered with loathing. "May the dark Gods be - "

"Soft, soft! Would you anger them now, with *that* on your back? Unwise."

Grumpily, like a thwarted infant, Elfloq followed his master across the smashed rocks of the plateau, seeking Thunderhammer. The curious blooms of the tree plants swung in unsettling unison, like crimson eyes that watched them, imbued with a suggested hunger.

A short while later they saw the smith not far ahead of them. He was kneeling beside a boiling pool, tempering yet another blazing weapon. But as they walked towards him they heard a piercing whistling from the skies. Looking up, they saw a fantastic figure astride a jet-black war-horse, the front legs of which swept out sideways and were thickly webbed so that they formed two great, bat-like wings. The back legs of the beast were shod with knives, and its face was encased in an ovoid mask that spat fire. This was the Deathmare, charger of the Warrior Goddess, Cellotristi. She sat haughtily upon its back, also in jet-black armour, and in her arms she carried a frightful triple-mouthed weapon that could vomit destruction threefold. Her face was angular steel, only her flowing mane of metal-blue hair streaming free of it. She laughed madly and her weapon spat out a gobbet of fire that burst over the plateau, an incandescent meteor.

"Thunderhammer!" she roared, and Elfloq was reminded of a hurricane stripping soil from the earth. "I have come back to you! I have come back to fulfil my promise." She laughed again, as the terrible Deathmare flew over the Voidal and Elfloq, neither of whom she had noticed, and the beast blew out a withering stream of vapour. The rocks that it touched cracked, as if gripped by the harshest of frosts.

Thunderhammer shook the newly formed weapon at her. "I'll not allow you to despoil my domain," he told her angrily. "Every stone that you break will exact a retribution."

Cellotristi flew directly above him. "I could eradicate you in the beat of a heart, my dear. But I have all eternity to torment you. Come, will you not give me what I desire?" Her rasping voice was like a fire, and Elfloq dropped to the ground, afraid of being scorched out of existence.

Thunderhammer roared his defiance anew. "I'll not place more destruction in your hands."

"Then feel my fury!" shrieked the Warrior Goddess. A bolt of fire leapt down at Thunderhammer and his weapon exploded into nothing. His hair was set ablaze, but he beat the flames out with a scooped fist of gray mud. Cellotristi turned her Deathmare and they tore across the skies like a comet, bent on unleashing havoc.

"Stars," gasped Elfloq. "These two were *lovers*?"

Quickly the Voidal pulled him to his feet and made a run for the infuriated smith. The latter did not realise they were there until they were before him. His eyes ignored Elfloq, but glared in hot recognition at the dark man.

"Have *you* come to aid that vixen?" he growled.

"Perhaps," said the Voidal coolly. "You have something of mine. Give it to me and I will thwart every trick she plays. Deny me and I will aid her. Your domain will go down to destruction. You will cease to exist."

Thunderhammer cursed roundly. "You expect me to grovel to you, Voidal? You want me to lick your hand like a dog and beg for salvation from you? I would rather embrace extinction. Stand aside, accursed one. I will not be mocked." Thunderhammer drew from the rocks near him a massive hammer, the head of which sparkled and gleamed like an incalculably precious gem. "I go to war." He strode past the Voidal and the cowering Elfloq.

"A proud and stubborn god," said the Voidal. "No doubt it is why he was chosen. We must follow him. He has no conception what the good lady of Ironwrath will unleash." He and the reluctant familiar followed the smith. They took up a position near to the edge of the plateau, raised on an outcropping of rock. "Keep away from the trees," said the Voidal. "They offer shelter, but you may not have noticed that they are carnivorous."

Elfloq flinched, but then wondered if he could tempt a blossom with the ghastly thing that he was carrying on his back.

Cellotristi, meanwhile, was winging her way around the skies above Firecrag, looking down balefully at the frozen host of murderers. Thunderhammer stood near the brink of the plateau, hammer poised. "Do your worst!" he shouted.

She laughed and aimed her triple-mouthed weapon downwards. Livid bolts of purple, green and scarlet fire roared from the mouths and splashed hotly against the squashed ranks of stone men. At once those daubed with the energy came to life. Scores of them awoke and laughed exultantly, howling their freedom to the skies. A host of a hundred or more quickly scrambled over the plateau lip and made for the lake.

Thunderhammer stood before them, determined not to let them pass.

Cellotristi watched, amused by the catastrophic results of her first brief attack. The smith swung his hammer and lightning bolts crackled from it, a living storm. A wave of the murderers was smashed back. They toppled over the lip as more came on. Over and over again the smith beat at the charging masses, but a few squeezed past him, then a dozen, then a score. They leapt into the lake, screaming in pain but determined to reach the mouth that was the gate. Both fire imps and Grabberlings attacked them from the sky and the noise of the fighting was terrible. Thunderhammer's blurring weapon sent thunder booming out over the pinnacles of his domain, its wild power an electric storm.

"How will you fare when a hundred thousand face you?" shouted the goddess. "They will forget the lake for a moment, long enough to tear your plateau stone from stone!"

Thunderhammer was too busy to reply. Countless dozens of the stone men were attacking and many of them were pulped by the awful hammer. Yet more escaped and swam the lake. Some tore their aerial attackers from the skies. Soon the first of the murderers had reached the gaping gate in spite of the barriers and leapt joyously through it. Thunderhammer aimed his weapon at the heavens and in a moment great storm clouds bent close to the rocks, unleashing fresh bolts of anger. The sound ands fury of the battle made the entire mountain peak shake.

The Voidal left the cover of the rocks and fought his way to the smith's side. A few of the stone men struck out at him, but Zargovyl's weapon rode the blows as if they were eddies of air. "Smith!" the dark man shouted over the din. "You are doomed! Already murder has been unleashed on the omniverse. Will you allow even more to be set free?"

Thunderhammer snarled a reply that was lost in a great roll of noise. Cellotristi screamed with joy and began firing successive bolts at the mountain. Thousands upon thousands of the murderers were revitalized by the hotly flowing energy. Thunderhammer could only gasp at the magnitude of the task set him. Soon the entire host of murderers, numbering millions, would be freed. His hammer could not be everywhere. In the raging sky, Cellotristi mocked the arrows of jagged lightning that forked for her, her black armour unharmed by their power.

The Voidal was beside the smith. He raised his arm-weapon and as Cellotristi flew overhead, taunted her. She spat fire at him, but the weapon easily absorbed the energy, pulsing with vivid life. Puzzled, Cellotristi passed again and aimed her own weapon down at the Voidal. The triple-blast showered him, but he was unharmed: Zargovyl's weapon sucked at the energy as though absorbing it and directing it into some other universe.

The Warrior Goddess wheeled away to puzzle over this phenomenon. The Voidal turned to Thunderhammer. "Well, smith? I can baffle her powers. And I can re-use it - thus." He turned upon the escaping murderers and directed his weapon at them. Spears of light crackled outwards and each man that was touched became stone once more. A wave of escapers was stopped in mid-stride, immobilized.

Thunderhammer gasped. "Your weapon can counter *all* this havoc?"

So it seems, the Voidal thought, only now understanding its real purpose. "Indeed. But it is yours to command if you give me what I ask."

Thunderhammer's face contorted with inner anguish. "Be reasonable! I cannot give you your soul! That would be worse than permitting Cellotristi what she wants."

"She will *take* what she wants," said the Voidal. But the smith's words disturbed him, for the god was dreadfully afraid of giving the dark man what he wanted. "Then what will you give me? What can you tell me? I must have something of value to myself."

Thunderhammer's attention was still focussed on the fleeing murderers and he yet used his hammer with hellish efficiency. He shook his head. "Only this. Your soul is no longer in this domain. I forged its prison, that much is true. But that prison is not here."

"Then where? *Where?* Give me some clue, or I will accelerate the annihilation of Firecrag. I'll drag up every last murderer from the lowest levels of your mountain and unleash them all upon the omniverse. I will be cursed by all the gods, but I will be no worse than I am now. So, speak!" The Voidal's voice his risen so that his words ended almost in a scream.

The smith lowered his hammer and ceased his labours. He stared at the Voidal, his voice dropping, his eyes smoky with suppressed frustration. "They did well to curse you."

"Tell me!"

"Very well. I hope that the gods can see that I am torn between inflicting the omniverse with one curse or another. You ask for your soul. Then look to the Swords. There are Thirteen. Gather them up, if you can. The Sword of Shadows houses them all. It is the key you seek." Thunderhammer sighed, watching the Deathmare circling as the enraged Cellotristi prepared to unleash yet more power.

The Voidal nodded. It was enough for him. A little knowledge. He went to the very lip of the plateau, spraying light at the stone men, petrifying them in the blink of an eye. Many fell backwards into infinity, shattering on the others below. Cellotristi fired and re-fired her weapon, as if endless stars of power were being born from the muzzles, but the Voidal caught each blaze with his own weapon and turned it back upon the murderers, reversing the charges, checking the flow of humanity. As each man was turned back to stone, he froze in a skyward-looking posture, hands pointing up accusingly at the Warrior Goddess.

She rose up over the Voidal and the hind legs of the Deathmare came down to crush him. But Zargovyl's weapon beat at them and the great beast bucked in agony as its power was turned back on itself. Cellotristi forced it to dive again, this time drawing from her belt a chain of blazing discs. She swung this at the head of the Voidal, but he brought up the weapon and the chain blasted into pieces so that Cellotristi almost toppled from the Deathmare. Still she rallied, firing the three-mouthed weapon not at the Voidal, but at the rocks below and around him. Part of that triple force smashed the rock like an earthquake, and too late the Voidal realised that he had been out-thought. The land crumbled like sand, sliding over the precipice. He tried to grip something solid, but all was collapsing as a whole shelf, complete with a hundred frozen murderers and the smashed pieces of as many more went spinning out into space. Cellotristi shrieked in victory and set to blasting at other parts of the plateau.

Staggered by the Voidal's fall, Thunderhammer tried to rebuild his storms, but their power was frail against the dazzling bolts of the goddess. Elfloq, meanwhile, had long since taken to the skies. He had a mind to rush on to the astral and rejoin his master later, once this whole dreadful affair had resolved itself. But in spite of the flickering storm, he waited. No one had noticed him, for he was high over the battle. And who would notice such a pitiful creature? He asked himself. However, he felt the stirring of the thing upon his back and again tried to shake it loose. Since it had been there, he had been in a sweat of terror, certain that it would close around him and squeeze him until he ran like juice through its fingers. Now it seemed to be goading him, almost like a rider, urging him to take up a particular aerial position.

After a token struggle, he realised what the hand was doing. It sought to manipulate him into a place above Cellotristi. Directly above her. But it was not easy for him to fly at such a speed, for the Deathmare swooped and dipped outrageously, whirling and rearing. Mercifully after a while Cellotristi temporarily ceased her destruction so that she could watch Thunderhammer helplessly trying to stem the flow of thousands released from the stone. Elfloq could see them coming like ants from the depths, endless as stars. Many of them were pouring through the mouth gate on the ash island, while others had set upon Thunderhammer's imps and were tearing them limb from limb, while yet more wreaked destruction on the smith's forges.

The black hand jabbed at Elfloq, who shrieked in alarm, but got himself directly above Cellotristi. If she saw him, she would blast him to atoms: the hand would survive. But he had no more need to worry about the hand, for now he felt it slip from his back and leave him. He watched as it tumbled through the storm like a glove tossed by the wind. But it dropped into the very lap of the Warrior Goddess. Immediately it snatched at the triple-mouthed weapon and bent it back on itself so that there came a detonating explosion. Out of the resultant clouds of smoke flew the Deathmare, riderless, and with its wings shredded like rotting sails. It could no longer fly properly and drifted ever downwards, seeking to avoid the hot gray lakes, but sucked at last into their deep embrace. Elfloq, tossed even higher by the blast, saw the Deathmare subside.

Cellotristi had been catapulted outwards, and her body fell, crashing down violently on the bare stone of the plateau, no more than yards from where Thunderhammer still swung his hammer. He saw the fallen goddess, who groaned but could not move, every bone in her body jellied by the impact. But the smith had no time to spare for her, for there was still so much to do.

For another hour Thunderhammer fought back the murderers. In the end, no more came, though the gods alone knew how many had escaped from this realm. Now the smith walked over to the still writhing goddess and stood over her. Thick blood seeped from a score of tears in her shattered armour, and her dulled eyes looked up at him. A brief flash ignited them, a reflection of the serene orange skies that had replaced the chaos of the storm.

"You brought this upon yourself," he told her sadly.

"Do I read pity in your stare?" she whispered. "Pity, where there should be only hate."

"I could never hate you, though you have given me cause."

"Then spare me this slow death. Or do you obey your masters implicitly in everything? Surely they will have me suffer eternally for my ambition. As I would have had you suffer."

Thunderhammer thought of the Voidal and the knowledge that he had reluctantly given to the dark man. "No. I am capable of making some decisions for myself. And I have no wish to see you suffer."

"Then finish what that foul hand began! Do what that treacherous black hellion could not do. End me!"

"Hand?"

"Yes," she gasped. "I thought to wipe out even his power, or that of his interfering masters. But I had forgotten the Oblivion Hand. You sank low, when you enlisted the aid of the Voidal."

"I was not given a choice - "

"Well, it is done. Use your hammer once more."

He shook his head. "I cannot."

"Then you must live with my pain forever. I cannot move from here. Do not touch me! The Dark Gods have transfixed me. While I live, here I must lie. You may enjoy my screams."

"This cannot be!"

"Then use your hammer. It is their way of punishing you for allowing this chaos. You told me that every stone would exact its retribution. It will. And no one avoids retribution."

He nodded with a deepening sadness. "But there must be a way to mend you - "

"No," she said faintly. "Else I would begin again. I die, or remain here in agony. Slay me! I want none of your pity."

"Pity? No, it is not pity that moves me."

"What then? Love? Your emotions are wasted. Slay me, for I never loved you, smith. I have betrayed you from the first. So you may use your hammer on me without remorse."

He bent to her. "It withers me to kill you, Cellotristi. But I cannot live with your pain. I will do it, but only if you give me the truth. Have you mocked my love simply to anger me, to fuel the killing blow? Or did you once love me?"

Her eyes flickered, her gaze not able to meet his. "You will strike?"

"Aye."

She emitted a deep sigh, as if exhaling her last breath. "Then the truth is this. I loved you and love you yet."

Sorrow closed around him like a fist. He closed his eyes and stood up. He lifted the hammer. "When next we meet," he said softly, "ask not too much of me and I will give to you the omniverse."

He brought down the hammer for the last time.

* * * *

Elfloq, tossed out into the distance by the blast of the explosion, righted himself and began the flight back to the plateau. Buoyed by the loss of the execrable hand, his first concern now was for the well being of the Voidal, whom he had last seen plummeting over the cliffs. He must find him.

The murderers were stone once more. The last of them had escaped that could, leaving bare places in the walls of Firecrag where naked rock showed through. Elfloq began his search, but it seemed that the Voidal must have fallen to the very base of the great cliff amongst the avalanche of broken humanity. Elfloq knew that this would not have killed the dark man, but his concern was nevertheless deep.

Near the bottom of Murderers' Mountain, where the mist was thickest, Elfloq saw movement. Looking closer, he saw that it was the Oblivion

Hand, scuttling down into darkness. He drew back in renewed revulsion. He could still feel its clammy embrace and would do so for a long time to come. In his mind he could hear the amusement of Darquementi.

Through the shifting vapours he was able to discern the sprawled body of the dark man, lying with arms outstretched, unconscious. The hand flopped down beside him and the mist rolled forward like a thick shroud over both of them.

"Master!" cried Elfloq. "The goddess has fallen! We have - " But as the familiar flitted to the floor of the ravine, he found himself talking to air and the shattered stone bodies.

A breeze curled from around the stones, seeming to whisper something to him. He cocked his ears like a hound, straining to hear the half-formed words that the air breathed.

"... Swords, Elfloq. Must find...Swords... Shadows. Sword of Shadows...key."

"Master!" he called again, but the air had gone still.

He began a search, but after a short period of squinting into the mist, he knew with a surety that the Voidal had gone. His purpose here was over

Elfloq muttered to himself. Swords? Made by the smith? He must yet hold the key to the Voidal's soul. Dare he go back and ask for it? What bargains had the Voidal made? What of the hateful imps? Many of them had died, but if there were any left. And then there were the Grabberlings. *No, no*, he mused, *I've done my part here. I've tempted the gods enough. And I'm lucky to be whole.*

Something shimmered in the mist. He came to it and grimaced. It was the smashed, oozing remains of Zargovyl's weapon. Elfloq shook his head at it. It had served its purpose. It had *drained* the power of Cellotristi and in negating it, had cancelled out its own powers. No sense in returning it to its creator. With no more thoughts on the matter, he slipped on to the astral and stretched his wings, relieved to be away from Thunderhammer's domain. For a while he would wander aimlessly, free of the crawling memories of this place. Later he would seek his dark master anew. The search for all that had been purloined was, he felt sure, narrowing.

The Sword of Shadows. His master's whispered words repeated themselves, exasperating but seductive.

PART FIVE

FAMILIAR TERRITORY

There are those who claim that the most powerful of all emotions is love, as it transcends all barriers, even death itself. I can believe this, for love brings with it a kind of madness that tends to sweep aside everything in its path. This is not always true, as the fiery affair of Thunderhammer and the Warrior Goddess of Ironwrath has testified.

The Gods, of course, would consider themselves beyond such emotions, but they only deceive themselves in this. And occasionally they let their veil of indifference slip and we may catch a glimpse, a hint, of their own humanity.

—**SALECCO**, who remembers such things with infinite sadness.

* * * *

Eye Patch of the Smile wiped spilled beer from the wide counter and watched the unfamiliar figure shambling towards him from one of Cloudway's many doors. The stranger wore an excessively voluminous cloak that failed to hide the fact that he was not very tall; his bearded features poked out from the hood. To say that the visitor wore an apprehensive look would have been a gross understatement. He positively dripped unease. Wary of the light, which was typically dimmed, for this was the deliberate nature of the inn at Cloudway, he came to the bar.

"I am to meet someone here," he said in a deep, hoarse growl.

Eye Patch poured a glass of beer and set it before the stranger. "It is why all my customers come to Cloudway," he smiled. His one eye twinkled knowingly, the other covered with a scarlet patch. How he had come by this, no one knew, though speculation was lively and exorbitantly imaginative.

"I am..." but the stranger paused, glancing around the hall. There were figures here, but they graced its shadowed alcoves, not the tables in the open areas. Apart from muted conversations, hardly a whisper could be heard under those tall beams.

"You are Ipsol," said Eye Patch of the Smile, leaning forward so that only his guest could hear him. "Formerly known as the Skulk of Illhallows."

The hooded one ducked down, sipping his beer. "Hsst! I was imprisoned for the crimes I committed under that title. I have but lately finished serving my sentence."

"On Murderers' Mountain," breathed Eye Patch of the Smile. "I think you mean, you escaped? No matter, I am the embodiment of discretion."

"Then you know who I am to meet?"

"Would I be correct in thinking that you bear with you, under that exceptional cloak, a certain weapon? A sword of a peculiar nature?"

Ipsol nodded, the hood almost flopping back from his face, which looked as though it had been carved from wood. Wood of a very hard and knotted nature.

"No need for me to know what it is," the host chuckled. "I was told that someone would meet you here. With instructions."

"I am to deliver the sword...the weapon...somewhere. And I will be glad to be rid of it. I would sooner carry a plague!"

"Of course. But don't think too badly of it. Its passage has earned you your freedom. Or would you rather go back to Firecrag? I gather that most of the runaways have been either returned or, well, let us not dwell on unnecessary unpleasantness. Tell me, would you like to eat? We pride ourselves on our fare."

Ipsol nodded, as if he had suddenly remembered hunger.

Eye Patch of the Smile indicated a table away in the shadows. "I'll bring food and some more beer."

Ipsol took his mug and shuffled across the wide room to the alcove, blending with its darkness, silent as a ghost.

After Eye Patch had arranged for Ipsol's food to be set before him, he returned to the bar and pulled a battered manuscript from under the counter, setting it down under one of the few pools of candlelight. Idly he scanned its poetry, whistling softly to himself. Some time later, a movement beyond the top of the bar caused him to raise his eyes. A diminutive figure was returning his gaze.

"Don't tell me," said the host, his famed grin widening. "You happened to be passing."

"Indeed," replied Elfloq, sitting on a tall stool, attempting to seem as relaxed and blasé as he could. "The thought of your excellent ale tempted me in."

"Ah, just as you say, Elfloq." The innkeeper slowly poured a small tankard of his foaming brew, which Elfloq accepted cautiously.

"Just passing."

"Not intending to summon your dark master, eh?" said Eye Patch jovially.

"Not this time," replied Elfloq uneasily, looking about him in a manner not dissimilar to that of Ipsol before him. He peered at the shadowed figures around the hall, but could make out no details. Probably just as well, he told himself. You never knew what monsters you would meet in Cloudway.

"Are you on a particular errand? I mean, outside of your calling in for a casual drink?" The irony in the host's voice was not lost on Elfloq.

He leaned forward. "To tell you the truth - "

"Careful! Truths are complicated things."

"I *am* on a quest."

"Ah, I had suspected as much. Perhaps you and I can exchange information. It is the coin I like best." Eye Patch nodded at the ale, which would not, of course, be on the house.

"Certainly. I am seeking some… swords." Again Elfloq looked around, but there was nothing to suggest that any of the secluded visitors were straining to catch his words.

"Swords," breathed Eye Patch. "No doubt their nature is specific?"

"It is. They are the Thirteen Swords."

Eye Patch began to chuckle, but put a hand over his mouth. "Forgive me, little familiar. *The* Thirteen? I know of only one set of Thirteen. Each weapon is in the custody of a Seneschal - "

Elfloq's batrachian eyes bulged. "You know their whereabouts?"

" - of the Dark Gods. Who would, I venture to suggest, be unlikely to render them up to you. Your master is, I further hazard, the last creature in the omniverse whom they would release them to."

"I can well believe that," muttered Elfloq. He frowned deeply. "So they are well protected?"

Eye Patch leaned even further across the counter, his scarlet patch a few inches from Elfloq's uncomfortable stare. "Well, *there's* a coincidence!" Eye Patch breathed. "But then again, that's Cloudway for you. We thrive on such things."

"What do you mean?" whispered the familiar, his heartbeat doubling its rate.

"You seek the Swords. And, lo, one of them is *here*, at this very moment!"

Elfloq gasped, almost toppling from the stool. "*Here?*"

Eye Patch tapped the bridge of his nose to indicate discretion. "Yes. Its bearer has come to meet a messenger from its masters."

Elfloq tried to turn and scan the guests discreetly.

"Over there," said Eye Patch, with a nod of the head in the direction of Ipsol.

Elfloq saw the figure in the shadows and for a moment deliberated with himself how to approach it. But the lure of the hunt was too strong. "My thanks," he said to Eye Patch, who waved airily.

As the familiar sauntered across the inn, it did not cross his mind that he had not paid for his ale, though his host did not seem to have noticed. When he reached the alcove where Ipsol had drawn himself into the shadows, he bowed.

"Your pardon," he said to the darkness. "Our host told me that we may have information of mutual interest."

Ipsol's hooded face loomed into the thin light. "Who are you?"

"I am Elfloq. I serve a dark master whose powers are too dreadful to describe."

"I think I have seen you before." The voice was a growl of intimidation.

Elfloq felt a shiver of apprehension. The face before him was too obscured to study properly. "Your name escapes me - "

"I am Ipsol, the Skulk of Illhallows. Are you the one sent to meet me?"

Elfloq felt his blood curdling in his veins. *This is one of the escaped murderers from Firecrag! Of all the unholy coincidences, to meet him so soon after that debacle! But, I should have expected no less! This is Cloudway, where nothing falls to chance.*

"I may be," Elfloq said softly.

"Don't you know?"

"I am discreet. There are certain questions."

"I am direct," snorted Ipsol. He drew from his cloak a long, broad scabbard and set it down on the bare table. From the scabbard, which was itself more ebon than the darkness, a haft of exquisite workmanship protruded, its silver gleaming with what appeared to be its own light.

Elfloq stared at it in a mixture of dread and fascination. This was undoubtedly one of the Thirteen Swords.

"So where am I to take it?" grunted Ipsol. "Tell me so that I can be rid of the accursed thing and away to my freedom."

Elfloq sat down slowly, trying to gather his wits. "Burden yourself no longer, worthy Ipsol. You are free to go."

"What do you mean?"

"I am here to relieve you."

Ipsol drew back slowly. "You? A familiar? I am to hand this weapon to you?"

Elfloq tried to laugh. "The gods are clever, and surpassingly cunning. This is, as you will have guessed, no simple blade. Its passage through the omniverse has to be clandestine. Thus, what better way to transmit it than by the simplest of means, the humblest of bearers?"

Ipsol, to Elfloq's huge relief, was nodding. "I see." He leaned back, taking from his cloak a second weapon. This was a long knife, the tool of his former ghastly trade, when monarchs had died at its touch; he jabbed it into the tabletop. It quivered, drawing Elfloq's eye like a serpent.

"You," said Ipsol, "are indeed a familiar. And I *have* seen you before. In the skies, above Firecrag. When I was freed, along with all the others, it was *your* master who helped Thunderhammer to rebuild the prison!"

"You are mistaken! This must be some other creature - "

Ipsol's knife had transferred to his hand as if by magic. Its point was no more than an inch from Elfloq's wide nose. "I think not. The truth, familiar, or feel the cold, cold bite of my revenge."

Elfloq was nodding his head frantically. "Yes, yes, it is so. I was forced to follow you! I had no choice!"

Ipsol gripped Elfloq's wrist, pinched a flap of skin and jabbed the knife through it, pinning the arm to the tabletop. Elfloq hissed at the pain, but could not move. Ipsol sat back in the shadows. "You thought to steal the sword from me," he said evenly.

"Yes," Elfloq gasped, staring in disbelief at the knife that held him fast, the blood that oozed thickly on to the tabletop. "For my master. What else could I do?"

"Just doing your job," Ipsol muttered.

"Where is the sword bound for?"

"That interests you?"

Elfloq nodded, tears squeezing from his eyes. Gods, but the blade of the knife *hurt*!

"I don't know," said Ipsol diffidently. "It does not matter to me. But since it is so important to you, and since I feel I owe you something for your pains - "

"Owe me? No, no, surely not."

Ipsol gripped the haft of the sword. "Oh, but I do. Your master tried to turn me back to stone on Firecrag. Tell me, have you any idea which sword this is?"

"One of the Thirteen," gulped Elfloq as Ipsol began to draw the blade out from its black sheath. It hummed as it came, the blade seemingly alive, *writhing* with forces that made the air throb.

"Indeed. It is called The Bane of Demons. If I draw it out fully, it cannot be slid back into its scabbard until it has fed."

"On a demon, surely. Not on a paltry familiar - "

"Under the circumstances," said Ipsol, with a hideous grin, "you would do nicely. Besides, you desire to know where it will go next. Why not go with it, *within* its heated embrace?"

Elfloq could see distorted faces peering at him from the uncovered part of the blade, their mouths twisting in hatred or agony. He had no wish to join them. With a final squawk of terror, he pulled at his arm, feeling flesh tear and blood spurt. But he was free, and within moments had taken to the air. He flapped up in desperation to the high rafters, gripping his damaged arm. Thankfully the wound was not too severe. Below him he could hear the muffled laughter of the assassin.

Eye Patch of the Smile stood beside the table where Ipsol sat. "I permit no brawls in Cloudway," said the host sternly.

Ipsol re-sheathed the sword. "Your pardon, good host. The familiar sought to cheat me. I was forced to teach him a lesson. He will not bother me again."

"Then the matter is settled. More food?"

"I thank you. And another tankard."

"As you wish. I will tell you when your contact arrives." So saying, he removed Ipsol's empty platter and returned to the bar.

A while later, a rueful Elfloq appeared cautiously at the counter again, clutching at his arm.

"Not a very successful venture," said Eye Patch. "Here, let me attend to that." He took Elfloq's bleeding wrist, grimaced at it and daubed something from a green jar upon the flesh. Elfloq winced, but was more intent on Ipsol's alcove. All was shadow there.

"Oh, by the way," said Eye Patch as he finished binding up the wound, "there is someone to see you."

Elfloq's face screwed up into a frown that would have made a gargoyle shudder. "Hmmph! You said Ipsol was here to see me - "

"I think not, Elfloq. I simply said that one of the Thirteen Swords was here. I did not say Ipsol had come to see you."

Elfloq thought better of retorting. On reflection, he knew that Eye Patch was correct. He flexed his arm. "My thanks, host. I am in your debt."

"Think nothing of it. Your being here is payment enough. I was growing bored, but you have made things interesting, as always. But see, over there. Someone who *does* wish to meet you."

Elfloq turned to look again into the hall. Eye Patch pointed to the opposite end to where Ipsol hid himself, much to the familiar's relief. At a lone table, obscured by more shadow, a wraith-like figure sat stiffly, shrouded in mystery.

"She means you no harm," said Eye Patch.

"She?"

"Go to her. Go on. Her time here is limited."

Elfloq slipped from the stool and cautiously approached the figure, which had the semblance of a ghost rather than a solid being. She sat motionlessly, draped in a gray cloak, her face hidden by a silken veil, through which only the dulled eyes showed. They were like the eyes of one dreaming, though they hinted at pain.

As the familiar came before her, studying her eyes, he felt a pang of recognition. "*Mistress*," he breathed. "But you are dead - "

The eyes turned to him as he spoke, their sadness welling. "Yes, little familiar. I am no longer of the flesh. The realms you frequent, the omniverse, are no longer for me. This shadow you see is the last memory of me."

Elfloq felt a stab of grief, far more acute than the sting of Ipsol's knife. For when he had last seen this woman, she had been stretched on the stones of Ludang, city of the Lamia of Lamias, Vandi-Nuessa. She had been the beloved of his master, the Voidal, who had slipped the Sword of Oblivion into her heart, deliberately shutting her off from the nightmare memories of her life.

"But, mistress, why are you here?"

"I have a simple message for you."

"For my master?"

"A warning, Elfloq. From the Dark Gods, to whom I now go. Your master must never seek me again."

Elfloq felt a surge of emotion and steadied himself with difficulty. "What must I do?"

"You seek the Thirteen Swords and the Sword of Shadows that houses them all. His soul. You must put this quest aside. The retribution of the Dark Gods is a terrible thing, Elfloq. Am I not testament to that?"

Elfloq could not speak. How could he deny her?

"If you must aid your master, there are other ways to do so. I risk much in sharing this with you."

"Mistress, you must not set yourself at risk - "

"My fate is sealed. But know this, you serve your master better if you seek the thing you fear most. Or that which it replaces."

Elfloq puzzled over this. "A riddle, mistress."

"It is all I can give you."

"But what must I give you in return?"

The eyes seemed to smile through their pain and the figure held out a pale arm. On one slender finger, a ring caught the light. It was set with a single, opaque gem. "You have already paid me," she said. "With the tear you shed for me in Ludang." And again the gem sparkled.

Elfloq was speechless. He drew back as the figure seemed to blur, swallowed by the shadows at the back of the hall. Their meeting was ended, as if it had been no more than a dream.

At the bar, Eye Patch was wiping tankards. "Well, Elfloq. I trust that was a more fruitful meeting than your first?"

Elfloq nodded, lost in thought.

"And you hand? It recovers?"

Elfloq held out his wrist, realisation suddenly dawning on him. "Hand? My hand, yes! That is what she meant. The thing I fear most."

"And what would that be? Ipsol's vengeance?"

"No, no, though that would be terrible enough. No, it is the hand of my master. The Oblivion Hand, that of the Dark Gods." He tried to reach round and touch his own back, hampered by his folded wings. He turned to his host. "Is my back marked? Can you see an impression upon it?"

Eye Patch studied the squamous skin, but shook his head. "I don't think so, unless, but no, a trick of the light - "

"What, what?"

"For a moment, it looked like the five digits of a splayed hand, but how could that be?"

"Exactly!" said Elfloq. "I carried the hand of the Dark Gods on my back. On Firecrag. Gods of the Abyss, but you cannot imagine the sheer *terror* of such a thing!" At once he launched into a lively and much embellished telling of his escapade on Murderers' Mountain, giving great attention to the incident with Cellotristi, when the Oblivion Hand had fallen from Elfloq into her lap.

"And I can tell you," Elfloq ended, some considerable time later, "that it was the most terrifying experience imaginable. The lady has pointed the way. What I fear most - why, it is that very same hand. But, what else was it she said? *Or what it replaces.*" He puzzled over this again.

"What it replaces?' repeated Eye Patch. "Surely that is your master's own hand."

Elfloq gaped. "Of course! His *real* hand!"

"It must be hidden somewhere," Eye Patch suggested.

"Yes," murmured Elfloq thoughtfully. "And we must seek that, rather than the Swords."

"There, you see, Elfloq. I am well repaid for my efforts. What a stirring tale! I will delight in passing it on to my guests. Cellotristi! What a stunning goddess! And her doomed affair with Thunderhammer. It makes an intriguing yarn."

"And my part in it was not small."

"Oh, yes, wonderful. Cloudway will resound to its re-telling."

"Well, I must be off. I have a clear path to follow."

"Good fortune to you," Eye Patch grinned, but Elfloq was already in the air, seeking a portal above and the astral beyond.

Eye Patch smiled a very personal smile, perfectly used to the impulsiveness of familiars. There was movement across the hall, where the wraith-like creature who had spoken to Elfloq yet sat, but the innkeeper turned away. Whatever further meetings took place there were private.

The figure who stood before the veiled woman now wore a scarlet robe and his long, jet-black hair framed him like starless midnight. He was Darquementi, the Divine Asker, and he bowed gently to the seated figure.

"Have I done well?" she said, her voice almost a whisper.

"Indeed. The familiar will take the lead you have given him. The Swords will not be paramount to him, for a while at least. Though, no doubt, he will be unable to resist a renewed search for them in the due course of time."

"Then I am to move on from this place? Oblivion will reclaim me?"

Darquementi sighed, an apparently genuine sadness in him. "That is so. But you have earned a last favour of the Dark Gods for your part in this."

"I will not ask for much."

"What shall it be?"

"Let me look upon the one you call Voidal a last time. Let his face be the last thing I see before I go on to the final darkness."

Darquementi drew himself up, nodding thoughtfully. "Very well." He placed his hands together above the table, as if in prayer, and then slowly pulled them apart. In the space between them, a scene hovered in the air, and the shadow woman leaned forward to study it with deep intensity.

It was a window on a world of ice and blizzards, a white emptiness, blasted by cold currents of air, thickly flecked with snow. Through this frozen landscape, a single figure trudged, head down against the blast. As the woman looked, the scene magnified, so that the solitary man filled the view. He paused, his keen eyes scanning the land ahead. Then he pulled down the muffle that hid his lower face, showing his entire visage. There was a pain in his eyes that equaled that of the watcher, an air of resigned despair about his mien.

The woman felt a hand upon her shoulder. It was the Asker. She pulled back from the scene in the snows, nodding again. "Thank you," she breathed. Something glistened on her cheek.

"Then it is done," said Darquementi, and the scene was gone as though it had never been. But behind the veil, the woman smiled.

Moments later the Asker was alone. He took a brief while to gather his thoughts, then went across the hall to another shadowed alcove.

A hooded face peered out at him from the edge of the candlelight. There was menace in that stare, the threat of anger.

"You are Ipsol," said Darquementi, unmoved.

The assassin's scowl deepened. "Speak your purpose! I've already dealt with one unwanted intrusion on my privacy."

"You bear a sword - "

"Perhaps. What's it to you?"

"My masters have a use for it."

Ipsol sneered and put the Bane of Demons on the table, as he had done when Elfloq had come to him. "You want to see it?" He began to slide the blade from its sheath.

"No. Cover it up," said Darquementi calmly. "I have not come to claim it. You are to take it to Alendar, a world far from here."

"Never heard of it."

"No matter. You are well wrapped, I see," said the Asker, referring to the thick cloak that still clung to the assassin. "That is as well. The northern snows of Alendar are exceptionally harsh. Leave the Sword there."

"In the snow? Anywhere?"

"It will be found."

"Then what?"

"Then you are free."

Ipsol looked at the Asker suspiciously. "As simple as that? Deliver the weapon, drop it in the snow and leave?"

"Your passage will be smooth. The Dark Gods pay their debts. Where are you bound for?"

Ipsol mused on this, unsure whether it would be a trap. But he had no choice. "I will go to Mindsulk."

Darquementi nodded. "So be it." With a final curt nod, he walked away.

Ipsol watched as the darkness claimed him, then slid the Bane of Demons back inside his cloak. He took a last pull at the excellent ale of Cloudway, and for a while remembered nothing more.

PART SIX

THE BURNING ICE, THE FREEZING FIRE

While Elfloq went his way, separated from his master by times and distances that are little more than a blink or a blur in the maelstrom that is the omniverse, the Voidal's destiny was again mapped out for him by the Dark Gods.

How the gods enjoy emotional turmoil, especially in those with whom they shape the fates of worlds! The weapons of Zargovyl, of Thunderhammer and a thousand other engineers are as nothing to love, anger, guilt, greed.

What follows is yet a further illustration of this.

—**SALECCO**, himself the plaything of cruel emotions

* * * *

Under the scarlet eye of Azadris, the Bloodworld, the cooler orb of Alendar spins like a solitary ruby, refracting the fires of its blazing parent. Men once bloomed in Alendar's tropical heat, spreading across this fertile world, raising their cities and towers in salute to the god that they made of Azadris. Those who turned aside from the divine face of the Bloodworld were sought out and put to a horrible death, or else given into the pitiless servitude of the Sangueen, the Crimson Priests, whose power was both omnipotent and omnipresent on Alendar. By their conjurations and necromancies, these Crimson Priests learned of the Bloodwights that thrived upon Azadris, demons that were merely the scions of the awesome deities of the Bloodworld. The Crimson Priests thought it in their interests to summon certain of these Bloodwights down to Alendar that the people could serve the Priests better. There were those among these Sangueen, ambitious men, who sought more, blasphemously desiring control and mastery of the demon spawn. It was through the machinations of these avaricious Sangueen rebels that the debacle on Alendar began.

Many Bloodwights were conjured to Alendar, some as intermediaries between Priests and gods, but those more vaulting Sangueen made slaves of their demons by the use of forbidden, powerful sorceries. Yet the renegade Sangueen were not alone in their desires for there were Bloodwights who schemed on no less great a scale. Foremost of these was Androzael, a demon whose true powers were kept shadowed from his aspiring masters. Androzael came to Alendar as a servant, but it was through his cunning and treachery that the fall of men truly began.

It was Androzael who sowed the seeds of conquest among the demons of Alendar. Now that they had been prized free of the Bloodworld's chains and their potent overlords there, they found it easier to revolt against mortals, for the Sangueen were far fewer in number than the Bloodwights and far less flexible in their movements. The Sangueen could cross the astral realms only at the expense of great effort and magic, whereas the Bloodwights travelled the astral realm at will. Androzael exhorted his fellow demons to join him in the overthrow of the Sangueen, and the conquest had begun.

Terrible conflicts ensued across the world of Alendar as the Bloodwights unleashed their realised potential. Cities fell like rotting trees and the very earth heaved in turmoil. Androzael enslaved as many of the deposed Sangueen as he could find and robbed them of their knowledge and more importantly of their gates to the Bloodworld. Having the keys to these gates, Androzael was able to draw through them whole armies of Bloodwights, and having overrun the entire civilized world with them, he sealed the gates for all time. Wisely, Androzael then had his human slaves build new temples to the glory of the gods of Azadris, so that he could rule on Alendar in their name and thus retain power. The gods were silent, which implied that they were not averse to the Bloodwights usurping Alendar. For certain the gods appeared to have no sympathy for the men who had tried to cheat them of their rightful obeisance.

Thus Alendar became a world of demons. Men remained, mostly as slaves, but there were yet isolated havens of resistance - remote, haunted places where the last of the free men hid, dreaming their hopeless dreams of wrenching control back from the Bloodwights.

One such lost haven was the serrated, ice-locked range of Bitterscarp, situated in the forgotten wastes of Alendar's remote north. There was little here in this blizzard-stung wilderness, even for Bloodwights, who could laugh at desert winds or parched landscapes. So for a time, men knew they would be safe here. From the upper crags of Bitterscarp they hacked the lonely retreat of Icehaven, where they dwelled for countless years, never venturing out into the world. They were rarely molested by the frightful new rulers of Alendar, who scorned the dwindling remnants of humanity.

* * * *

Qundquek's sleep amongst the royal pelts was light, uneasy, fraught with evil dreams. An ice worm wriggling across his gloomy bedchamber would likely have woken him, so tormented was his sleep, but the din that assailed his ears from without woke half Icehaven fortress. The monarch sat bolt upright, bloodshot eyes staring at the carved doors as if they would burst inward to reveal some awful nemesis; the doors threatened as much for all their runes, their massed sigils against evil, for beyond them the noises shook the very walls. Qundquek had stationed his two favourite snow jaguars out there, as he did each night, preferring their strength over his human guards, the Starwatch, for there was not a man the king could trust completely.

The shrieking screams of the snow jaguars ripped along his nerve edges; he could hear the frantic rattle of their silver chains as both lithe beasts rolled and slashed, fighting something that must have been as powerful and savage as they were. Qundquek's veins stood out on his face, embossing the bizarre tattoos that covered it, further runes against dark forces. Sweat and terror blotched his features. Only a Bloodwight dared attack the snow jaguars, though it would have to be colossal. But how could one have got into the castle, past the killing spells that guarded it? The spells that clung to Icehaven choked the very air. Qundquek shook his head. No solitary demon could have breached such a defense. Then what was it that came closer to him each night?

A week ago it had eviscerated a sleepy troupe of guards as they dozed before their brazier several floors below. The next night the intruder had wreaked even more havoc a floor above and closer to Qundquek, and the pattern had not changed. Night by night this unseen horror drew closer to the king's chambers, its purpose clearer with each bloody murder that it perpetrated. It came for Qundquek. The monarch could not believe that it would best his snow jaguars, for they were kept hungry and thus ill tempered; even if a Bloodwight had breached Icehaven, it would surely be no match for two of these ferocious beasts.

Yet the battle raging without grew in volume, though the snarls of the snow jaguars became less frenzied. The doors shook, the walls rang to the crash of heavy bodies; yet the assailant was as silent as the frozen air. Had it been seen at last? Why had no one been able to describe this interloper? How had it evaded the magical traps set for it, the age-old workings? Qundquek watched the doors shake, himself muttering a string of protective cantrips.

A shrill whimper pierced his ears. In horror he realised that one of the snow jaguars must be dead. Blood seeped like a dark carpet beneath the door and Qundquek shuddered as it licked at his discarded robe on the stone. Another frightful roar from outside heralded the death of the other snow jaguar and Qundquek echoed the last screech with a choked groan. Now, surely, his ensorcelled doors would part like silk and whatever monster had marked him out for death would come to claim him. He fought to cling to his sliding sanity.

Silence gripped the castle, focussed on the doors. Qundquek could hear nothing, not even the rasping breathing of demon or beast as he would have expected, for the battle must have been exhausting. If anything, the silence deepened. Qundquek felt his nerves burning. Tension twisted him, squeezing his heart until it forced a shout of terror from his lips. It rang out down Icehaven's rune-daubed corridors, but as it died, silence fell again.

No further attack came. Whatever had killed the snow jaguars had had its sport for the night, for cruel sport it was, and had withdrawn. Qundquek fell, shaking, into his pelts as he realised he had been spared, at least for the moment. His Starwatch, beating on the bedchamber doors, waited long for his answer. The monarch finally opened the door to the armed warriors, and his face was deathly, his skin a sickly gray, his eyes the eyes of a man condemned to a hellish death.

"You are safe?" breathed Elovar, sergeant of the Starwatch.

Qundquek nodded, but his wild eyes were staring at the havoc outside his rooms, at the torn and mangled carcasses of the once white snow jaguars and at the pooling lakes of their blood. The king turned away, sickened. "*What has done this?*" he breathed.

There were no replies. Once again no one had seen the intruder, but in truth, the guards had not been standing in waiting for it: their own terror had kept them well away. Had the king known that his corridors were unarmed at night, each guard would have been executed. Qundquek gestured them away and shut himself once more in his gloomy chamber.

"What monster stalks our halls?" said Elovar to a fellow guard. "See, it has not eaten of its kills, as before, nor has it left a drop of its own blood. Can a Bloodwight have breached us? The spells were tripled. The magic is of surpassing power."

His companion shook his head. "No Bloodwight could do this! But it has the humour of those vile creatures. Did you realise, Elovar, that the *heads* of the snow jaguars have been taken?"

* * * *

Qundquek stared out of his barred window at the smashed rock terrain of Bitterscarp, fanged with dawn's shadows, icy and indifferent to the monarch's anguish. His guilt tormented him as it had since the day he had usurped the kingship of this remote place. Had he been wise? Had his ambitions been justified? To be king of these god-spurned ice fastnesses, so far from the once-proud cities of men, that had once ruled all of Alendar? It would be a beginning, he had thought, a first step towards marshalling the pathetic survivors and making something of them before going out to challenge the Bloodwight dominion. But his people feared him and sensed a bane upon him, for no *man* had ever ruled Icehaven before him. He had changed ancient traditions, and some whispered that he had fractured old powers.

He felt the onset of the past yet again: would it ever seek to remind him of his treachery? But had it been treachery? He had tried to act in the interests of his people. Yet he knew in his inner heart that his own ambition had prompted him, too. As he looked out from the ice tower now at the sun-bloodied snow, he thought of the grim deeds he had set in motion to make himself lord of Icehaven.

There had always been a queen in this fortress, since its very first, Zarochti, whose wisdom, vision and strength had made her subjects strong in their isolation. Sorcery such as the Sangueen had once misused was no longer tolerated, for it had betrayed mankind. However, the queens of the castle did have purer powers, which men were forbidden to possess. Only the queen could retain the witching skills. Queens had used these beneficially throughout Icehaven's history. Qundquek's mother, Sheshquari, had been queen, and had ruled with a confidence and strength that even her predecessors had rarely possessed. The people of the fortress and its outposts grew in number and there was serious talk of hewing other castles from the crags of Bitterscarp, where once this had been no more than idle dreaming.

Yet a curse came upon the castle, for Sheshquari's destiny was not to be one of glory nor of rebuilding the fallen empire. She had chosen her mate, a typically strong warrior, who excelled both at weaponry and administration, but before the marriage ceremony could be conducted, terror struck Icehaven. A deceitful pack of Bloodwights lured with rich promises of power several of the Traders of the castle. These were itinerant men who journeyed deep into the northern snows to barter goods with other minor castles, men with no true homes. Through these Traders the Bloodwights gained ingress to Icehaven. For a while, before they could be driven back, chaos reigned, and in that short season of madness, the Bloodwights killed the queen's loyal bodyguard and despoiled both her and her servants, thus negating her sorcerous powers. They themselves were cornered and killed, strung from the battlements as a warning to other Bloodwight war parties.

The fall of the queen had been a secret well kept, and none but those closest to the throne knew of the dreadful acts that had been perpetrated. For it was feared that the people of Icehaven would have fled out into the snowy wilderness, thinking themselves no longer protected by the high magics of old. But order was restored, though Sheshquari had never been the same woman. Her powers had been drained and she bore hard the frightful stigma of the Bloodwight raid. Even so, she had married her mate and for a time it seemed that Icehaven had recovered. Men prospered, as much as they could in this closed community. Sheshquari was silent, withdrawn, and when she gave birth to the child, a girl, the castle rejoiced, even though the birth taxed the queen almost to death.

The girl's life was sheltered, but the queen insisted on this, saying that she must learn all the ways of witching so that her powers would be even greater than those of former queens. Sheshquari secretly encouraged her child to delve into certain sorceries that had long been discarded as dangerous and that could bring a blemish to the soul. She told the child that only such forbidden lore could truly defeat the Bloodwights.

Perhaps only Huak, consort of Sheshquari, knew that the girl was not his own daughter, but the result of that terrible Bloodwight intrusion, that she was part human, part Bloodwight. If he did know, he did not demand her death, as custom would dictate. Nothing tainted by the Bloodwights could be allowed to live. But the girl's secret was hidden from everyone, even herself. Huak was loving and understanding, and his deep love for his queen, mirrored by hers for him, finally bore fruit in a son, Qundquek. The boy grew up to be aggressive, determined, and full of wild dreams for bettering the lot of his people. When his father died, he became the great strength of the queen, often supplanting her waning witchery with the strength of his arm and the many guards who flocked to him and his iron principles.

I ruled in her place for years, Qundquek told himself for the thousandth time. *She was ailing, and that endangered all of us. I did no more than my duty. Icehaven loved me for it, and so did she.*

He had rarely been allowed to see his sister, and then but fleetingly. But he sought to know more of her, for she would be queen when Sheshquari died, and he had wanted to be sure he would remain as powerful under her as her mother. But it quickly became clear to him that there was some dark secret surrounding his sister. In time he had uncovered it: one night, as Sheshquari lay in a fever, the garbled truth dribbled from her lips. Qundquek, appalled by this outrageous knowledge, called the Lawkeepers of the castle to him and demanded immediate action. Their terror of the Bloodwights worked like a poison against the daughter of the queen. They abjured her.

Qundquek would have slain the girl at once, but his ailing mother begged him to spare her, saying that she knew nothing of her real identity. Reluctantly Qundquek agreed that the girl should not die, but he had her taken deep below the roots of Icehaven to the caves that led far under Bitterscarp to the glacier-wrought maze beyond. There she had been cast adrift, left to the mercy of the legendary ice ghouls that legend had it haunted these extreme reaches.

After that, Qundquek set to courting the support of the Lawkeepers, saying the he was all that was now left of the royal line. The queen was too old to bear another girl-child and indeed, her age hinted at her own death soon.

In the end, they made me king, the monarch told the scarlet dawn. *I, who have no sorcerous powers, but whose arm is yet stronger than that of any other man in this northern wilderness. They made me king, though they had no choice. But what else could I do? Should I have let the people disperse, cursing Icehaven as doomed?* But he knew that since he had become king, the people were divided. There had always been a queen, the source of all magic. It was a bad omen for a man to take the crown. The spells that protected the castle would be weakened. Qundquek had laughed such words to scorn, for no Bloodwights had been near the place since the disaster of years before. Why, he had even sent out skirmishers that had harried the Bloodwights from the edges of Bitterscarp, and no queen had ever done as much. Yes, he had been a powerful monarch and Icehaven had never been stronger. Its numbers were still waxing.

He turned from the stark lands outside with a bitter glare. A strong king, yes, but he bore his own curse. He had taken a wife, Usquem, a beautiful, strong girl, who would have given him many children and surely a daughter fit to rule after him, who would restore all the old magics. But fate had been unkind, for Qundquek was sterile and could sire no children. He would be the last of his line and would sire no dynasty. The people had learned of this, guessed it, for it had been another of Icehaven's darkly guarded secrets. There were renewed murmurings of evil omens. There had never been a king before. The faction against Qundquek gathered support. And he knew it.

And now something had entered the castle's inner heart and skulked closer to him nightly. Had the people themselves conjured up some eldritch horror and sent it against him for his sins against tradition? Had the castle's women tapped their combined powers? If so, it would indeed be no Bloodwight, for nothing sowed more terror in their hearts than that. No, this was something else, though just as evil. Tonight it had reached his doors. How soon would it breach them?

* * * *

Azadris shed crimson sunlight: it slanted down from the high windows of the Audience Room, splashing ominously on to the shoulders of Qundquek. His worn face spoke of deep inner turmoil. Before him stood his worthiest Starwatch guards, men whom he knew were rigidly loyal to the safekeeping of Icehaven, if not to his personal cause.

"I *must* know what this terror is that stalks me by night. Every person in the castle must be interrogated. Every child also. Speak to the lowest menial, and even speak to those serving sentences in the cellars deep below, even the outcasts. Every Trader that has ventured here in the past three months must be doubly questioned. I will have an answer! And if none is forthcoming - if no one brings me word of what it is that threatens us - I shall resort to using the women and whatever witchery they have. I will fight vile sorcery with sorcery."

There were none of the Lawkeepers at this private hearing, or else they would certainly have protested this last, for the women's powers were only used in binding the protective spells, no more. As it was, a murmur ran through the ranks of the normally stoic warriors.

"Aye!" snapped Qundquek testily. "Icehaven is in danger! Our very unity is imperiled. We must spare no efforts to seek out and destroy this fiend." He dismissed them, slumping back into his seat with exhaustion when they had gone, brooding long thereafter.

For hours the guards brought no word. They questioned everyone they could find. Many had heard the frightful screams of the men and the beasts that had died at the hand of the intruder, but none had seen it and lived. By night the people of Icehaven had shut themselves away in their chambers from the bitter cold, redoubling their spells against evil.

The day wore on without result. Qundquek sought oblivion in the insipid wine of the castle, a remnant of years long past, but it did little to blunt his anguish. Drained, he watched the huge red eye of Azadris passing beneath its zenith as the afternoon began. And tonight? What then?

A discreet cough broke into his melancholia and he looked up to see three of the Starwatch before him. In their strong hands they held a squirming bag of bones that could have been an old man or a child. It squealed like a piglet about to be butchered. The guards tossed the filthy creature to the foot of the throne, where it sprawled over the etched runes.

"Have you word?" said Qundquek, his voice a death rattle.

"Naught save this imbecile, lord, whom we found tittering below the castle in the pits where the ice bricks are quarried. He tends the outcast caves that lead beyond into the very entrails of the mountains. Some say he is mad and toss him food scraps out of pity. They say he roams many parts of Icehaven freely, for most fear him and think him tainted by the ice ghouls. Others say he is the carrier of a disease. Certainly, lord, he has about him the reek of decay."

Qundquek studied the bundle of rags, which was idly tracing the curled sigils on the stone. The king knew that a few diseased ones and certain criminals had been banished to the lower pits, and this indeed had the appearance of one.

"They call him no more than Babbler, lord, for his wriggling tongue shakes loose every shred of gossip that ever passed through the walls of Icehaven. Or so the old wives say."

"A madman who wallows in castle gossip!" Qundquek snorted. "Yet every other soul remains tight-lipped. What can this poor fool tell us?"

The Babbler had curled into a ball and hidden his head under his rags. A guard kicked him. "He was blind with drink when we found him. Singing like a child. But he spoke of you, lord, and of some vengeance that is to be directed at you. It spoke a strange name, and not one that any of us recognize. That of the Bane-Witch."

The lines about Qundquek's tired face tightened and the king emitted a short gasp, as if he had been stabbed. He stared at the bundle of humanity before him. "All of you - leave us!" he snapped. "Go. I will question this fool myself, and alone. Go from me!"

They hesitated an instant, but seeing the grim mood of the king, did as they were instructed. The tall doors of the Audience Room boomed shut behind them. Only then did the Babbler look up, speaking in a grating voice.

"I see you bathed in blood where you sit, Qundquek. Yet even should you move from out of the Bloodworld's rays, that scarlet stain would remain upon you."

Qundquek stood up slowly and drew out his stabbing sword. "It will be *your* blood upon me if you mock me further. But before I gut you, tell me what you mean by the Bane-Witch. What is that name to you?"

The Babbler snickered, sitting up and crossing his legs, unafraid of the king and his blade. "I am the worm that crawls through the icy walls of your castle, lord. The stone elementals have shown me every cranny, every loose rock. Long ago I heard them whisper of the coming of the Bane-Witch. I heard another name spoken . *Scyllarza*. A name once spat out by Starwatch bent on murder. Down in the glacial caves. There I have my simple den. Only there can a half man such as I - a poor halfling who could not even sire stunted children or halfwits, they say - find a quiet place to sleep, with only the keeping of my fire's life to fret over. Ah, the decrees of the Lawkeepers are hard on lesser mortals such as I. Even more so, it would seem, lord, than they are to those who can produce no issue at all."

Qundquek's face drained at the pointed words, but he was immobile.

"Down in the ice, wrapped in my pelts, I heard of Scyllarza."

"*What did you see?*" said Qundquek coldly, his memory sharply in focus, distant days brought before him.

"I saw a girl - a young beauty she was, and fit to be a *queen's* girl - marched brutally by the Starwatch. Your Starwatch, lord. Marched to her death, she was. Child of Bloodwights they called her. Cursed among men, the brat offspring of the queen, your mother. She who would have been queen, save that her own brother lusted for her throne. Child of demons, they called her, taunting and teasing. Walk in hell, they told her, laughing. They ignored her screams. If you are a demon Bloodwight, then the ice will give you a quick death, they scoffed. So saying, they tossed her into a subterranean river that flows icily from the upper glaciers at the pole."

Qundquek closed his eyes tightly, his sword falling on the steps, his fists balled, drained of blood. He shook. "I had to do it," he breathed. "She had to die. If the people had known of her, they would have fled Icehaven forever and the last real bastion against the Bloodwights would have fallen into ruin."

"Die, my lord?" echoed the Babbler, chuckling. "Would you toss a fish into water to drown it? Would you kill a worm by burying it? Would you destroy an imp in flames?"

Qundquek glared down at the Babbler, fear blotting out his anger. "What are these riddles?"

"A fish will swim. How little you knew of your mother's teachings! She learned everything that she could of the sorceries that flourish on Alendar. We dwell in the realms of *ice*. There are beings here to be won to the cause of men. Your mother knew them and taught her daughter of them and their ways. And of their alliance."

The king sagged back on to the throne, gripping its arms, his tattoos writhing. "She is alive?"

"Why, yes! Into the withering current she was cast, but after your lackeys had gone, having noticed me not at all, I gazed down into that whirling torrent, and I saw her rise again. On the back of an ice elemental she rose. He shook her off his great back so that she fell beside me on the black rocks of the cave. With fire I warmed her and revived her, though she thrives on both ice and fire. They are all the same to her!

"She was confused and bewildered, but I fed her. I knew who she was, and her history, and in time I taught her all that I knew, which was much. Your subjects say that I have the longest ears in Icehaven. I can tell you the very movements of the ice worms - "

"You dared to interfere!" hissed Qundquek.

"I acted only from pity, lord," said the Babbler mockingly. "I have lived a loveless, spurned existence, and understood well the girl's plight. And she was little more than a child. She lived with me in the deepest of the ice caves, and we both knew the ice elementals. She is there now. But no longer a child, for that was ten years since. She is a woman - more than a woman, but you, I think, must know that."

"Then it is she who is responsible for unleashing this ice elemental in my corridors?"

The Babbler tittered. "The ice people could not do the things this prowler does! But, yes, it is Scyllarza who has unleashed it. She has thrived for ten years on a diet of revenge. She has perfected her art for ten years. Now she is ready to give to you your doom. Perhaps also the doom of Icehaven, for how could she love its people?"

Qundquek shook his head. "One woman? Even one with Bloodwight tainting? Destroy me and all this with her arts? Then let her send her horrors. I will finish the bloody business I left undone. There are powers that *I* can yet turn to. And you, who think it fitting to spit at me, will feed the eagles that soar about Icehaven's highest spires!"

The Babbler merely laughed. "That will not save you. I am ready to die, having served my part. But I will be sorry to miss your meeting with your sister."

Qundquek nodded. "Is that so? Then you shall remain, and see her die slowly for her ill work."

* * * *

The two guards at the bottom of the stairway snapped to attention as they saw who it was that approached. Qundquek rarely came to the Tower of Sighs, the remotest and coldest in all Icehaven, yet its stairway was always guarded. Twice a day food from the kitchens was brought up, together with the luxury of fruit, though none of the guards knew who it was that was imprisoned up there, the food itself being brought by a mute. Qundquek climbed the spiral stairs wearily, his mood draped about him like a chain. At the top, he took from his belt the only key to the tower room and unlocked the door. With a last glance behind him, he entered the room and re-locked its door.

A single, slitted window admitted bright rays of sunlight, and silhouetted there was the lone occupant of the tower. His apparel was luxurious, his chamber sumptuous. Many books lined its walls and there were countless phials, retorts and tools suggestive of sorcery about the tables. Yet as the man turned, there was a clinking of metal, for he was chained by the foot to a central ring in the chamber floor.

"Another visit to the Tower of Sighs, Qundquek?" said the prisoner smoothly. His hair was iron gray, sleeked back over a high, domed forehead and down his back in curling tails. "Are you so eager to discover the lost arts? Do your people still go in ignorance of what transpires above their very heads? One day they might call for your head - "

"No one knows, nor needs to. They think they know who is incarcerated here, and the rumour is enough to keep them at bay. They have no inkling that it is you, Eordred."

"Else they would seek *my* head? Yes, they came close enough to wiping out my fellow Priests to a man. I may well be the last of the Sangueen. But you did not come here to discuss my status, or lack of it. Or did you? Have you considered my last words to you? Are you ready to release me from this pretty dungeon and let me serve you? Have you come to your senses and realised that it is only I who can rid you of the Bloodwights?"

Qundquek was distracted by other thoughts. He picked up a piece of fruit from a dish on the table. It was always so fresh, one of the miracles that his growers still wove. Eordred always had the best. Qundquek had always intended to find a way to use him. It was only the foolish superstition of his people that forced him to incarcerate the Sangueen here.

The monarch sighed. "Aye, there may be a way you can serve me, after all."

Eordred's eyes narrowed. "No need to mask your thoughts, O king. I am not easily deceived."

Qundquek snorted, tossing away the fruit. "I merely choose my words with care. There is no need for deceit between us. And you know I am a cautious man."

"Given your past, that is as well. Your people are not united under you."

Qundquek's face soured. "I know that! I have striven to weld them for years. Yet still there are dissenters. They want a *queen*, damn them!"

"Do not ask me to make you fruitful again," said Eordred softly, tired of this worn conversation. "I have explained that it is not within my power to work such a miracle. You must accept that you cannot sire children. The gods are adamant."

Qundquek stared out at the frozen wastes, thinking of the Babbler's veiled taunt. He spoke through closed teeth, biting down on his frustration. "I have accepted it. Do you think I have not!"

"Then what is it you ask of me?"

The monarch turned sharply, the runes on his face dancing. "There is a particular plot - one of real substance - to unhinge my mind. You remember Scyllarza, the first child of my mother, who had Bloodwight blood in her veins - "

"The girl you had murdered, yes, of course. You did well to kill her, for the powers sleeping in her would have far exceeded the magics of your other women."

"Powers that she would have eagerly turned against me, and possibly all in Icehaven. I know that. Well, it seems that this Bane-Witch, as she is called, is not dead. Her hell creatures walk the corridors by night, killing my guards. Preparing to add me to her tally."

Eordred could smell the king's fear. He resented the man for making a prisoner of him, but could still find a morsel of respect for his bitter determination to serve his people, the last feeble men of Alendar. Yet how much of the coward hid behind the warrior? "You go in fear of your life?"

"Aye, but more than that. If my people are left without a monarch, even one of whom they are uncertain, they will perish. Other men on Alendar are scattered, wasted. All will cease to be. And so, my friend, will you. The Bloodwights will overrun this place, never mind its cold, and when they find a *Sangueen* here - "

Eordred nodded soberly. "I know what that will mean."

"Then help me. How can I rid myself of this Bane-Witch and her vile servants?"

The Crimson Priest looked thoughtful, then smiled. "There is always a way to dispose of such abominations. I will soon have it. But if I do - my friend - surely you would reconsider all the things I have said?"

Qundquek nodded. "Aye! Rid me of this curse and I will release you from this prison. You will accompany me in the castle, and I will let you stand beside me in the Audience Room."

"And when your wretched people cry treachery?"

"As long as they are assured that you obey my will and that you work in the interests of humanity and not the Bloodwights, they will accept you. I will see to that. You will have to trust me in this matter. But understand this, Eordred, you *will* obey me. Forget any schemes to further your own ends. Do as I command, work for my cause, and you will better your own cause. I will reward you well. Your power and stature will grow under me, just as you would wish. In time, when Icehaven is strong enough, we will flex our power together."

"I see. Then you would trust me, knowing my ambitions?"

Qundquek stood close to him and stared at him in both defiance and a desperation he could not hide. "Fail me and I will kill you - or give you to the women. Or better still, stake you out for the Bloodwights."

Eordred smiled mirthlessly. "Then I had better do what you ask. After all, as you say, we have so much more to gain if we combine our talents."

"Give me of your knowledge, and I will give you asylum."

"Agreed."

They spoke then of the Bane-Witch and of how her creatures terrorised the castle by night. After a while, the Sangueen consulted his grimoires while the monarch fidgeted impatiently. It was an hour before Eordred closed one particular tome with a grunt of satisfaction.

"Well?" said Qundquek, who had found wine to sip. It had done nothing to calm him.

"There is a way. Dangerous, perhaps. But effective. There are pitfalls, but they can be sidestepped."

"What is it?"

"There is an ancient invocation, little more than a legend. It may even have originated in some other time plane, and certainly in another dimension, for there are many. I will not detain you with details, although the history itself is incomplete and very fragmented. But there is a being, one who is said to walk in a void, a limbo between universes. If he is called, he can perform tasks of the most puissant nature."

"Such as the destruction of the Bane-Witch and the things that serve her?"

"Yes. But we must exercise the greatest of caution. This being, this Voidal, as he is called, can be as much a curse as a boon, for the book warns of a severe penalty. He who invokes the Voidal must pay a fee. And it is not one that a man would relish paying."

Qundquek shook his head slowly, mulling this over.

"There are ways," said Eordred, "to force another to invoke the Voidal."

"Enough men have been sacrificed - "

"No, no, not a man. My advice, O king, is to capture a Bloodwight. Make *it* invoke this wanderer from the void. Ensure that it relays the commands we wish carried out to the Voidal. Then he can mete out whatever damnation he desires to the Bloodwight."

Qundquek nodded with relief. "And you are sure of this?"

"Yes, quite sure. These are powers beyond measure, unrelenting."

The monarch studied the scarlet sunlight outside. "Then I myself will take a party of Starwatch out at once. The Bloodwight Xarbial has been seen abroad with his scavenging pack of vermin. I will harry them in the eastern passes. And before Azadris sinks into twilight, I will take one alive."

Eordred grimaced. "Excellent."

"When I next come to you, be ready to supervise this invocation. When night comes, we must hold ourselves in readiness."

Eordred watched the monarch as he began to leave. "So, Qundquek, you will trust me?"

Qundquek frowned. "When you give me proof of your loyalty - "

"Have I not already done so? Consider this: I could have allowed you to invoke the walker in the void. You would have known nothing of the penalty. Yet I have spared you an unpleasant fate."

Qundquek paled, but then smiled grimly. "Aye, you spared me. But it would not be well for you if I were to perish. No matter what hell I fell into, you would soon follow."

* * * *

The skirmish had been short, well executed. Xarbial's Bloodwights, hampered by their armour against the bitter cold that they so loathed, had been taken completely by surprise and had been blocked into a cul-de-sac high up in the crags of Bitterscarp. Qundquek's Starwatch had loosed a small avalanche, burying most of the enemy. The few that survived had been put to the sword, save one, and this had been chained and dragged back to Icehaven.

Qundquek took his success as a propitious omen. He stood now among the guttering firebrands that threw the deep dungeon under Icehaven into garish relief. Hewn from the iron-hard ice, this was a grim place, featureless and bare, its cold biting at the bones. It had been deserted for centuries, being considered far too cruel for human criminals. This was the first Bloodwight to have graced its raw mercies in living memory.

Eordred, thickly robed and cowled so that he would not be recognised, was brought under heavy escort to the steps that led down into the dungeon. In the writhing firelight he could see the central floor area.

For a moment he stood still, gazing down on his detested enemy. It had been long since he had seen a Bloodwight, but he knew their savagery well enough.

The creature had been spread-eagled on an iron grille, its wrists and ankles chained securely to the metal, a thick loop of steel around its waist, bolted to the grille so that it was impossible for the beast to free itself. It had been stripped naked, exposed to the cold that burned it, for the air in here was little warmer than that of the blizzard slopes outside Icehaven. Bloodwights feared such cold, and this one exhaled clouds of white breath that dissipated slowly.

It had been motionless, having initially spent an hour hissing and spitting at its captors, the dozen silent guards warming themselves at the firebrands. They had ignored it with the stoicism of their breed, other than to toss buckets of icy water over it from time to time, as Qundquek had instructed them to. At length the Bloodwight had subsided, but now its head jerked up and its bestial glare fixed on the covered Sangueen, instinctively knowing who it was that stood there above the steps, scenting it. The demon features were mannish, though chiseled from hate and malice, its teeth sharp, eyes slitted and bloodshot.

"We thought you were all dead or enslaved," it hissed.

Eordred began to descend the steps with deliberate slowness, savouring his triumph. He could see Qundquek in the shadows below.

"Here's one who's had his fire cooled," the king said to him. "Luck rode with us in the eastern heights. We surprised this scum and his rabble. They don't enjoy their sorties into these icy lands. It makes them careless, sluggish."

Eordred slipped back his cowl. His eyes were wide, feeding almost hungrily on the prostrate body of the Bloodwight. He nodded diffidently at the monarch, going to the very side of the prisoner, looming over it like a predator about to strike.

"Yes," said the Sangueen softly. "I should be dead, as most of the Crimson Priests are. Your barbaric masters practiced a very thorough genocide."

"Your own kind ended you," retorted the Bloodwight. He shouted out to the guards. "See what festers among you! A Sangueen! Have you set them up once more? Only to be betrayed again!"

Eordred took from his robe a talisman that had been carved from pure ice. He placed it with slow deliberation on the Bloodwight's forehead. Steam hissed and the creature shrieked. "The ice that burns," said the Sangueen.

The guards remained motionless, but shock flickered across their faces.

Qundquek turned to them. "The Sangueen is our ally. Icehaven is relying on his help now, otherwise it is doomed. So be easy, and watch."

No one demurred. Qundquek had picked them carefully. They were his most loyal men, and they had no love, no pity for the Bloodwights.

Eordred removed the ice talisman. He knelt down, keeping far enough from the Bloodwight to ensure that the creature did not spit upon him. "I seem to have wounded you," he said, but his words were chilling. He took a ladle of icy water from a bucket beside the grille. "Let me attend to it." Slowly he poured the cold water over the face of the Bloodwight, which emitted another shrill cry of agony. "This is simply the beginning. I need to teach you a complete understanding of the nature of pain. Beneath this grille is a river that is fed by the upper snows of Bitterscarp. The water is cold, and I do mean *cold*. You have felt the ice that burns, but it was no more than a taste of what it will be like to *bathe* in the glacial waters."

Involuntary shudders jarred the body of the captive. Nothing could be a greater torment to it than this. "Kill me now," it spat. "I have nothing to give you."

"You are too modest. Are you so willing to cooperate?"

"Say what you want." The creature had no wish to be immersed. Eordred knew that the Bloodwights were fickle and selfish, their principles weak. Terror prompted them to betray any cause.

"You must perform a small service for us," said the Sangueen gently. His patience fascinated Qundquek, who knew the hate that must be blazing inside him, consuming him. "You must invoke someone for us. A demon, of sorts, so you should have no qualms. Someone who will be pleased to answer. So pleased, in fact, that he is sure to demand your freedom for having called him."

The Bloodwight was immediately suspicious. "A trick!"

"We want you to summon the Voidal. Invoke him. Use those words."

The Bloodwight tried to writhe, swearing profusely, issuing a stream of Bloodwight profanities. But they were of no use here.

Eordred motioned to a guard. "Lower him, slowly."

The Bloodwight screamed, but the grille was lowered on creaking chains into the freezing waters below. After this had been done several times, the prisoner had almost screamed itself hoarse. Its whole body steamed as if the skin had been attacked by acid.

Qundquek breathed in Eordred's ear, "Be swift, for it dies, and night approaches."

"When it reaches his bones, he will obey," Eordred said mildly.

After another immersion, the Bloodwight's body gave a convulsive jerk and the screams were inaudible, the babble of words making no sense. But the creature was invoking the Voidal. Over and over again, until the last gasps died away.

"Is it done?" said Qundquek, appalled in spite of himself.

The Sangueen nodded, his eyes roving over the Bloodwight's ravaged form the way a lover looks upon the object of his desire.

A sudden movement of the guards drew Qundquek's attention. They had unsheathed their swords and formed a line, facing the far end of the dungeon, a cleft in the ice, a black fissure. Qundquek went to them as their captain pointed into the shadows. Someone was stepping out of that darkness.

It was the Voidal.

Hesitantly he walked towards the men. "I dreamed I was crossing a sea of snow," he murmured. "Who has brought me here?" He stared around in confusion at the figures in the torchlight.

Qundquek and his guards were too bemused to speak or move, but Eordred showed him the Bloodwight. "The creature invoked you."

The Voidal walked past the men and stood over the prisoner, who now seemed frozen in a rictus of pain. The dark man frowned deeply. There was a mystery in this hellish work.

Eordred smiled calmly. "He has work for you. A moment while I speak to him." The Sangueen again knelt by the creature, so close now that he could whisper in its ear. No one else heard what was said, but the Bloodwight's half-crazed eyes looked up at the Voidal, as if beseeching him for salvation. "You will have to lean close," said the Sangueen to the dark man.

Still puzzled, and somewhat irked at the calmness in the other's tone, the Voidal bent down and put his ear to the bleeding mouth of the Bloodwight. Eordred evidently wanted to catch the words also, but could not. The Voidal alone heard the rasp. He straightened up.

"Is your duty clear?" said Qundquek. He did not trust this dark being, for it seemed in no way subservient.

The Voidal eyed him coolly. "Perhaps."

Qundquek nodded and fetched a double-headed ax from a weapon stack. Quickly and unexpectedly he brought it down on the Bloodwight's neck so that the severed head sprang away. The king retrieved the bloody object and raised it by its straggling hair. Eordred gasped as if the death had been too sudden, too merciful. The Voidal looked upon the head with disgust.

"The creature had suffered enough," said the king. "Here, your tribute."

The Voidal remained motionless. "Why should I wish for such a vile thing?"

"The Bloodwight summoned you. Let this be his fee. There is no need to take anything else from him."

"You misjudge me. I have no need of either. I had no quarrel with the wretch you have executed."

Qundquek handed the head to his captain. "Have it displayed up on Bitterscarp for curious Bloodwights to see."

"Who are you people?" said the Voidal. "Who is the Bane-Witch that the dead one spoke of?"

Qundquek shot a troubled glance at Eordred, but the Sangueen looked composed.

"There is much to explain to you," he told the Voidal. "Let us discourse somewhere more salubrious. The smell of that carcass offends me."

* * * *

Fifty of the king's most trusted Starwatch lined the curtained walls of the vast Hall of Law. Herein were the runes and pentacles of protection most prominent in Icehaven, the warding spells most potent. The floor was polished, inscribed with powerful glyphs from the days of man's supremacy on Alendar, and the very walls reeked of sorcery. The king's advisors, his Lawkeepers and many of his subjects were gathered here, most of them armed and all wearing small chains about their necks that bore talismen against the Bloodwights. The women had bathed every wall in their magics. A bright circle of letters had been carved in the ice rock around the raised throne, and other talismen had been placed around its rim. Then the women had been taken to a safe place and locked away with the children from the pending terror.

For evening had seeped over the sky, like a thickening bloodstain. Qundquek sat on the throne, himself carved motionless by his thoughts, brooding again on his sister. At the foot of the dais, outside the pentacle, sat the Babbler, his face fixed in a smile.

The monarch rose and called the gathering to order. "Men of Icehaven! I have summoned you all here because this is the hour of our greatest challenge. We are under a curse. I know that many of you think that I am the focus of that curse. But it is nevertheless a curse that implicates you all. It must be exorcised, for if it is not, we shall all perish. The Bloodwights will then have Alendar to themselves. I have learned from a prisoner that I captured today that a Bloodwight army plans to assault us at last, led by the monstrous Xarbial. I have gone to great lengths to make our fortress secure, and there are those among you who think me rash and foolish - even ambitious - in my desire to make Icehaven secure. But understand this, all of you, we *are* secure! Not only will we put down this night stalker, but we will blunt Xarbial's attack. Having done that, we will harry the Bloodwights in their own lands. Yes, make no mistake, I *am* ambitious. For you, for the last men on Alendar, for humanity. Man should rule Alendar, not the vermin from Azadris."

Heads nodded generally, though there were the inevitable scowls. The king was by far the most forceful man among them, but they all saw the dangers in his fanaticism.

"Behind me you see two figures," Qundquek went on, indicating the two who stood in shadow just within his pentacle. "You view them with suspicion. I tell you they are allies. Strong allies, with vital powers. The type of powers we *must share* if we are to triumph. Dark powers, perhaps, but ours to control, chained to our cause. We have the tools that will bring the downfall of the Bloodwights. We stand on the brink of extinction. Will you reject the weapons of your salvation?"

One of the Lawkeepers stepped forward boldly. "The women should be here. They wield the only powers in Icehaven other than the force of arms."

Qundquek smiled patiently. "Aye, but this is a greater power by far, and one which our women would envy. You are the men, the warriors. You must decide."

"Then let us see into this darkness," replied the Lawkeeper sceptically, and there were murmurs of agreement.

"You shall. I hide nothing." The king turned to the first of the figures and summoned it to him. Eordred revealed himself and there were instant gasps of astonishment, for the Crimson Priests had been loathed almost as much as the Bloodwights. But Eordred knew that he was safe within the confines of the pentacle. He smiled down at the hostile gathering with remarkable coolness.

"This is Eordred," said Qundquek. "Yes, a Sangueen. Probably the last of them. A man - a man, mark that - who has spent his life repenting the folly of his brethren and their irresponsibility in bringing the Bloodwights upon us. He longs to atone for the sins of his nation. They weigh heavy upon him, and he feels keenly the barbs of your hatred.

"We are living in terror by night. Yet Eordred can rid us of that curse in a stroke! Would you reject him? Cut him down where he stands? I say, this would be foolishness. Let us feed on his power. He is not here to betray us, for how would that benefit him? Does he not dream of the warm lands, as we do?"

Eordred bowed deferentially, kneeling before the king, taking his hand and kissing it. He then stood back with bowed head in a gesture of servitude. Many of the assembled men were stunned, and it was clear that most of them were in favour of this suggested alliance, in spite of the ancient taboos. Yet there were those who shook their heads. And these Qundquek marked well.

He now indicated the Voidal. "This is the second of our weapons."

The dark man stepped forward, masking his views on the oratorical delivery of the monarch, which to him had bordered on desperation. But he had now been told the history of Alendar and understood better the dilemma of its people. Yet he knew that he was again being manipulated, which galled him. He intended to move with caution and obey his own dictates first, if that were possible. The words of the dying Bloodwight still rang on his inner ear.

Qundquek was speaking again. "I can tell you little about him, for he is a wanderer of worlds, seeking an identity for himself. His knowledge is remarkable, for Eordred has recruited him to help rid us of this night demon. He owes us nothing and wants nothing from us. Would you reject him?"

After this there was much discussion, for it was clear that the king wanted to shatter more than a few of the old laws. But his intentions were creditable. It was his methods that were questionable. Would they succeed?

Qundquek paced up and down irritably while the Lawkeepers went among the throng, listening to the debates, encouraging full discourse.

At length their spokesman came forward. "Lord, you are the voice of Icehaven. We understand your ambitions and what prompts them. We will not oppose you, for you are the strongest. Do you command us, or do you ask us what we wish?"

Qundquek struggled to find an answer that would not destroy his integrity and yet sustain his control. He could not allow them to reject the two men. Without their help, the vengeance of the Bane-Witch would engulf Icehaven. "I ask for your judgement," he said sternly. "But I also offer you advice. It is meant for the best. I do not want to see Icehaven die."

"Then we are in your hands."

Qundquek could not help but sigh in gusty relief. A great weight seemed to lift from him. "Then I thank you all. Our only hope lies in unity. That will grow."

"What do you wish us to do?"

"Remain here. We will await the night as one," Qundquek told the entire assembly. "The ill that comes will be vanquished, I promise you. I want you all to witness its eradication."

Those of the Starwatch who were not present had already been sent to search the castle's every recess, high and low, instructed to find Scyllarza before she could work her mischief. Every stone in Icehaven was to be lifted in an effort to find her.

As twilight shifted into night and the first of the big braziers in the Hall of Law was being lit, a party of Starwatch entered the hall.

"We have found no more than a single person, lord, outside the chambers of the women. In the lower corridors. We thought all the women and children had been secreted well away from danger, but one young girl has fled in terror and confusion. She was distraught, but we have calmed her. Other than her, Icehaven's corridors and deep caves are lifeless."

Qundquek nodded restlessly. "A child? She should be with the women, but it grows late. Bring her here to me, where she will be safest."

This was duly done and the meek, tear-stained girl stood in the flickering shadows before the throne, clutching a grubby sack to her still heaving breast. Her head hung down, face obscured by her tangled hair. She was very young. To many of the men she symbolised the plight and vulnerability of their own lives. Her clothes were little more than rags, his frame spare.

"Whose child are you?" said Qundquek softly.

"No one's," she whispered. "For no one wants me." There were a few illegitimates in the castle, but they were always cared for, as numbers were essential to the prosperity of Icehaven. "I have no one and nothing," went on the girl. "This is all I own, and I give it gladly to my king." Slowly she undid the string that tied the neck of her sack. She turned the sack upside down and two objects fell out and bounced over the floor, rolling into the pentacle, coming to rest at the foot of the dais.

Firelight speared from the dead eyes of the heads of the snow jaguars, which looked up at Qundquek in mute astonishment. The company drew back from the girl in sudden horror.

"Where did you find these?" gasped the king, his face ashen.

The Babbler's tittering laugh cracked the silence. "Mistress!"

Qundquek stared at the girl: some strange transformation was taking place. Her rags shook as though a wind clawed at them, then split and parted, sloughing off like the skin of a snake. The child lifted her shoulders and stretched out her arms like an emergent moth. A unified cry went up, for this was no child, but a grown woman, and one fitted with burnished armour. It clung to her body like a thin metal skin. Her hair fell back from a proud face that had been chiseled from scorn and her eyes glared up at the king. An ominous hate filled them.

At once one of the Starwatch cast his spear and it whistled as it sliced through the air, but by an impossibly fast movement of her forearm, Scyllarza struck the missile aside. No human could move so swiftly. Her head never turned, her eyes locked on her half-brother's: in the brazier glow they were crimson.

Qundquek swung round to the Voidal. "Do what you must! Do as the Bloodwight commanded you! Kill her!"

The Voidal stepped forward calmly, but ignored the king's outburst. He looked down at the woman's almost feline power with interest. "Is this the one who holds your fortress in such despair?"

Scyllarza's gaze wavered under his stare. There was something infinitely forbidding about this black-garbed stranger, a power that radiated like heat from the sun.

"Yet she is not a Bloodwight," said the Voidal, his gaze unflinching. Something about the hate emanating from the girl moved him, for he recalled only too clearly the frightful things he had seen in Ludang, where his lover had been the victim of a terrible punishment.

Scyllarza spat. "I have no love for the Bloodwights! I will be a bane to them."

Qundquek grew impatient at the exchange. "Why do you hesitate, Voidal? You were brought here as a destroyer. Fulfil your obligations."

The dark man turned to him calmly. "The girl has powers, so you tell me. And she would be a bane to your mortal enemies. Perhaps she would make a better ally than foe. Will you not hear her speak?"

"She is demon!" insisted Qundquek. His eyes appealed to the gathered men of the castle and their fear and revulsion of Scyllarza was apparent.

Scyllarza laughed, the sound like a wind of disdain gusting through the Hall of Law. "I am neither woman nor demon, brother. I can be a girl, meek and tearful as you saw, or a warrior as you behold me now. Or would you have me as an old hag?" At once she had transformed herself into a bent crone, face magically raddled, lined with age, hair like straw and bones twisted back on themselves. The watching host was too stunned by the speed of the change to act, other than to draw back.

"Shape-changer!" said Qundquek. "This is evil witchery."

The Babbler giggled. "It is no worse than the witching powers that your own queens have sought to master, as far back in time as the first, Zarochti."

Scyllarza was a warrior woman once more. "I can be many women if I choose. And as a woman, I can step across your simple pentacle and stand beside you, brother."

"And die by steel," said Qundquek, his sword ringing from its scabbard.

"It would be murder, though you are no stranger to that. Do your subjects condone it? Will you kill me openly before them, or in secret as you murdered my mother, Sheshquari, whose food you had poisoned?"

Qundquek's face was drained of all colour. "You lie!"

Scyllarza shook her head. "Your impatience to be king prompted you to kill her and take the throne that should have been mine. The Babbler hears everything. He speaks to the crawlers in the ice, the snow bats. You cannot deceive me, brother. You tried to make an end of me. Those who cast me into the waters under Icehaven are not here to tell of it, for they, too, sickened and died in mystery. You paved the way to that seat with corpses."

Qundquek looked to his appalled subjects, seeing their changing mood. "It was necessary! I saved Icehaven from dissolution and decay. I had to cut off the withered arm that my family had become - poisoned as it was with the Bloodwight taint. My duty came before my family."

The Voidal addressed the men no less calmly than before. "If this is the sister of your king, perhaps she should stand beside him. Should you not unite against your common foe? She wields great powers. Obviously she would set them against the Bloodwights. Together you would be a strong alliance against those who have usurped Alendar. Destroy each other and you strengthen them."

At this, Eordred could no longer contain his anger. "This is madness! You speak of a demon, sired by Bloodwights! She is the result of a violation, the worst possible insult to the queen. She has stalked Icehaven by night and unleashed unholy terrors to decimate its people. She has made her quest clear and will not rest until she has had us all cut down! Would you tolerate that? Make an ally of her? Ludicrous - you must end her now!" The hate that gleamed in the Sangueen's eyes was far more livid, molten, than that burning within Scyllarza, clear for all men to view.

She pointed scathingly at Eordred. "My brother speaks of serving and saving men. Yet see how he sets about his task. He cares only for his own power. His ruthlessness has brought you a Crimson Priest! As evil as any Bloodwight. It was his like that brought the Bloodwights from Azadris. Perhaps this Sangueen is allied to them? Is it not strange that the demons seek Icehaven, so deep in the winter lands they so abjure? What guides them here?"

Eordred swore crudely.

Qundquek's face clouded in fury. "I labour for the good of Icehaven!" But he could see that the woman had prodded a nerve among his men. All the old doubts about the Sangueen were in their eyes. Fear rippled among them, a palpable wave. They needed to see that their monarch was true to them and their trust in Eordred wavered.

"She speaks like a Bloodwight," said the Sangueen. "Nothing but deceit and malice."

"You would make a puppet of Qundquek," she laughed. "I see you are half way to doing so. How long has he sheltered you here? What other sorceries have you been party to?"

Qundquek shook his head violently, blood rushing back to his face. He could see the tide ebbing away from him. "You question my worthiness?" he shouted to his people. "Then I shall give you an answer!" Turning, he made one savage lunge with his weapon. He was yet a strong man and it tore upwards in a ripping motion that sank deep into the Sangueen's belly before the Crimson Priest was even aware that the king had swung round. Eordred choked on a scream and sprawled backwards, gushing blood as the sword came out. He writhed, groaning in agony.

The gathering let out a great gasp of shock. Qundquek swung back to them with bloodied sword. "There's an end to confusion! Since you cannot accept him and since you question my motives, you have his execution. Is that more to your liking? Well? He cannot harm you further, and thus cannot control me." He was shouting this as much to his sister as to the crowd, his manner wild, hysterical. To the Voidal, Qundquek's greatest ordeal was with himself, riddled as he was with guilt.

The dark man gently touched the sword arm of the king. "Put up your sword. You have disposed of your real enemy, though you do not seem to know it."

Scyllarza glared at the king. "Would you cut me down so readily?"

"You have the evil blood," Qundquek muttered, bewildered by the violence of his own outburst. Still his people waited. They seemed in shock, unable to call out advice.

"No demon could defy such magic as this," replied Scyllarza, indicating the sigils and the runes in which the hall of Law was so steeped. She lifted one of the golden talismen. She crossed over the markings of the pentacle without a tremor of reaction. As she climbed up the steps to her brother, she smiled. "You see, I am as human as you."

The people murmured as though some of their fears were abating. They saw not a warrior woman, but a young woman in an unostentatious robe, beautiful and at the mercy of their hard king. Surely he could not strike her down in this guise. In truth, he had wronged her already.

"What is it you want?" the king hissed, so that only the girl and the dark man could hear.

"To amend the wrongs that have been done. To do what this traveller suggests."

"He was brought here to destroy you - "

"To destroy the *threat*," said the Voidal. "That has been achieved without the destruction you demand." Though he turned to the stiffening corpse of the Sangueen. Qundquek gestured to his nearest guards and at once they covered the body and dragged it away.

"Elevate me, brother," said Scyllarza. "Place me beside you. Make me queen. Our people will be safer than they have ever been before."

"And stand down for you?"

"There is no need. We will rule together. Will you not embrace me? Will you not kiss me before your people and seal a new bond?"

"You would forgive what I have done?" he said uneasily.

She nodded.

Qundquek shuddered. "If I refuse?"

"Then you betray your people, for I will have no other choice but to unleash that which has visited Icehaven each night. Be assured, brother, it will rip out your soul."

Qundquek felt the acid of fear biting into his bones. Darkness hung, poised, outside the castle walls, and all within had become purple shadow. He looked to the Voidal, but the dark man seemed to be wrapped in private thoughts.

"I had not expected the things you offer," said Qundquek.

"You live in greater fear than do your subjects."

"Very well," he breathed. "I will embrace you."

He reached for her and she placed her hands on his shoulders; her eyes came close to his as her mouth sought his cheek. He had a fleeting impression of something behind the crimson eyes, like a landscape over which something loped. Her hands dug into his flesh and her teeth were of diamond. But she kissed him lightly and drew back, laughing, a young woman again. The brief horror had flashed past. The people sighed as if they, too, sensed some passing shadow. But Qundquek's inner fears had not subsided. Scyllarza's body felt warm, but his soul had been held in a freezing grip by its touch.

"It is you," he whispered. "There is no other intruder."

It was too much for him, would never be possible for him to have that terror always at his side. Instinctively he brought up his sword, meaning to open her as he had Eordred, but she moved in a blur. Laughter crashed on his ears as she disappeared, re-materialising behind the throne.

The Voidal gasped, realising that she had danced on to the astral realm and back again. He stepped forward, puzzled by the exchange, unsure how to act. The dying Bloodwight had told him with its last breath that they wanted him to destroy this Bane-Witch, but the Bloodwight had gasped out its own wish, which was for him to kill Qundquek, Eordred and every man alive in Icehaven. If the dark Gods had any part in this, the Voidal wanted nothing to do with it. Rather he would let events unfold as they must. Significantly, his right hand had not stirred. He watched.

"Since you yet spurn me, brother," cried Scyllarza, watching the guards, who were immobilized by fear, "I shall take one last kiss from you." Her transformation began anew, for her hair blazed in tresses of gold fire like a bloody halo; her eyes were icy with fury, her body like beaten iron, writhing with frightful powers. Terrible hands reached out for Qundquek and sank into his flesh like curved knives. The king rammed his sword upwards, but it disintegrated on her abdomen. She forced him to his knees and then lowered her mouth to his face, sinking the diamond teeth into his throat, tearing it out in ruinous triumph. Then, with amazing strength, she picked up his gargling form and hurled it far out into the Hall of Law. It fell among the horrified men, who staggered back from it in sheer terror and confusion.

A rain of spears flew up at the monstrous figure of the Bane-Witch, but she laughed them all to scorn as though they were corn stalks. Her demon arms were longer than any human's and as Elovar and the Starwatch rushed upon her with pikes and longswords, she used her slashing talons to fend them off with ease.

The Voidal pulled Elovar back. "Get away from this chamber! Take everyone with you, before she unleashes carnage on you all. She will bring ruin on you before you can finish her. I alone can prevent this. Do as I say! Use the power of the women to protect you."

Elovar, bewildered by the abrupt death of three of his colleagues, nodded and waved the Starwatch back. The Hall was quickly emptying of Lawkeepers and men while the bemused guards covered their retreat. It was a matter of moments before only the Voidal, the Babbler and Scyllarza stood in the hall. Several dead guards littered the steps to the throne and the king's corpse was like a broken doll out on the polished floor, leaking pools of blood.

Scyllarza stared at the Voidal, her demonic shape flowing back into that of a warrior woman. The dreadful killing lust seemed to have left her.

"Who *are* you?" she said, wary of him.

"I do not belong on Alendar," he answered. "But I will not watch the killing of these people. Is that your purpose? To slaughter them, just as the Bloodwights seek to? Are you, after all, their harbinger?"

She shook her head. "I have already said that I would be the Bane of the Bloodwights. Their blood may be in me, but I despise that part of me, even though it will strengthen my vengeance. I am the Bane-Witch to *them*."

The Voidal reached for the haft of his sword for the first time. "Before I was brought to Icehaven, I dreamt I was out on the snows. I met a lone traveller there, and he gave me this. It is the weapon of the Dark Gods, whom I am fated to serve, though I do not relish this service. You call yourself Bane-Witch." He pulled the blade from its sheath. "This, I was told by the one who met me in the snows, is the Bane of Demons. It seems there are two of you."

Scyllarza drew back slowly, for something in the sword, some suggested movement, filled her with an instinctive dread.

The Voidal studied the blade, the twisted faces that shifted like shadows along its length. "I do not know why the Dark Gods allowed me to be invoked. I only know that Qundquek and his Sangueen forced a Bloodwight to summon me and charged me to destroy you. With this weapon, that would be the simplest of tasks. I think you know that."

Scyllarza nodded, tensing as if to meet an attack that would be swifter than light.

"Yet I have no desire to destroy you," said the Voidal. He slid the sword back into its sheath. "If the Dark Gods have given me the sword to that end, they have not indicated that to me. And I will not slay you unless you force my hand. I will not allow you to take revenge on the people of Icehaven."

Scyllarza sat down heavily on the throne, making no attempt to cover her exhaustion. "They are like sheep. The wolves among them are dead," she added, pointing to the dead king. "Why should you or your gods of the night aid them? They showed me no mercy. I was a child and they allowed me to be tossed into an icy river to drown, as they thought. Only this poor creature below us took pity on me. The people of Icehaven are hardly worthy of saving. They cannot save themselves from the encroaching Bloodwights. They needed a beast such as Qundquek to rule them. Do you regret his death?"

The Voidal shook his head. "He was even more alone than you. No one will mourn him. He wove his own fate. But I agree, his people are like sheep. Must they be torn apart by the Bloodwights, who seem to kill merely for the pleasure of it? Would you see this place an ossuary? You say you are the enemy of the Bloodwights. If that is truly so, then you should remain in that seat and weld these people into a weapon to smite at the spawn of Azadris." He went to her and lowered his hand so unexpectedly that she did not jerk away. He touched her face.

"There is room in you for kinder emotions than the hatred I saw. Hate kills all it touches. It would engulf you." The words echoed within him, an omen.

"You ask me to do more than spare these people. You ask me to love them?"

"They deserve your compassion. Love may come from that, in time."

She stared at him. "Is it your purpose to bend me to this?"

"I would prefer you to exercise your free will. It is something I seek, though rarely with any success. But I will prevent carnage here."

"What would you have me do?"

"The Bloodwights have amassed a small northern army, under their commander, Xarbial. Icehaven's spells will not be sufficient to hold it back. Stand with the defenders, and they will have a chance."

She snorted. "You think they won't cut me down themselves?"

"I will not permit it. I will stand with you. We will conjoin our powers. The Bane of Demons will account for many of the Bloodwights. The people will look to you and I to champion them, at least for a while. Once the Bloodwights are repulsed, then the people of Icehaven will believe in themselves. They will find other champions, but I think they will make you their queen."

They stared at each other in silence for a moment. Again he found himself thinking of his lover, destroyed in the hellish Ludang. A pang of guilt stabbed him as her face superimposed itself over that of Scyllarza.

"What do you offer me?" she said, but she could see that his mind was troubled by something. Is there a way of destroying him? She asked herself. Is that what I want? What is his weakness? He seems to pity me, or does he possess deeper emotions? Her own thoughts disturbed her. Could he feel more than compassion for her? No one had done so before, apart from the Babbler, whose love had been a beacon in a sea of despair. Could this dark man of power love me? No! she told herself. He may desire me, or seek to use me. *But I would be foolish to expect anything more. Well then, I shall find a way to turn his desire against him and learn how to kill.* But the angry thoughts lacked conviction, warring with other emotions she did not understand.

She stood up. "I know nothing of love or compassion," she said abruptly, breaking into his mood. "In such things, you will have to be my guide." She came to him and leaned towards him, her lips parted innocently. He yet saw his lover's face, and for a moment time warped. Then he had bent to the girl and put his lips to hers as though kissing the shadow from the past. Scyllarza softened as he kissed her, and he felt something within himself, some fresh power that had been veiled, perhaps by the Dark Gods that used him.

Scyllarza felt his resistance ebbing, her own control waxing. The Bane of Demons was forgotten now. She tightened her hold, her fierce instinct for survival mastering her. The abrupt transformation began. Her arms clawed, her body like iron, her teeth about to make the fatal bite. It must be done quickly.

The Voidal knew instantly that she meant to destroy him. The fear in her body had transmitted itself through her embrace, just as the

Bloodwight in her fuelled itself and gripped him like talons of fury. His own powers responded and welled up, so that the two figures remained locked about each other, wracked by the spasms of the bizarre conflict. Below them, the Babbler saw what was happening, at once assuming that the stranger was attempting to kill his mistress.

He rushed up the steps and picked up a fallen sword. Without hesitation he thrust it into the Voidal's back, again and again, but it was like driving the blade into a stellar void. There was no effect. He tried striking with the cutting edge, but nothing he could harmed the dark man. It was like trying to slice up a shadow.

Scyllarza felt something vast smothering her killing lust, deflecting it like a passionate surge of energy that could not be dammed. She focused her hate, but it broke under that tide. Her strength waned, changing, running with the flow of new power, growing in the running.

Something within the Voidal was opposing her treachery, but whatever power had been channeled through him to shatter that deadly embrace had also cracked the walls of the vessel that held those killing desires. He had no control over this terrifying surge of energy, which was made more terrifying by the fact that it was not totally poured into him by extraneous gods, but had part of its source within him. He tapped depths to his own core that had been locked away from him. And Scyllarza, he knew, was going to die, imploded by the destructive madness that threatened to burst. But he must not let her die!

He fought himself, fought to contain that inner power, to warp it to his own use, to shape, direct and adjust it. And he knew that it was a war with the Dark Gods, their will against his. Yet, little by little, he brought the explosive energy to heel, as he would have a savage hound, curbing its malice.

Scyllarza hung limp, as if drained of blood, energy and will. The Voidal set her down carefully, ignoring the curses of the Babbler, who thought her dead.

In a moment, her eyes opened. They were soft, free of hate, as if it had been drawn from her like puss from a wound. The demon in her had subsided.

"I tried to kill you," she breathed.

"Something else did. It is not what you want."

She shook her head. "You spoke of unity. It seems as though we talked hours since - "

He lifted her up easily in his arms. The Babbler watched, shut out from their existence for the moment, as the dark man carried his mistress to another part of the castle.

For a long time the Babbler stood, only the fading embers in the braziers keeping back complete darkness. Something probed furtively at his foot and he hopped back, staring down in horror. The Crimson Priest was still alive. He had crawled agonisingly across the stone, smearing it with his blood. The Babbler raised his purloined sword to strike, but the Sangueen began to speak in a croaking, dying voice. He dipped his finger in his own blood to write a single rune on the steps to the throne. Soon after that, he was dead, but on the face of the Babbler a smile broke out at last.

* * * *

Secreted in a place between stone walls that only he knew of, the Babbler listened.

To begin with there was little to hear, but he knew that his mistress and the black garbed man were sharing something utterly private to them. Love? But this traveller could not possibly feel the anguish of love as understood by the Babbler! His life owed itself to his own love, and fed upon it, thrived on it alone. This accursed outsider could have no more concept of love for Scyllarza than for a single dawn, which could be savoured and remembered but never cherished to the exclusion of all others. Scyllarza was the Babbler's life and he did not look beyond her. This outsider would lie if he said as much of himself! Aye, his transient ardour mocked Scyllarza. Yet the Babbler could do nothing. Only listen.

They spoke of many strange things, the Voidal of his erratic destiny, Scyllarza of her intense loneliness and of her hate for all the beings of Alendar. But she spoke kindly of the Babbler and told of how he had saved her and nursed her and given her the will to rise up and destroy those who had rejected her. These words did little to ease the growing sorrow of the Babbler, who saw himself in their light as no more than an instrument. Even so, better that than to have earned the hate that she had meted out to all others.

The Voidal spoke again. This time his words cut deeper than the frosts of Bitterscarp. "Your hate comes only partly from yourself. Much of it comes from your strange squire. He has fostered the loathing in you. It is a mirror of his own. It is a mirror that must be shattered if you are to save yourself. Alone against Alendar's denizens, you would soon perish."

Alone! The word roared in the Babbler's ears. She will never be alone, not while I breathe.

"Am I to be alone then?" Scyllarza said.

There was silence for a moment. "Not by my choosing, for between us we could do much to free Alendar of its burdens. But it will not be permitted. Those who use me do not veer from their course. And they mean *me* to walk alone."

"I am not bound to Alendar. I have small powers. I traverse the astral at will. The many dimensions are open to me."

"You would accompany me?"

She laughed, surprised at herself and the warmth of the sound. "I would."

"The Dark Gods issue dreadful forfeits to those who share themselves with me."

"You loved," she said, her hand lifting his. "I know it. I have seen that in your face. You were punished for that."

"More so was she. I would not see such cruelty again."

"These gods deny you such things?"

"While I am chained to them, yes, it seems so. I am plucked up and set down erratically, or in no pattern that I can fathom. There is a familiar who serves me." A smile brightened his sombre face. "And he would bide with me as a tic to a sheep. But our meetings are by chance only, or by the whim of the Dark Gods. Our meetings suit them before him, though he does not always grasp that.

"I fear for you," he told her. "I would not have you suffer the same fate - "

She put her fingers to his lips. "Keep her secrets to yourself. There may be a time when you can speak of them to me. But, if you ask it, I will leave Alendar with you."

"I have a mind," he said grimly, "to stand against these Bloodwights and see that the people of Icehaven defeat them. Who knows if that is what the Dark Gods wish? I think it unlikely that they would want to promote the cause of the Bloodwights. Let us at least give the people here hope."

"Very well. I can bring other powers into the battle. My Babbler is not the only being who serves me. There are ice elementals here that I can call to me from the glaciers and the northern peaks. They will strike terror into the Bloodwights."

"Then we must use them."

After this, the Babbler left, his heart pounding. She would *aid* the people of Icehaven! After a lifetime spent preparing their fall. What must be done? This dark demigod must be destroyed, but such a thing would encompass extreme danger. He had stolen Scyllarza's reason. It must be returned to her. Icehaven must fall. The Babbler sighed. He had been patient for so many years. Now he must apply that inexorable patience once more.

* * * *

The men of Icehaven feared Scyllarza, the Bane-Witch, but they feared the Voidal more, who had no fear of her, indeed, who controlled her. Her vengeance, the dark man told them, was complete, for Qundquek had been her foe, not them. Their fear led them to obey him and they felt its cessation when he told them he and Scyllarza would stand against the Bloodwights. Even the women, preparing their ancient spellcraft, were relieved that there would be unity following the king's death.

On the outer walls of the castle, the defendants readied for the Bloodwight siege, knowing from scouts that Xarbial had followed through his promises to harry them and had drawn up an uncommonly large northern host. There had never been so many of the demon spawn in the northern lands before, but the forays of the Starwatch had angered them to madness. They rode at midday, hopeful to catch at least some warmth, and they came storming down the wide canyon that led to the gates of the fortress.

The defenders unloosed showers of arrows, but these were of little use against Bloodwight armour. The Voidal called for the men to ready their swords and wait for the Bloodwights to come scaling up the walls. This was not long in happening, for the demons were remarkably agile, hot with confidence. Their numbers were frightening.

On the ramparts the resultant fighting was a grim affair. Men grappled with fanatic Bloodwights, often going down to the slash of a talon, for the demons were far stronger than the humans and possessed of a maniacal love of war, almost mindless in their killing frenzy. Scyllarza and the Voidal, twin spears of opposition, pressed back many, though, being more than a match for them. The Bane-Witch gave blow for blow, madness for madness. And the Bane of Demons was justly named, for the supernatural sword drank deep of Bloodwight life. The Voidal felt it shudder as it carved a swathe into them and knew that the Dark Gods had blessed its crimson crusade.

In spite of the carnage that the dark man and the Bane-Witch wrought, Xarbial's army continued to pour over the ramparts like a swarm of bees, determined to sack Icehaven at any cost. Scyllarza dismayed many with her own demon guise, but still they came. She summoned from the winds the ice elementals and from the glaciers and snows more of the same. These creatures, some small, some far larger than man or Bloodwight, flew, hopped and crawled into the battle, searing Bloodwight flesh with bitter cold, whipping up blizzard winds that forced even the men to draw back. Countless scores of Xarbial's warriors toppled to their doom, or were ripped apart by the claws of the wind.

The Bloodwights still pressed at the foot of the walls hesitated, seeing the monstrous forces of the ice realms that hung over them like clouds of death. Xarbial himself made a frenzied attempt to drive his forces on, but the Voidal smashed a way through his immediate guards until he stood before the demon lord. They exchanged mighty blows, on the highest of Icehaven's battlements, with the forces of the blizzard screaming about their ears in a white vortex. It was as if the ice elementals sought to drive them both out into the abyss.

The men were finding it impossible to fight in this bitter wind and slowly drew back into the castle, sealing what doors they could, while the Bloodwights had become so numbed by the power of the storm that they fell back, watching the heroic contest on the battlements. Xarbial realised what weapon it was that the Voidal carried and it filled him with fear. His attack became wild defense, fraught with errors. The dark man alone was impervious to the elemental storm, his green eyes fixed on the great Bloodwight, the lights of doom. At last he drove home the Bane of Demons and Xarbial screamed above the storm's glee so tormentedly that every man and Bloodwight felt that scream, like the tearing of a knife.

Xarbial crashed down and lay dead across the upper parapet. It was enough. His minions immediately swung back over the walls and flung themselves into the drifts below. They closed ranks for warmth, turned and fled back down the canyon in search of any cave or fissure in which to hide from the pursuing storm. They had left innumerable dead, their army massacred. By the new day, the survivors would be frozen, none surviving.

In the upper corridors of the castle, the Voidal met the Lawkeepers. "The Bloodwights will not return to the north," he told them, warming himself by a cresset. Already the storm was abating, the elementals flowing back into the remoter fastnesses. "They will shun this place now, knowing that its magic is far stronger than theirs. Use the future to grow strong."

"We are indebted," murmured the spokesman, Nanchook. "Your part in this victory was formidable. We misjudged you."

"You must choose a leader," the Voidal told him.

Various things were said, or shouted, and it was clear that a unanimous choice had already been made. But the Voidal shook his head. "It cannot be me. I fear my time here will be short. Other powers call on me. And besides, I have no link with your royal line. It is not fitting that you should elevate me above the true heir to your monarchy. Has not Qundquek's sister proved herself in battle? It was she, not I, who called up the ice people, without whom Icehaven would have fallen. Their continuing protection will be vital to you, and it is she who commands it.

"Scyllarza is the heir. Your tradition demands a queen. It was her crown that Qundquek took for himself."

Clearly there remained a few doubts among the people, but none could dismiss the furious onslaught Scyllarza had made on the Blood-wights, both personally and through the elementals. Her utter loathing of the Bloodwights had been evident. The Voidal left the Lawkeepers to discuss it and went up to the walls in search of the girl.

He found her alone on the battlements. The storm had completely abated, the last of the ice elementals returned to its home, and the sky was streaked with the red pennants of Azadris's light. Below, the white snow mirrored the sky, rich with the blood of the fallen. Scyllarza embraced the Voidal as he came to her, relieved that the fury was over.

"They will make you their queen," he told her.

"But they do not love me. They saw the Bane-Witch, the beast."

"Yes, they fear you, as they feared your brother. But rule them wisely and fairly and they will accept you."

"I am not sure that it is what I want," she said, staring out at the bleak terrain, its cold emptiness.

"Go to them. Show them your humanity, as you have shown me. Let the other side of your nature subside. Use it only when you make war on the Bloodwights. There is nowhere else for you."

"And you? Can you not stay? Have you not won that freedom?"

He sighed. "Perhaps I have. I will stay as long as I am permitted."

She smiled. "Could it be that you humour me, and would rather leave?"

He hugged her to him. "No, but I would not have you share my curse. I will not have you suffer as she suffered. But I could find contentment here. I will stay, until they have more bloody work for me. Go to the people below. Face them without me, for they fear me the most. They will accept you, for they know you have won them this day, and their future."

She nodded.

He unstrapped his scabbard, the powerful blade within it. "Here, take this. You are the Bane of Demons, and this will be your strength. The Dark Gods meant it to be your banner."

She took the weapon and strapped it to her, going to the stairs. "Come to me soon," she called, descending, and he nodded.

As he turned to look out over the heaps of the slain, he was troubled. He knew that he had been right, for the Dark Gods would never allow him to stay here with her. They would send him out into the omniverse once more, though he would truly have been content to stay. He knew that they would never permit him to regain what they had taken from him. The Swords of the Seneschals were scattered. To regain his soul, he would need them all, but how could he hope to bring them together? Like the Bane of Demons, they would be needed in their own worlds. If he united them, what damage would he wreak, what worlds would fall?

"A pretty victory, master," said a hoarse voice behind him. He turned to face the grinning Babbler.

"A beginning, I trust," nodded the dark man.

"Have you made my mistress a queen?"

"It seems so. And you would be a knight, eh?" the Voidal smiled.

The Babbler bowed. Secretly he was smiling, for the dark man could not have noticed his attempt to strike him down when he had first fought with Scyllarza.

"A poor knight I!" he laughed. "Such finery!" He indicated his rags.

The Voidal bent down and picked up one of the many fallen swords that littered the parapet. "Here, then. Let this be your first tool of office." He tossed the sword to the Babbler, who caught it clumsily and tried its balance. He hunched forward casually. He had seen the Voidal hand the Bane of Demons to his mistress. He carried no other weapon.

The dark man absently slipped his right hand inside his shirt. "It is cold. Let us go in."

The Babbler's mind was churning, thrilling to the dying words of the Sangueen, recalling vividly what he had said about the words of power, and of the bloody rune daubed in scarlet on the steps of the throne. By these words and rune alone could the Voidal be returned to the place from which he had come. The Babbler straightened abruptly and spoke the words with stumbling hesitation, then repeated them with more confidence.

The Voidal gasped as if he had been knifed, and lurched backwards. He tried to speak but could not, a sudden dizziness rocking him. At once the Babbler used his advantage and darted in close. He made two sweeping strokes with his sword, cutting a rough symbol on the chest of the dark man: Eordred's rune. It wept blood and the Babbler said again the words spoken to him by the dying Sangueen.

It was as though a sudden mist had enveloped the Voidal. The Babbler watched in amazement and relief as the mist started to dissolve. With it went the dark figure. In a short while he was gone, no more than a memory. No one had seen. The Babbler laughed, tossing away the sword guiltily, and scuttled into the castle.

He would tell his mistress that the dark man had drawn a pentacle about himself, spoken certain potent spells and taken himself far from Alendar, without as much as a backward glance.

PART SEVEN

THE EXILE OF EARTHENDALE

And so to what became of Elfloq after his unsettling visit to Cloudway.

Retribution, the gods would say, is an art. Men generally assume that physical pain is the worst form of suffering, and as a consequence have devised unlimited means of inflicting physical pain on each other.

The gods certainly recognise the effectiveness of physical pain (especially when dealing with mere men) but they use far more subtle methods of punishment.

Who knows this better than I?

—**SALECCO**, the tormented and long-suffering.

* * * *

Through the shifting mists of the astral realms flew Elfloq, relieved to be away from the perils that had lately beset him while following the cause of his chosen master. His arm throbbed from the nerve-wracking encounter with the assassin, Ipsol, and in spite of the attention given to it by Eye Patch of the Smile, Elfloq knew he would have to spend a while resting it. Even so, he kept his eyes and ears constantly alert for any word or revelation that could strengthen his bond with the Voidal. He was wary, too, of the machinations of the Dark Gods, who desires could never be fully understood. Retribution would always be a threat, but for the moment his many qualms were yet overridden by his ambitions.

As he flew through a particularly murky patch of the astral, he heard a nearby flutter of wings and then a piping hail. "Elfloq, is that you I spy?"

Elfloq's own wings thrummed as he steadied himself. From out of the surrounding miasma materialised another familiar. This was Troldo, a waggish youngster who was at least as fond of gossip as was Elfloq. They exchanged greetings and agreed cheerfully to fly on together for a while, speaking of various intrigues and plots. Elfloq proudly displayed his wound, describing with considerable excess his 'conflict' with the Skulk of Illhallows.

Shortly before Troldo was due to veer away on his own master's work, the two familiars heard a doleful pulsing sound emanating from the near distance like the boom of a great dying heart. Its source was invisible, but it broke over them like the billows of some melancholy sea, full of immense sadness and despair.

Elfloq reeled, astounded by the depth of the anguish in that sound. "I have never before heard such sorrow," he commented. "Who suffers out there in the emptiness?"

Troldo snorted derisively. "Ah, pay no heed! 'Tis only the Old Man down on Earthendale. They say he is crazed. He must be if can bemoan a sojourn there. Fool! 'Tis a bright, healthy world, full of harmless beings. Why, even the witches there would rather kiss than curse!" He attempted a lecherous wink.

"Does no one listen to the Old Man?"

"Not any more. He is so tiresome and his moaning has become an un-witting beacon, warning astral travellers away, not to him, as he wishes. Well, I must away myself. Duty calls. Until we meet again, Elfloq. You might try bathing that arm down in Earthendale's waters, but - " He laughed and was gone.

Elfloq, distracted, muttered a goodbye. He felt drawn to the mournful call of the Old Man, whose sorrow must be fathomless if he could voice it up from his world into the very astral realms. The familiar saw again the sadness in the eyes of the beautiful woman who had been the lover of his master, who in Cloudway had shown him the ring that she had made of a tear. His tear.

Now, feverish with curiosity, he flew closer to the source of the puls-ing sorrow. Soon he had detected the proximity of the world of Earthen-dale, and with a last shrug, popped out into a clear blue sky and sunny, invigorating climate.

Far below him the contours of Earthendale stood out like an embossed map, the hills and dips rich in greenery, voluptuous and alluring. Elfloq sensed the nearness of the Old Man of sorrow and swooped downwards. Presently he found himself confronted by a towering wall of stone, a huge, living crag that rose up uniquely from the surrounding dales. It was set here like the castle of a god, and from it one must be able to see half the world. It was upon the top of this gigantic outcrop that the astral voice of the Old Man had its source.

Elfloq flew over the mossy rim, marveling at the small meres and waterfalls and sprawling floral groves that adorned the crest of the crag. A miniature paradise, he thought, and more salubrious by far than many grim divine retreats he had seen, notably of late. He espied the Old Man by a glittering pool, sat upon a rock, head in his hands as if sobbing in great distress. Yet he was silent, though Elfloq knew that his voice reached out into the astral.

Gently the familiar alighted on the springy turf beyond the pool, putting the placid water between himself and the Old Man. Scintillating butterflies fluttered away from the movement in a brilliant cloud. The Old Man looked up at once. There were no tears in his eyes, but unspeakable pain resided there. He seemed amazed by Elfloq's presence and for a moment struggled to find words to express his confused emotions.

"I heard your distress," said Elfloq. "It seemed only courteous that I should visit you."

This only served to promote the Old Man's dumbness, as though he had received an even greater shock. His silence had started to become a source of minor embarrassment to Elfloq and the familiar began to fidget.

"Have you come to laugh at me, as did all the others? I had thought they had ceased coming. It has been so long," said the Old Man at last, his words laboured, almost too much of an effort.

"Laugh? Nay. Curiosity brought me, sir, of the idle kind. You seem to be suffering greatly. I interpreted your sorrow as an appeal, a plea - "

"Indeed!" cried the Old Man. Elfloq found himself gazing into twin prisms of hope that sparkled almost as intensely as the sorrow. "A plea it was, and always is. Is it foolish of me to suppose that you have come with the intention of aiding me? I had thought myself denied pity."

Elfloq sniffed nonchalantly and began examining certain of the exotic blooms around him. He must discover what advantage he could gain here before making any commitments. "I have a master, of course, being a familiar. His work is my only calling. You appreciate that I cannot step outside the bounds of my duty to him."

The Old Man's hope began to fade visibly, like winter sunlight at dusk. "Yes," he sighed. "As I feared. As you say, it is curiosity that has brought you, as with others. The best I can hope for is ridicule. Best be on your way, familiar! You are too painful a reminder that other worlds beside this one exist."

"Oh, I have a little time to spare at present," replied Elfloq. "And it may be that I can be of some small service. My master, I feel sure, would be glad to spare me for such, provided, that is, it would benefit him in some small way." *Or myself*, he thought, though it would have been imprudent to have said so. "If you understand me?"

The Old Man sighed, his body trembling. "A small service? If you could aid me, familiar, I would certainly aid your master."

Elfloq tried not to appear too eager. "How? Are you a god?"

The Old Man shook his head. "No! Nor have I ever sought godhead. I have a few simple powers, though like me, they are dying. I have so little time left. You may have all that is mine, all my waning power, all my small secrets. I gladly promise you that. But is it enough to win your help?"

"If the task you set me is not too vast or inconvenient, then we may well be able to do business. Tell me more about yourself and your plight here. Is this not the beautiful world that it seems?"

The Old Man nodded. "Oh, it is." His skin, Elfloq noticed, was dry and cracked, parched as a desert, his brow scored with channels and lines as if scorched and worn by terrible heat. Did he not bathe in the soothing pools here? There was grime and loam encrusted in his pores. Why should he torture himself with such uncleanliness?

"My name is Mermerides. This is not my native world, although it is beautiful and fair, and more so than a thousand other worlds. I am from the oceans of whispering Mare Serenis. How far away that is, I cannot say. Many universes, many dimensions, perhaps the width of the entire omniverse.

"How did I come here? Willingly. It was so long ago that it seems I must have lived out a hundred lifetimes here. As a young man, I lived in the warm waters of Mare Serenis, for I am a sprite (though to you I must seem more like a withered tree spirit). Hot-blooded I was, too, for the sprites are not the cold fish others sometimes think us. I loved and honoured my mistress, the boundless ocean, and she gave herself freely to my fellows and me. Our desires lacked nothing. Our lives were full, joyous.

"One day there came to the golden beaches of Mare Serenis a young witch from this world, Earthendale. She was gathering shells and conches and bright pebbles for her simple spells at home, for they are compulsive hoarders, you know. They love beautiful things. At once she wove a spell over me - oh, it was no intentional thing! She had no inkling that her strange and alien beauty captivated me - not until I stepped sleekly from the sea and walked with her. Ah, but how blissful that day was! I knew instinctively that the magic worked in her also. We spoke nothing of it, except with our eyes, with embarrassed movements of our hands, but love had netted us.

"Later, when we had learned more of each other and at last spoken of our mutual love, I walked with her to the edge of the sea, asking her to let the waters soothe her feet. But the salty spray hissed in anger and jealousy! Mare Serenis was not to be placated. I was a sprite, she said, and I belonged to the sea. The witch was of the earth, alien, to be tolerated but not to be worshipped. My own anger was huge! Such is the impetuosity of young love that I turned my back on my mother sea. I told my beautiful witch, Lissild, that I would return with her to her world. She was torn by her love for me and her fear for my rash decision, but in the end our love rejected all cautions, as love often will. I see now that it was foolish of me, but I went with her - yet I would not change that. I would not alter a moment of her nearness.

"Mare Serenis whispered to me as I walked away across her wide sands. 'Go!' she cried tempestuously. 'No good will come of your bond. As you spurn me, so do I you. Never return! You will die alone, far away.' I was young, ablaze with love, which laughs at fear. I must have thought that I would live with my Lissild forever.

"She worked the magic that brought us both through the astral realms to this world. At first I was overawed by the undulating dales, the rounded hills and verdant forests. They made me giddy as I could not and I could not dwell in such confusion. Lissild found this high place, where I can yet watch the clouds chasing each other like surf and study the blue depths of the sky, so reminiscent of the sea. We were so happy. In time we had our first child, then more. They were sturdy, content, but such high isolation became too restricting to them and they begged us to let them descend the crags and go out into the world to seek their separate destinies. Painful departures they were, for the children were a great strength to me, but they went, ablush with hope. Their earth called, their god.

"There were seven, and all have long since gone, even our raven-haired daughters. High places were not for them and they were happier climbing down to be one with the bosom of the earth. Their mother and I never stayed them. Later we wept. It may have been those sad departures that began my witch's decline. Earthendale's children do not live long, you see, although they believe it is forever, as they go back into the earth and are reborn. Lissild died and I wrapped her small form in thick leaves tied with vines and watched her plummet over the crag to a long overdue reunion with the earth so far below. Does that sound a cruel way to part?

No, I should have released her sooner. She should have gone with the children.

"I expected to live but a short time after she had gone from me, but to my horror have lived on. It has been the promised curse of Mare Serenis. Her water children live short, youthful lives (as do the earth children) but my life has dragged on, reluctant to free me of its grasp. I thought of leaping from the crags, but could not face such an end. The water? No, it is not the sea. The sea birthed me and must be my grave. I will not live forever - I am indeed no god - but am to die very soon.

"Before I die, there is one burning dream I must fulfil. I must go back to Mare Serenis. I must stand one last time upon her whispering shores. I must go down to the laughing waters and feel their silken touch, their goodness, and pray to the sea mother to be remembered, for I do not expect forgiveness."

The Old Man had been staring at the clouds. His eyes turned once more upon Elfloq. "No one has offered me hope of such a return. Will you? I have no magic, no spells to take me across the astral."

Elfloq cleared his throat, in which some inexplicable lump had wedged. It had been a touching story. "I may be able to work a few magics, I think. I once had a master who was a sorcerer. Quite notorious he was. You may even have heard of him - "

"Say what you require of me," said the Old Man breathlessly, leaning forward, desperate to be able to give something useful to the familiar.

"Oh, a little knowledge will suffice," Elfloq sniffed. "Nothing extravagant. You must think me impolite to ask anything of you. Well, I'd help you for a smile, but my master - "

"Yes, yes. What knowledge?"

Elfloq had hopped around the pool and stood close to the Old Man. "There are certain gods at work in the omniverse. In truth there are many, but these are malicious and particularly terrible. Their purposes are shrouded in secrecy, often in pain, always in fear - all seem wary of them, even other gods. What can you tell me of them? They are known simply as the Dark Gods."

Mermerides gave this some thought, nodding. Elfloq had expected an answer garbed in horror, but there was none as Mermerides spoke. "I know a little of them. Glad I am that it was only Mare Serenis that I offended and not the Dark Gods, for they would doubtless have punished me far more mercilessly than the sea mother."

"They are evil?"

Mermerides shook his head. "Oh, not truly so. Cruel, perhaps, but not evil. They war on evil and their methods are often what we might consider evil. But the Dark Gods are just. Fire against fire, fury against fury."

"Their purpose?"

"They are the Punishers. The gods of justice. I know very little, but they serve some supreme deity, I think."

"They do? Not evil," breathed Elfloq. "The darkness that hides them is the darkness of mystery, enigma. Gods of retribution. They would not destroy or chastise or punish for a mere whim or for spite, but for valid reasons? They act purely by design?"

"In justice, yes."

Elfloq clapped his tiny hands. "Then I am satisfied. It is enough. A little knowledge. I shall treasure it, Old Man. Uh…that is, my master will be pleased, and in his pleasure lies my own." He was indeed pleased, for it painted the Dark Gods in a less awesome aspect and suggested that they would have little time to seek out a minor recalcitrant as himself.

Mermerides stood up, tears welling in his eyes. He shook, his body tired, enfeebled by the colossal weight of years. "Then…you will take me from here?"

"If I can. It is not common for a man, uh, that it, a *sprite*, to journey through the astral realms. Mages, necromancers, sorcerers, yes and witches - they all do so at will, though none with ease. It will be difficult for you."

"I have nothing to live here for. If I die here, the earth will not have me. Work your spells."

Elfloq nodded. He possessed a remarkable memory and from it was able to tug innumerable cantrips, spells, workings as well as information about the omniverse that would have filled whole libraries. He sifted this and took from his trove a working that might help Mermerides across the astral. Then he began to murmur and make passes. Habit forced him to dramatise the whole procedure, as it gave him a heightened sense of self-importance.

Mermerides felt a roaring sensation in his veins: the sky went very black and rushed down like the fall of a mountain range to squash him. Winds tore at him but then thrust him forward like a tide. Oblivion claimed him for a while.

Elfloq guided the apparently lifeless Old Man across the astral at great speed until satisfied that he was near the world of Mare Serenis. The familiar worked more sorcery to bring them through into light.

They were standing between two tall dunes, the breeze lifting a sheet of sand from the wide beach before them. Mermerides stirred and swayed on his feet. Elfloq, half his height, steadied him, squinting into the distance for a glimpse of the sea. "Is this your world?"

Mermerides gazed at the lapping waters so far away. Their greens and blues fused and rolled as waves raced eagerly shoreward, expending themselves happily in sighing surf that bubbled up the beach. The Old Man gasped, his hand slapping his chest. He drew in the air as if taking a powerful anodyne. "Mare Serenis!" he whispered, his voice thick with emotion. It was as if all his early memories raced up the beach with those sparkling waters, coming to meet him mirthfully. But they teased, receding, leaving the sands damp and gleaming, empty.

Suddenly Mermerides collapsed, face grey, eyes misting. He could barely speak.

Elfloq quickly knelt beside him. "What is it, Old Man?"

"Heart…about to beat…its last. No matter. I have seen."

"The water," muttered Elfloq, staring in angry despair at the remote tide line. "I will take you to it."

"I am too much for you…"

"Nonsense!" Gamely Elfloq put his tiny arms about the back and neck of the Old Man and managed to raise him to a sitting position. His ragged shift parted and fell, leaving the worn husk of body naked, corpse-like. Elfloq began the immense task of dragging him through the resisting dried sand and on to the firmer sand of the upper beach. As he did so, his wounded arm reminded him that it was far from recovered. Groaning, the familiar knew that his task was impossible. The sea was so far off. He could never manage so great a weight as Mermerides, however frail, though a normal man would have picked him up like a doll. Yet Elfloq continued to try.

The Old Man wheezed a faint, final thanks and Elfloq sensed his life trickling away. Defeated, impotent, Elfloq cursed, for he had to lower the dying sprite to the sand. There were tears in his own eyes. He looked at the sea and shook a tiny fist. "May the sun dry you up for this! May all your children leave you!"

As he spluttered his anger, he saw another wave about to break, but one that was fuller and taller than the others. It began to race unnaturally up the beach, churning the sand, flinging high white spume before it. Afraid now that he had infuriated the sea mother, Elfloq took to his heels and scampered off for the dunes. Half way there he turned, smitten with horror and guilt, for the body of the Old Man was stretched upon the open sands like a corpse upon a bare catafalque. Too late! The wave boiled over him in a cascade of erupting surf.

"Mermerides!" cried Elfloq. "I did not mean to desert you - "

The wave had broken; no more than a few drops splashed over Elfloq's in a faint drizzle. The familiar felt the air vibrate with a sudden stab of great *joy*. He saw the waters recede and in their embrace was the body of their prodigal child. Mermerides was floating out upon the now calm waters. Elfloq could not see the face from here, for it gazed down into the deeps, but the familiar knew somehow that it smiled its first smile for countless centuries.

He rubbed at his arm subconsciously, then, glancing down, realised that the fine drizzle of sea spume that had fallen on him had seeped into the wound. And in that touch, a delicate caress, the wound no longer throbbed. It was mended.

And somewhere far across the omniverse, in Earthendale, voices murmured under the earth, enriching the soil with their echoes of Mare Serenis's contentment.

PART EIGHT

THIEF OF THIEVES

There can be few more potent punishments than loneliness. To be alone is one thing, shut away in a barren stone prison where the rest of the omniverse is little more than a vague memory, a hint of reality. But not to enjoy the company of others, share their lives even when travelling the omniverse, that is loneliness indeed.

When the Dark Gods set the Voidal on his erratic path, which took him repeatedly into the worlds of men, they cursed him with loneliness, saying that no man could be a friend to him without dire penalty, and well they understood the frustrations and melancholy this would bring him.

Perhaps this was why they permitted him his strange relationship with Elfloq the familiar, who otherwise must surely have been subjected to the most dreadful of reprisals. Certainly, in charting their history, it is clear to me that the dark man did come to rely on Elfloq, and drew more than a shred of comfort from his dubious companionship.

It is a theme I will return to.

—**SALECCO**, the incarnation of Loneliness

* * * *

A traveller, straying to the limits of any of the many dimensions, might find himself, somewhat bemusedly, standing upon a particular dead world, the surface of which is raddled and pocked like the face of one suffering from the Great Wasting Curse. This dead world is not so dead as its much-cratered surface would suggest. The more knowing traveller would recognise this grim outpost as Intercelestis, which is sometimes referred to as the 'grandfather of boltholes.' It lies in no single dimension but in the very interstices of many (if not all). Its outer surface is but a guise, a façade affecting old age, even decay and extinction, like a meteor-blasted moon. Yet should the traveller investigate those broken-rimmed craters and venture down into their apparent darkness, he would find himself stepping into another domain altogether.

In this inner world, the first wonder to light up his eyes would be the innumerable spans of glistening rock that arch out over a gulf to the blazing core of Intercelestis, which itself is like a colossal aerial hive, an orb of fused buildings, the architecture of which implies the melding of countless cultures, which indeed it is, for the worlds that open on to this place would require the age of a god to list. Many of its abnormal structures are, in fact, prototypical designs of the gods, tossed aside in favour of more artistic or functional constructs: they have been fused together in Intercelestis in a kind of celebration of architectural disaster. They more than hint at lunacy, but it is a guise that suits well the singular inhabitants. Those who cross to Intercelestis may return by any of the many spans: each leads out into a dimension other than that from which the traveller came.

Who has adopted such a baffling retreat? Not the gods, who would be far too embarrassed to admit to having created it, and it is from them that the dubious rabble of Intercelestis hide, generally speaking. Demi-gods and demons, mages, renegade elementals, masterless spirits - all have played their part in the continuing construction. And of course, Man has laboured hard here, too, ever anxious to mask himself from the power of the gods and even to compete with them. Nothing is more covetous of the gods' power than Man. Naturally, the gods know of this place, yet they have never tarried long to study it, for they know that those who hide here cannot do so forever.

The central citadel of Intercelestis is perhaps as unusual a conglomerate of beings and creatures as may be found anywhere else in the entire omniverse. Yet there are certain mores adhered to by the majority, for the safety and sanity of the community, although for the most part laws and regulations are touchy subjects. Those that choose to dwell here for a while, though, do pay tribute to the mores: after all, they would not be here without very good reason. Ejection could lead to something far worse.

Primarily Intercelestis serves as a retreat, a sanctuary. It does have other purposes. For example, its markets and bazaars are fabled. There are items to be bartered for here that would be found, indeed shown, nowhere else.

* * * *

The Heaving House tavern was living up to its name and reputation, crammed to capacity, as ever. Here, in this sweaty, smoke-hung, low-roofed dungeon of a bar, enough wine and ale flowed to launch a fleet of war galleys. Noise was more than a bubbling blur: it pressed down like an open hand over the squeezed revelers, though their ears had long since become deaf to babble, ears that somehow picked out the individual messages bawled at them by associates and companions. All manner of beings pressed together in that seething amalgam of flesh, bibbing and ale-swigging. There were mostly men here, as well as hybrids and half-breeds; there were scaled Ellyx (the imps from Zyreve), stocky elementals, cloven-hoofed rock demons from Phesmir; there were women, too, though none foolish enough to flaunt their beauty, or lack of it, save the torrid Firerider from stormy Emberdoom, whose laughing eyes (and singing sword) mocked even the tough mercenaries from Snarlgard. Three Sacred Hags from Thaumatand sat in a corner, pulling threads from the effigy of a doomed monarch, teasing from the mock king a cruel fate. Few had want of business with these, so none pressed close. A tall dryad from the Waterworlds drew tighter her leafy cloak as she nodded silently to the silent Ax-Bearer beside her, listening patiently to his tale of how he had almost won a crown from Prince Gedyrak on war-riven Toomeraf.

In this entire hubbub there was scarce room to spare for a fragile familiar. His delicate wings folded neatly to his shoulderblades, his back pressed firmly against one of the thick timbers supporting the roof, Elfloq grimaced as a burly crewman from one of the docked frigates, a winged whippersail from the luscious dimension of Elberdale, home of many forbidden spices and unguents, brushed by with a belch and much slopping of ale. The two men with Elfloq were no better mannered, guzzling from their heavy goblets while drenching their shirts as though they had had no ale for half a lifetime. Elfloq would have deplored visiting such a tavern as *The Heaving House*, quite the most notorious in all Intercelestis, where taverns were as frequent as lice under tree bark, but only here could he expect to meet those whom he must speak with. However, his desired conversation was faring badly.

He had bought drinks for the two men, and although for a familiar to be in possession of silver coins was most unusual (even in the service of a master) the dark-skinned feline girl behind the bar had passed over the brew without question. Most of the loot exchanged in here was not honestly come by. If it was real, that was enough. (As an aside, Elfloq had acquired the money through the unscrupulous act of pocket-picking and as the contents of the pocket he had pinched were from that of one of the men he sat with, he felt little remorse, given that he had spent the money on the very same man and his fellow.)

The two men were scarred, indeed, boasted emotional wounds a-plenty, too. They had crewed reivers' vessels most of their lives and had the stench as well as the look of brigands about them. Elfloq had engaged them with money, but now they were growing interested in a group of mistresses of the house, of which there were always a plethora on call. Elfloq attempted to snatch back the conversation before it disappeared. It was not easy, for the burly ruffians were twice his height.

"Will you win ought at the Fair?" shouted the familiar, almost chok-ing on the smoke. He would have to leave soon, or asphyxiate.

One of the men focussed an eye on him as though he had forgotten he was there. "We'll win a few small trophies to take away with us. As for this season's Definitive Challenge, our master, Pulgrave Pelodorian, has no stomach to stand against the celebrated Jakodark. No matter, we have wares enough in our hold to trade for what we need. Our master is no gambler. Thrifty is Pulgrave."

"Mean, is the word," corrected his companion, with a swallow.

"He'd not risk his cargo for all the treasures Intercelestis can offer! Safe bets only, that's our Pulgrave. We trade our wares and go back to Elberdale, and there we'll trade what we take here for a new cargo...then we'll sail away elsewhere and trade that for something greater..."

His companion delivered an elegant belch as if to summarize his opin-ion of the lack of inspiration in the leadership of Pulgrave Pelodorian.

Elfloq fought his way into the discussion. "Tell me, who has come to this place for the first time, who is this Jakodark? A fellow, perhaps, whose participation in the Definitive Challenge you feel will result in triumph?"

The pirates scowled, then laughed. "Not heard of Jakodark? What realms do you familiars inhabit? Jakodark is unquestionably the great-est thief that ever drew breath! We would gladly sail with him - as who among the reivers of the omniverse would not! - but he picks his crew for himself. Brave men or fools follow that one, for he thinks nothing of daring places where even those hotheaded rock demons yonder wouldn't go. For the last two seasons, Jakodark has been the victor at the Defini-tive Challenge. One more victory would make him the Thief of Thieves, a title not won since the forgotten days of Darsynocci the Reckless. And what a man that one must have been, though some say he is no more than a legend. Jakodark is real, though!"

Elfloq had heard only smatterings of this, in spite of the incalculable mass of knowledge stored in his tiny skull. But it was exactly what he had hoped to hear. He hid his smile behind his tankard, which required both his hands to raise. The ale was not to his taste, but he sipped.

"There is little doubt that Jakodark will triumph again, for he is without peer among the reivers. He lacks nothing of the cunning, wit and ruthlessness needed to succeed. Not to mention daring," said the reiver. "Of course, there is always Bulgarst," he added, though scarcely as more than an afterthought. "He is Jakodark's only serious rival. They have been set against each other for many a season."

"I see," mused Elfloq, masking his thoughts. "And who is to issue the Challenge?"

"You *are* a stranger! Why, it is free to anyone. There are judges, of course. Five of the Oligarchs of the Hive. Should anyone issue a Challenge, they judge its merits. Too trivial a task is rejected. Once the most difficult Challenge has been chosen by the judges and pronounced the Definitive Challenge, it can be taken up by those eager to try for the victory. Those that fail to win the prize, forfeit their stake to the Oligarchs, who use it to replenish the troves of Intercelestis, from which we all benefit (the Oligarchs having first taken their share). Sometimes all fail to win the prize offered up and thus the Hive wins all. This is not uncommon. Otherwise, the victor wins the title of season's Champion, which grants him many boons, including the freedom of Intercelestis until the next season. But to become Thief of Thieves, that is to win the freedom of Intercelestis for always."

"And the prize that is won?" prompted Elfloq, though he had to repeat himself.

"Oh, that goes to whoever has suggested it. So there are several parties who stand to gain by the Definitive Challenge and several who stand to lose! Not our master, though. He'll stand by what he holds and risk none of it."

"It seems you wish it were otherwise," said Elfloq.

The pirates both shrugged. "We have both served under men who sought prizes at the Challenge. Fate spurned their efforts. I recall one quest, five seasons since, on the dark world of Hadrasm, seeking the idol cast in Graakshik's blood, worth a fleet stowed with rubies. The storm elementals wrecked us and the djinns picked the bones of most of us clean." They began reminiscing on their misfortunes. Elfloq had heard enough. It was not difficult to slip away from them and leave them to sift through broken dreams.

Outside, the little familiar stretched his wings and flitted up to a stone roof, sitting with his legs dangling, glad to suck in the magical air of

Intercelestis. He watched the gentle drift of the ships on the enchanted currents that enclosed the citadel. Most of the things he had heard about the seasonal Challenge had been true, then. The Definitive Challenge would be the one chosen by the Oligarchs. And this season, Jakodark would endeavor to win himself the title, Thief of Thieves. Had anyone yet hinted at what challenges might be issued? He must find out. There was so much to do.

* * * *

Elfloq watched the ship come in from a tall spire. It was the most remarkable vessel he had ever seen, if vessel were the correct word to use, for it was a nothing less than a living creature. Not a Snapwing from the Universe of Islands, nor one of the more common whippersails, this was a beautiful gliderorchid, a hundred feet long with bright green skin and two huge, purple wings that scarcely seemed to beat as they rippled with the invisible thermal currents of this inner world. Long ago the gliderorchids had been all vegetable, loosening their seeds that floated on the air, but they had evolved to become more animal-like, with an enhanced intelligence. Now they could take on the appearance of a huge bloom, or use their exotic wings to tug them across the skies like giant aviators. Using its trailing fronds as a rudder, this magnificent, docile creature guided itself down to one of the thickest of the bridges to the outer world, where many other craft, large and small, had been tethered. They bobbed on the invisible breezes like drifting islands.

As the crew of the gliderorchid disembarked, some of them seeing to the needs of the creature, which required water and a kind of mulch, Elfloq took to the air and drifted as close as he dared to the curved back of the creature, which in recline reminded him of a long fish. In the shadow of the vast petal-wings, spread wide like trembling sails, the familiar picked out the man who must be the captain, the celebrated Jakodark. He was a tall, thin fellow with laughing eyes that seemed to miss nothing. He wore simple garb, though his thick belt sported an impressive array of knives. Elfloq had learned that Jakodark was more expert with these weapons than anyone else alive, man or demi-god.

Perched high up on one of the many spine-like projections that grew from the central trunk of the gliderorchid, Elfloq studied the activity below. It was over quickly. The men were anxious to get to the taverns and their various contents, having doubtless been journeying long. Jakodark was the last man ashore, carefully checking to see that everything was as it should be. Elfloq was impressed. He waited until the captain had secured a last vat of oatstraw for his ship, then drifted down to within a few feet of the man's head.

Jakodark ducked, span and almost cast a spiked weapon in one silver movement.

"Belay that, sir!" appealed the familiar, assuming a nautical turn of phrase. "I am on no evil mission. I wish a few words with you before you enter the citadel."

Seeing that it was no more than a small familiar above him, Jakodark laughed. The knife was back at his belt before Elfloq had even detected its movement. This was no man to make an enemy of. "Be swift, familiar, for I've a raging thirst to quench and many mistresses to visit."

"I will be brief." Elfloq hovered closer as Jakodark began to walk briskly along the arch that served as a quay. His eyes were always alert, his whole manner suggesting hair-trigger responses, his ears attuned to every breath of air.

"You will be at the Fair?" said Elfloq. "To take up the Definitive Challenge?"

"Of course. I have waited long for this!"

"And you have no doubts that this season you will take the coveted title, Thief of Thieves?"

Jakodark stopped, staring sideways at the familiar, but he snorted, though with a shade more curiosity. "But of course. Who can prevent me?"

It was a question that demanded an answer. "I gather that there is only one headswollen enough to think he can."

Again a knife was miraculously in Jakodark's hand. But he tossed and caught it playfully, chuckling with evident merriment. "Ah, so that muscle-bound lout, Bulgarst is here, is he? He'll provide a worthy Challenge, no doubt, but a rock has more brains! No, I fear him not at all."

Elfloq had expected to hear such confidence. "As I would have thought. Yet I must assume you would rest more confident should Bulgarst happen not to appear at all this season."

Jakodark caught his knife and stared at the blade thoughtfully. "Not appear?"

"Word is," exaggerated Elfloq (who had already put the word about) "that Bulgarst has a number of Imric Zealots working for him." These Zealots were purely the products of Elfloq's imagination, but Jakodark was not to know that.

"Indeed? He means to resort to some dubious sorcery, then. Well, Bulgarst is certainly an irritant, though a source of amusement to us all. Perhaps, this year, it would be better for me if he did not attend. Unless my ears translate falsely, familiar, your words contain the hint of a bargain."

Elfloq smiled, his batrachian features widening. "I was not incorrectly informed that you were a man who knew his wants. Yes, a bargain. My part of the bargain - "

"*Your* part?" cut in Jakodark, surprised. "Surely you mean your master's part? I never yet heard of a familiar working for his own ends."

"Quite so. A slip of the tongue. *Our* part of the bargain, and for the moment my master wishes to retain his anonymity, will be the elimination of Bulgarst from this season's Definitive Challenge. Before you reply to that, I must assure you that your rival will not be clandestinely murdered, nor will he be disposed of in an unsporting manner. But I promise you, he will not rise to the Challenge."

Jakodark nodded, face serious. "And in return?"

"This season's Definitive Challenge will be *exceptionally* hazardous. However ominous it may seem to you, you must accept it."

Jakodark stared, waiting, but the familiar had evidently finished. "I do not follow. You say I must accept the Challenge? But that is precisely what I came here to do!"

"Are you inferring, then, that there is no Challenge that you would be capable of rejecting? There is nowhere you will not venture, no god that you fear to offend?"

Jakodark threw back his head and laughed aloud. "To the Abyss with them all, little familiar! Hah, they've singed my buttocks before now and put many a curse on me, but I've outrun them all. No, I'll not flinch from any Challenge. If I become Thief of Thieves, Intercelestis will always harbour me. But wait…you speak as if you have advance knowledge of this season's Challenge. Is that so?"

Elfloq smiled again. "My master will throw down a Challenge and it will surpass any other, that I also promise you. It will be the one chosen."

Jakodark nodded. "Then tell me no more! This intrigues me deeply. You think I will fear to take up this gauntlet? Not I! Jakodark? Turn down a Challenge? After last season, when I cut off the head of Inkhitamun the Deathless, whose breath made ghouls of men? And this season, when I *long* to be made Thief of Thieves? No, no, if I fail to win it, then let the damned gods have me!"

The man's bravado sent a shiver down Elfloq's lumber region, though he did not show it. "Then we have a bargain? I will - that is, my master and I will remove Bulgarst from among your rivals, and you will take up the Definitive Challenge, whatever it may be?"

"Indeed! I'll not flinch. Come, let's find a tavern and I'll drink to your health, for this pact between us surely leans in my favour."

"My thanks, but I cannot tarry," smiled Elfloq. "I have much to attend to. Not least of which will be the problem of the Imric Zealots. But we will meet at the Fair."

Jakodark grunted, vaguely suspicious, but nodded as the familiar winged away. It had been a bargain abruptly struck, which was not his usual way, but what had he to lose? He had forsworn all gods long since.

* * * *

Elfloq coughed and blinked his eyes several times: the fug in this bar was even worse than that in others he had had to frequent in Intercelestis. But again he told himself it was necessary, between racking coughs. At least this time he had found a number of thick beams overhead and had been able to get up here without drawing undue attention to himself. There were several winged beings squatting on another beam opposite him, drinking and buzzing cheerfully. The bar below was packed, which seemed to be a permanent state of affairs in Intercelestis.

Elfloq had been doubly fortunate, for now, beneath him, a group had gathered, swashbucklers all, bawling and belching out ballads and obscene stories, laughing heartily at each others' deliveries. Central to this group was a giant of a man, a beefy barbaric colossus with bulging muscles and a thick neck that looked strong enough to withstand the hands of a dozen simultaneous strangulation attempts. This was Bulgarst, himself captain of a reiving band, whose craft was moored somewhere outside on the spans. Elfloq had quickly discovered that where Jakodark used principally his wits to achieve success, Bulgarst used his undeniable brawn.

The giant pounded his chest like a bull ape of Gargantuama and bawled for more ale. Several of his underlings barged to the counter to see to their master's bidding. Three mistresses of the house sat near Bulgarst's side, eyeing him a trifle apprehensively, hoping he would intoxicate himself with ale before attempting to do so with them. He had no reputation as a lover, for all his bluster.

"Come!" shouted Bulgarst above the din. "Before I carry these three wenches upstairs, who'll try me out at a test of strength? Come - the Grip Game! Who'll try me? A barrel of ale to anyone who can best me!"

There was a lot of laughter, most of it uneasy, but no one ventured to accept. Bulgarst looked around angrily. "Come, you vermin! Give me a test, I say! Two against me, then. A barrel to each of you if you win. Come on!"

After a good many exchanged glances and much muttering behind hands, two of Bulgarst's crewmen shuffled forward, smiles worn thinly. Better to appease Bulgarst than aggravate him, even if it meant a few bruises. Bulgarst took the challenge and sat down at a wooden table, his elbow crunching down on it, palm outspread to receive their two fists.

The struggle was brief. Bulgarst's immense strength was too much even for the combined efforts of the reivers. He forced their fists backwards until they thudded flat on the table. A roar of nervous approval went up, and the two defeated men went to the bar, glad it was over. Bulgarst laughed bombastically. "Any more? Come, come, one more test. They never tried me! By the Abyss, I swear the very gods would shy from taking me on!"

This last brought more than a few reproving looks, for no one had any desire to tempt the gods more than their wayward lives already did.

Elfloq used the sudden drop in the hubbub to flutter down and stand on the table where lately the Grip Game had been played. Even standing there, his batrachian face was some way below that of the hideous smile of Bulgarst.

"What's this? An imp from the rafters!" Bulgarst laughed. "Surely you don't mean to try me! I'd crush you like a gnat, little imp." The audience joined the giant in his mirth.

Elfloq waited, indulging the mob in its fun. "Not I, worthy Bulgarst. I am no warrior, as you can see. But I can assure you of a test that will require all your famous strength."

Bulgarst leaned forward, beery breath like a cloud of poison air. "Is that a fact? A true test? I have not been stretched since my two-day bout with Pugnax the Swamp Troll. You have a master, is that it? I see now that you are a familiar, not an imp. Who is your master?"

Elfloq trusted now to his gamble: if it failed he would be kicked, probably brutally, out of the building. "My master is called Voidal."

If there were a few indrawn breaths or nervous coughs amongst the throng, Bulgarst either failed to notice or else he paid them no heed. His hand reached out and clasped a huge tankard as he gulped his ale. "Voidal? Never heard of him. Is he a sorcerer? One who seeks to test me with magic, eh? Trickery?"

"Not at all, master. No sorcery. Just a traveller."

"And where is this monument to strength?" The words prompted an outburst of laughter, though not everyone was laughing. Indeed, there were those who had already begun to quit the building, discreetly.

"You have only to summon him, and he will come promptly. I promise you a test of strength such as you have never had before."

"Why? Is your master so anxious to win himself a crushed hand? Or does he lack the coin to buy himself a barrel of ale?" growled Bulgarst contemptuously.

"It is a matter of prestige," replied Elfloq. "You see, my master has never been bested in the Grip Game."

Bulgarst threw aside his tankard and bellowed joyously. "Is that so? Never been bettered, eh? Why, then, bring on your champion. I'll gladly put him to the test. There could be entertainment here tonight after all!"

"You have only to summon him, merely to invoke the Voidal."

The three mistresses of the house quickly disappeared. Bulgarst rolled up his sleeves and grunted approvingly. "Then I invoke the Voidal!" he shouted to the audience. "Man or demon, I fear none. There's many across the omniverse will tell you why. Let your man step forward!"

Silence fell upon the throng, everyone now fascinated by the turn of events. Heads turned, but otherwise no one moved. Bulgarst glared about him. "Is he here, or hiding outside? Has he changed his mind?"

Abruptly two men parted and a dark figure stood before the table, eyes lidded as though the man had been sleeping quietly in a corner. No one had noticed him before now, as if he had materialised like mist, but they all studied him intently. He dressed somberly, in dark shades, his hands encased in black leather gloves.

Elfloq had skipped to one side, out of view of this quiet stranger.

"So you think you can beat me, eh?" said Bulgarst, unmoved by the solemn demeanor of the dark man.

"Was it you who summoned me?" said the latter coldly. His eyes were slitted with green anger.

"Aye! What is wrong? Will you not try me at the Grip Game? Now that you are before me, do you tremble?" growled Bulgarst, fearing that the man would back down.

"You called upon me, knowing that there is a penalty for doing so? To play at some *game*?"

"Penalty? Pah! If there is to be one, then *you* shall pay it! Come, sit at the table. Try and best me. I hear you have never lost. Well, neither have I! Sit, I say!" Bulgarst slammed his elbow on the table, ready for the Grip. The drink had excited him. The lust for victory blazed hotly within him.

Annoyed, the Voidal sat on the chair that had been pushed forward. *"You would try me at this?"* he said incredulously. His head turned and caught sight of a scuffling movement nearby. Elfloq was trying to squeeze himself between two onlookers and away.

"Elfloq!" snapped the Voidal. "Step into the light!"

Elfloq would have demurred, but the pirates laughed and swung him easily into view. The eyes of the Voidal settled on the diminutive figure, but there was no humour in them. "This is your doing."

"Forgive me, master, but I thought only of your reputation."

"You still insist on calling me master, after the disaster on Firecrag. I recall only too well that foolishness, and the burden you bore for a while."

Elfloq grimaced, his back giving a sudden shudder.

"As for my reputation," the Voidal went on, "I would trade it for a song. You know that." He looked across at Bulgarst. "You do not know me, or of my fate?"

Bulgarst laughed coarsely. "I know you not, but as to your fate, why, that is to surrender your unblemished record!"

Everyone laughed at that, except the Voidal and his familiar. They stared at each other, but the familiar quickly looked away.

"Come, stranger!" insisted Bulgarst. "I am impatient to test your great record. Your hand!"

The Voidal placed his left elbow upon the table, but Bulgarst knocked it aside roughly. "None of your warlock trickery here! Your right hand!"

Reluctantly the Voidal did as he was asked. "Don't begin this," he said under his breath so that only Bulgarst heard. For the briefest of moments the big man looked as though he would take this advice, but then another contemptuous laugh broke from his lips.

The two hands locked, elbows firmly on the table, as the rules demanded. The mob pressed in as close as it could. Bulgarst winced, for the grip of the dark man was much firmer than he had expected from so thin an opponent. Presently sweat stood out on Bulgarst's brow. The Voidal closed his eyes, muttering something to himself. Bulgarst emitted a gasp: neither hand moved from over the centre of the table. The grip of the dark man tightened, tightened.

Suddenly Bulgarst had gone gray. Something clicked. No one was sure what was happening, except that Bulgarst was not crushing his opponent at all. Of the two men, he looked to be suffering the most. He brought up his left hand and used it to aid his right - the audience let out a uniform cry of objection. But Bulgarst's fingers began scrabbling at the hand of the Voidal, trying to pry it loose. Fear coated his face.

The Voidal shook his head. "I cannot stop this now."

Bulgarst sought to speak, but could not form words, his tongue clotting. Only pain squeezed out of his mouth in another gasp, then a cry. Amazed, the audience echoed his gasps. Elfloq was able at last to slip away outside, knowing full well what the outcome would be. At least Jakodark would be pleased.

A crunch came from the locked hands. Bulgarst actually *shrieked* in agony and aimed a blow at the Voidal with his free hand, though it was weak and ineffectual. Something dripped down the bare arm of the giant from his hand. Blood. The men nearest to him drew back in horror: the dark man's hand was *squashing* the hand of the pirate captain. Relentlessly the grip went on, until several streams of blood ran thickly down on to the tabletop, forming a tacky pool. The Voidal looked impassive, almost detached and people quickly moved away, fearing sorcery of the direst kind.

Whimpering, Bulgarst slid to his knees, eyes appealing for release. No one had ever seen such a thing before. For all his colossal strength, he was helpless. With a final moan, he slumped to the floor. The Voidal released his ruined fist with a shudder of revulsion. Men rushed forward to attend to Bulgarst, covering the bloody horror that his hand had become, hardly believing what they saw.

At once the Voidal rose. No one stood in his way as he made silently for the door, needing air. Two of the reivers of Bulgarst stared at each other as the dark man left. "Who in all the hells is he? Bulgarst's fist is pulped as though it had been a beetle!"

"Then he's crippled his last victim, and I for one will drink to that," came a voice from the stunned audience. Others murmured agreement.

Another pirate rose from the crumpled body of his captain. "The damage is worse than that, lads. Bulgarst is dead!"

This brought a mingled cry of horror and anger from the men. United, they overcame their terror and made for the door. But the false night had already swallowed the enigmatic figure of the dark man.

* * * *

In another part of Intercelestis, the Voidal and Elfloq met. The dark man's green eyes flashed with renewed anger. "Why did you bring about that wretched contest? You must have known the reiver would perish." His right hand was thrust guiltily inside his cloak.

"I had to bring you here, master. For here you will find the key to part of the things you seek. There is one here who will help you to recover what has been usurped from you."

For a moment, Elfloq's words distracted the Voidal from his anger. "As Thunderhammer was supposed to be the keeper of my soul? That was a trick. It is housed in the Sword of Shadows. Is the person here able to lead me to it?"

Elfloq swallowed hard. "Uh, no, master. It may not be wise to seek the Sword of Shadows just yet - "

"Oh? I thought you bent your every effort towards recovering my soul?"

"Of course, of course. But, but, there are other things. Your own hand, for example. Especially in view of what has happened. Would you not prefer to recover it at the earliest opportunity?"

The Voidal glared at him suspiciously, but could not help grimacing at the thought of the abomination inside his cloak. "Aye. To be rid of this monstrous burden would please me well."

"Then have faith in your familiar," Elfloq grinned hopefully.

The dark man towered over him. "I see you have not lost any of your ambition. Still as unscrupulous as ever, eh? And the reiver, Bulgarst is dead because of it. Tell me, does his death mean nothing to you?"

The question took Elfloq by surprise. "But...but he was an evil man. A bully, a killer. A man not loved by others. I have heard many speak of how he left a wake of ruined victims in his path. And he mocked the gods - "

"Something you would never consider?"

"They were evidently displeased, master. Surely Bulgarst deserved to die, even by the Oblivion Hand. I suspect many will rejoice the fact."

"No man deserves to die as he did," said the Voidal coldly. "You make too many decisions on my behalf. If you are to call me master, then obey my commands, curse you! In tricking that witless buffoon into summoning me, you gave him a cruel death, and it was no whim of mine that he should die. By your actions you have undoubtedly served the Dark Gods. Or is that your desire? To win their favour?"

"By no means!" gulped Elfloq, shocked by his master's anger. "I thought only to aid you. There is a purpose behind what I do - "

"Yes, I'm certain of it! You act for me, but be wary, Elfloq. The Dark Gods move us all like pieces in a game. You may be more of a pawn than you think."

Elfloq looked slightly crestfallen. "I seek only to aid you."

The Voidal sighed deeply. "Yes, I see that. But have a care how you use my powers. You must not sit in judgement over life. Bulgarst may have deserved his fate, but I will not be instrumental in casting men's destiny. So, what have you been up to while you have been here? Why did the reiver have to die?"

Elfloq shrugged off his complicity and grinned. For a long time he explained, silver-tongued as ever, the wider issues of the Definitive Challenge and all it entailed. And for all his frustration, the Voidal took some pleasure from the machinations of the tiny being.

* * * *

Intercelestis's renowned, or rather, notorious seasonal Fair was a splendid example of organized confusion and chaos. Focused in the great central plaza of the citadel, it managed to overspill itself in the form of tents, bazaars and countless stalls and booths down many a sidestreet and alley. The colors were gorgeous, ranging from one end of the spectrum to the other in every conceivable shade and hue. The variety of merchandise here likewise sparkled - there were rare spices, gems, exotic fruits and foodstuffs, strange artifacts, priceless works of art, and others far less so; the valuable vied for success over the fake, and in truth often came off second best. Sorcerers' tools and warriors' blades, both fabled for their infallibility, were sold alongside charms to protect and ones to immortalize or make potent.

While the interminable bartering and trafficking went on, there were scores of games and contests in progress, many of which entailed heavy gambling. Mistresses of the Fair were always in abundance, and the Fair boasted that this abundance of feminine charms could be found nowhere else. Here at the Fair, it was said that a man could find anything he desired.

Many of the pedlars and mendicants and reivers had their private entourages of muscle to protect them, but for good measure the Oligarchs had peppered the main plaza with a noticeable array of their own experienced Brawlers, hired warriors chosen for their skill in quickly dealing with disputes, especially the physical kind, of which there were always many, this being one of the most enjoyable parts of the Fair. The Fair was a timeless occasion, lasting for as long as there were those who had a mind to buy or spend. But at last the Oligarchs themselves made a grandiose appearance, standing pompously in their regal robes of gold upon a balcony that overhung the main plaza. By and by, all heads turned to them. There came a rumble of trumpets, deep and sonorous, followed by three sharp blares from similar instruments. Silence reluctantly settled on the seething mass below. It was the time of the Definitive Challenge, the culmination of the games, and no one ever missed it, unless he was dead or dead drunk.

Firstly, those who had a mind to participate boldly stepped forward into a space that had been cleared by the Brawlers under the balcony of the judges. There the participants announced themselves and their pedigree and declared what goods they would offer as security for their participation. The judges were allowed to inspect the goods to see that they were not paltry and were indeed worthy of the Challenge.

Some dozen warriors, reivers and merchantmen announced themselves and were passed. Last to stride forward and loudly pronounce his interest was Jakodark. There was a roar of approval from the crowd: his proffered goods were the richest. The judges nodded their approval.

"Strike the gong."

This was done, three times. The last reverberations died down and no one else stepped forward. No one else could now compete. Jakodark noticed a tiny figure sitting cheekily astride one of the parapets above the judges: the smiling familiar. Bulgarst, notably, had not appeared. Evidently one half of the bargain had been adhered to.

"Who will deliver the first Challenge?" called out one of the judges. Soon the first of many Challenges was issued. Some had no merit and were evidently shouted for amusement, such as that bawled by a drunken wit to the effect that the participants should attempt to steal the virtue of a certain mad Beast-Queen said to rule in one of the more unhealthy dimensions, but many were worthy enterprises: a search for the missing ears of Pazildzil, a frightful demon who had been able to hear sounds in every dimension before being robbed of his ears by the gods; a quest for the Secret Talisman, Lovehallow, which was said to make a man capable of seducing any goddess; a raid on the fabulous wealth of the Black Gatherers, the nebulous monster-lords of the dark world, Ottoomikhaab, where the very castles were hewn from rubies; and others equally as inspired. Several of these the judges accepted. Later they would weigh them and select the Definitive Challenge.

When it seemed that no more Challenges were forthcoming, Jakodark looked up enquiringly at the familiar. Yet the impish fellow did not seem prepared to offer a Challenge himself. That was just as well, thought Jakodark, for none of the Challenges yet offered up had deterred him: indeed, the best of them offered great excitement and adventure.

Nearby in the crowd stood the Voidal, arms folded across his chest. He had not seen Elfloq for some while and knew that the familiar must have been attending to further business. The dark man had been persuaded to go along with the familiar's suggestions. Although Elfloq was as persistent as a dung-fly, the Voidal could not help but smile at his ability to engineer events, something that he envied. He just wished that the familiar would have more care for and be a little more compassionate toward men, whom he seemed to have no regard for. As for the Voidal, he considered himself a man, whatever he had once been, and it seemed that the gods alone coveted the right to kill.

While the dark man watched, an elderly mendicant pushed weakly by him, staring briefly at his face before going towards the front of the throng. The crowd made way for him, calling to the Oligarchs that here was another, possibly final, Challenge.

With difficulty the mendicant spoke above the muffled silence. "Your Challenges are trivial things!" he began. Mingled laughs and jeers rebuffed him. "Your quests are all too mortal. None of you entreats the questers to dare the wrath of the gods."

"Well, Bendoshaar, oldest and arguably most knowledgeable among us," called down the first of the judges, smiling patiently, "deliver up your Challenge. What would you win? A cure for excessive age, perhaps? Or a treasure of rare wines for your depleted cellar?"

It was some time before the crowd ceased guffawing at this rare jest from an Oligarch. Bendoshaar's comical scowl deepened. "My Challenge is no jest. I speak to you of the Voidal, he who has been cursed by the Dark Gods. They have stolen much from him."

This silenced the crowd effectively, for talk of the Dark Gods was enough to sour any proceedings. "Know you that the Voidal is here, among you now." Those who knew little or nothing of the Voidal murmured questioningly. Those who knew of him looked about them uncomfortably. "My Challenge is on his behalf."

The Voidal was surprised, never having had any dealings with the aged mendicant, but he guessed that Elfloq had made some pact with him.

Bendoshaar raised a twisted stick to emphasize his words. "The Dark Gods have cut off the true right hand of the Voidal and hidden it away. In its place they have burdened him with another hand, a hand more terrible than any other. The aptly named Oblivion Hand. The work it does is cruel, singling out those who are to be punished. On the very eve of this Fair it smote down the mighty Bulgarst. You must not blame the Voidal for that, pawn that he is. But listen! Who will challenge the Dark Gods? Who will dare go forward and take back the hand of the Voidal - his true hand - and free him of his curse?

"There is my Challenge to you. Find his true hand. Once the Dark Gods held me in their confidence, but they punished me for using my powers falsely. I destroyed a world by seeding it with plague. Now I am forced to live in this husk that passes for a body for as long as it pleases them, and it has been *eons*. Thus I strike back! Who will accept the Challenge?"

The Oligarchs considered his words, talking agitatedly among themselves. Then at length, they nodded. "We consider your Challenge worthy. We will retire for the customary hour. After that we shall declare which quest is to be this season's Definitive Challenge."

Several of the questers had already blanched. Who in his right mind had ever gone against the Dark Gods? There were only rumours, all unfavourable. One of the questers called over a bailiff of the Brawlers. He pointed to his goods. "Take my stake. My cause is withdrawn." The man left hurriedly and the bailiff signaled his men to take the goods into the keep of the Oligarchs, thinking to himself that there would be more withdrawals yet.

An hour later the crowd reassembled as the judges emerged once more. As many had suspected, it was the disturbing Challenge of Bendoshaar that had been nominated. At once three more participants declared their withdrawal and shortly thereafter another two. The remainder had an hour to decide if they would accept the Challenge, or withdraw and forfeit.

Jakodark's crewmen muttered uneasily. "What of this quest, Jak? To take it up is madness, surely."

Jakodark said nothing, searching the roofs for signs of the familiar, but Elfloq had disappeared. Yet a bargain was a bargain. Although there was much at stake. Jakodark had been told of the grim death of Bulgarst, and he did not like the sound of it. He turned to his men, though, swallowing the queasiness that threatened to embitter his humour. "Lads, this year we seek the ultimate title, Thief of Thieves. It will make legends of us all until all the suns are dead. To win such a title, we must achieve something miraculous! We have never asked for kindness or sympathy or an easy passage! Gods of the Abyss, we seek immortality in our exploits! Shall we win it with petty voyages, stealing worthless idols and mindless aphrodisiacs? Nay! Let us go forth and beat upon the doors of hell! This Challenge offers glory such as no one has ever earned before. If we succeed, think of the songs they will sing of us down the ages!"

"And if we fail?"

"Ah, but even then, they will speak of us as long as men have tongues." Jakodark's words were always infectious. A few dozen jugs of ale would set his men a-boasting again. He had covered up his fears. "When the judges ask us for the last time if we accept, then we shall! In the meantime, we have an hour to devote to our amusement."

A further hour later, Jakodark kept his promise and returned to accept the Definitive Challenge of the season's Fair. He was, understandably, the only one who did.

* * * *

Elfloq presided over the introductions, and if it had been possible for a familiar to sweat, he would have done so. He had secured a booth in yet another bar, getting an empty one with difficulty. (This had involved some spurious rumours about a certain Purple Infestation, brought to Intercelestis by a genuinely disreputable troupe of acrobats attending the Fair.) When Jakodark entered the booth, he saw that the dark man was already here, sipping from a glass of bright blue slumberwine.

"I believe I have you to thank for the disposal of Bulgarst," said the reiver. "Though it was an ugly death. In some ways I will miss that buffoon."

The Voidal's face clouded and he glanced at Elfloq. "The deed warrants no thanks. A curse, perhaps."

Elfloq interrupted. "So you will fulfil the bargain and seek the, uh, object in question?"

Jakodark nodded. "Aye, though my crew are troubled. What are these clues you promised us, familiar?"

"Unless my ears lie," said Elfloq, "you shall have them in a moment, for I hear the wheezing of the mendicant." He pulled aside the thick curtain of the booth. Bendoshaar stood there, coughing. He shuffled in.

"Well?" said Jakodark.

"Tell him where the hand is to be found," Elfloq prompted Bendoshaar.

The mendicant nodded, blowing his nose noisily. "My debts to you are paid. And I have cocked a snoop at the Dark Gods," he grunted.

Elfloq chuckled and turned to Jakodark. "You'll have to pay him for what he knows."

Jakodark returned the grin and haggled with the old man for a while, at last agreeing terms. Bendoshaar then switched his attention to the Voidal. "Before I tell you where the hand may be found, Fatecaster, will you not tell me what my fate is to be? Doubtless the Dark Gods will learn of my treachery, but will they repay me with death? That is all I seek now. To be at peace."

The Voidal stared into the eyes of the oldster with pity. "Don't ask me to dispatch your fate, old man. I do not have that power. But if the Dark Gods have allowed you to carry such a secret as the location of the hand for so long, they must have known that one day you would relinquish it. Perhaps they even planned it, for they do nothing without purpose. Therefore it may well be time for you to rest. Put down your burden."

"I am satisfied," sighed Bendoshaar. He turned to Jakodark. "Very well. Listen well, for after this I go out to oblivion. Do you know of the dimension of Warrior Stars, where the heavens burn with a million internecine conflicts?"

Elfloq nodded at once. "Where no world is secure, shaken by the reverberations surrounding it? It is said that a legion of the most ghastly demons has taken root there and that no other creatures survive. Even the gods shun the place, fearing that too long a time spent there infects the visitor with howling madness. Well, that is how the poet-mage Scriventorini from Pompasto puts it. A little floridly, if you ask me."

"All this is true," nodded the old man. "With the exception of Krogarth. He rules now, after a fashion His volcano spews its everlasting fury up at the very stars that war. And in his fires are forged the weapons that may lead his demon swarms elsewhere to conquests."

"Remind me not to read any Scriventorini," snorted Jakodark. "What about the hand?"

"Oh, Krogarth has that. He and his legions. Shut away somewhere within that seething cauldron. Seize Krogarth, best him, and you may wrest from him the hand."

The Voidal nodded. "The Dark Gods protect him?"

"Perhaps not, for he worships only himself. But he is formidable, as is his volcano world of Vyzandine."

"We will put it all to the test," said Jakodark, though his confidence in the matter was by no means assured.

Elfloq's smile had become a grimace. He already had more than a few doubts about this quest already. Krogarth and his hordes sounded, if anything, even more hideous than the celebrated poet-mage had intimated.

"Let us drink to my success," suggested Jakodark.

"Our success," corrected the Voidal. "The familiar and I will be there."

Jakodark did not object, smiling acquiescence. Bendoshaar shook his head. "I wish you all fortune, but I will burn incense and recite your names aloud as I pass over. There may be a god somewhere merciful enough to grant you a swift demise."

* * * *

If Jakodark's men were squeamish about the voyage into the dimension of Warrior Stars, they made light of it. It was said that only a handful of mages and ambitious sorcerers had ever been there, but nothing was said of their condition on return.

As the gliderorchid drifted into the peculiar dimension, both Jakodark and the Voidal stood near its living prow, staring at the incredible spectacle around them. The skies of this dimension were lit up by crossfires of shooting stars, as though each were a flaming cosmic ship intent on blasting asunder any other in its path. Like mad gods they clashed. Bright trails of sun-white fire followed each star, forming curled patterns that interwove in some divine tapestry. When these searing balls met in full collision, they burst apart in scintillating showers that began the process anew on a smaller scale. The worlds of this dimension were constantly lit up by the spectacular explosions in their heavens, and the surfaces of many were charred and gutted by falling stellar debris from the eternal chaos around them.

Jakodark shook his head. "Passing through such a realm as this will be utterly hazardous. My gliderorchid can survive in the most extreme conditions, but these flying embers - the very dust is made up of fiery particles. We must breathe with caution."

The Voidal agreed. "Yet we are small things, Jakodark. The heavenly titans that clash so violently are vast bodies. Although they cram the very sky, they are not so close to us as our eyes would have us believe."

Jakodark gave this some consideration and his usual grin returned. "Well, perhaps you are right. There is air to breathe in this weird place, even if it tires the lungs. But where is your familiar? He should be guiding us to Vyzandine."

"Elfloq makes use of the astral realm wherever he can, particularly when there are signs of trouble in the realms we pass through. This time, though, I suspect he will find Krogarth's retreat more readily from the astral."

Only moments later the little familiar popped into being, his face strained with fright, eyes rolling, seeking evidence of enemies. The Voidal went to him but pulled up short as two more shapes flapped into view from the astral. These were scarlet, scaled and hissing steam furiously, eyes like miniature furnaces, fuelled with malevolence.

"Quickly!" yelped Elfloq, darting for cover. "Krogarth's lava wights, out to fry me!"

Jakodark moved speedily. He confronted one of the demons with a smile. The lava wight reached out a wicked claw for him, but in a flash it had been severed from its arm. The Voidal's sword whipped through the air, spitting as it sliced the other wight clean in two. Jakodark's knife flipped up and over into the throat of the first wight. Now both corpses smouldered at his feet.

"Bravo!" cried Elfloq from a safe height. The Voidal stared at his sword. He had used it instinctively. This time the Dark Gods had allowed him a weapon that could kill, though it was not the Bane of Demons. It did not seem to be one of the Thirteen at all, but an ordinary blade.

Jakodark waved Elfloq down to the deck. "What did you learn?"

"I found Krogarth's world of Vyzandine." Elfloq went to the edge of the vessel and pointed down. The Voidal and Jakodark leaned over the rail and looked.

"I see only an abyss, no worlds, not even stars," said Jakodark.

"Other worlds and blazing stars are blotted out by what lies below. What you see is the black surface of Vyzandine. It stretches infinitely. We are in its upper atmosphere," said Elfloq glumly.

The two men contemplated Vyzandine's immense size in amazement.

"It is riddled with volcanoes," went on Elfloq. "As a dog has fleas. And it is crawling with lava wights like ants over a fresh carcass."

Jakodark chuckled. "A challenge, then! So, we go down."

* * * *

As the uniquely hardy gliderorchid drifted close above the surface of Vyzandine, the crew could see scores of the demonic lava wights moving about on its heaving surface. The volcanoes had countless vents and most of them vomited cinders and fire up at the sky. It was with difficulty that the gliderorchid wove a path through the black clouds laced with scalding rain, and even this resilient creature trembled. The light here was scarlet, flickering, the light of gushing lava, ruptured magma, not the light of the Warrior Stars, which now seemed so remote.

Jakodark had to shout to be heard. "Did you find out where Krogarth is? If we confront him and best him, we'll take what we want and quit this hellish sink."

Elfloq looked troubled. "You see that vast peak that dwarfs the rest? Krogarth dwells inside it."

"Inside?" echoed the Voidal. "But it is brimming with molten lava. See, a dozen white-hot rivers course down its slopes to the ash plains. Krogarth dwells within? What is he, a fire elemental?"

"More than that," sighed Elfloq.

"So how are we to confront him?" said Jakodark. "I dare not land the gliderorchid near that summit. Its skin resists fire, but to risk immersion in this lava would be foolhardy."

"You could lower yourselves on vines," suggested Elfloq. "Keep the ship circling above until you have what you seek."

"Spoken with true confidence," said the Voidal with a rare laugh. "You will, of course, descend with us?"

"But...but...surely you have no further need of me," Elfloq spluttered. "I am far too small to be of use."

"You are far too modest. Make ready!" the Voidal told him with another laugh. "Since I am your master, that is an order."

Elfloq muttered something inaudible, but prepared to obey.

Jakodark pointed. "There is a place where we can set ourselves down. The climb up to the rim of the volcano from there is fee of chasms and lava streams. It seems the best route, though hardly a comfortable one."

Moments later the majority of the crew were swarming down long vines that had been hung over the sides of the vessel. The Voidal and Jakodark were the first to alight. The ground was hot, spongy, trembling as if alive. At once they were set upon by a flight of lava wights. Swords sang in the shuddering gloom as the reivers leapt down from above, etched against a bloody backdrop. Presently a score of twitching demon corpses littered the broken earth. The ground moved gently as though in protest, portending a small quake. Quickly Jakodark led the run up the tortuous slope to the brink of the heaving volcano. It was like a monstrous beast, palpitating and undulating, its belly full of pain. The roar was deafening, the air thick with smoke and sulphurous fumes. Upward the party climbed. More demons erupted from crevices, screaming furiously as they launched into the affray, while from out of the swirling ash clouds came a host of their winged fellows. Madness spurred them on like hurled missiles, their purpose singular. Heedless of death, they screeched into the assault, intent on blanketing their enemies by sheer force of numbers. Many of the horrors were destroyed, for they fought with no other weapons than their claws. Yet, inevitably, they took several of the valiant reivers with them.

The path Jakodark had chosen was narrow, which was well, for the demons could not attack with more than a given number at any one point, else they would have slain the entire party in a moment. Showers of hot embers rained down and the men ducked, fighting off the flames that licked at their clothes as well as the clutching talons of the aerial horrors. The Voidal and Jakodark were first to reach the summit. A fresh swarm of lava wights came screaming at them and they were almost forced back into the lava flow, but their combined swordsmanship wreaked havoc. Once the entire party had assembled at the summit, the men were able to group defensively and ward off the attack better, and although the numbers of the demon throng were now staggering, crimson steel rang and flashed in a pattern that kept them at bay. Heaps of demon dead piled up on the high slopes, making the summit difficult for others to reach.

"Let the men cover us," suggested the Voidal above the terrible din. "I will go and confront Krogarth."

"And I," cried Jakodark. "I came here to win the prize. You'll not find me wanting now."

"You don't understand," shouted the Voidal. "Whatever this Krogarth is, he cannot destroy me. I am not mortal in any normal sense. It is part of the curse that claims me. But you - "

"I'll take my chances! Lead on."

The Voidal nodded. "Elfloq!" he called.

The familiar appeared at once. "I was merely surveying what lies ahead," he blustered.

"Where is Krogarth?"

Elfloq led them further beyond the lip and they looked down. They both gave voice to cries of alarm. A well of fire plunged before them. Deep down in that bubbling volcano was a brilliant, seething mass, an amorphous *being* that heaved and boiled as if it were a very part of the lava cauldron.

"Krogarth," gasped Elfloq, eager to dart back to the safety of the astral.

Jakodark's sweat-smeared face clouded. The creature was titanic. What sort of weapon would they need against it? A simple sword or dirk would be useless.

"And the hand?" asked the Voidal. "Where has Krogarth secreted it? Break your cursed silence, Elfloq, speak!"

Elfloq's expression suggested that he would rather not answer, but the Voidal repeated his demand.

"Yes, I have ascertained that unfortunate fact," replied Elfloq, though the noise almost drowned out his words. "The hand resides in...uh, in Krogarth's belly."

The Voidal again stared down, and as he did so, he saw that the awesome bulk of Krogarth was rising up like a tide. Jakodark drew back.

"May I now be excused while you resolve this dilemma?" piped Elfloq.

The Voidal waved him away and the familiar was gone in the blink of an eye.

"We cannot best that thing!" cried Jakodark despondently. "I should have commissioned sorcery, though I love it not." Behind him the battle among his men and the lava wights waged furiously. The scarlet fiends were almost demented with frustration, their dead piled about them.

"There is a way," said the Voidal. "But it will test both your courage and your reason to the full. Would you win the prize?"

Jakodark managed a smile. "If there *is* a way, show me!"

The Voidal watched the slow but inexorable rise of Krogarth. The noise was frightful, the heat intense. Sweat poured of them as they waited. Several of their fellows fell from above, together with tangles of the demons and all disappeared into the rising lava creature, absorbed into it. Something beneath the surface threshed as the bodies hit, receiving them with evident glee.

"If Krogarth has a stomach," said the Voidal, "then he has a mouth also. We must entice it open and you must prevent him from shutting it."

"*Entice* it open?" gaped Jakodark, wondering if this strange being had totally succumbed to insanity. "Then what?"

"I will find the hand."

Jakodark was totally bemused. Yet he was ready to obey. He knew the dark man was more than human, for no man could possibly face what was rising without fear. The Voidal was unmoved. In silence they watched as Krogarth's impossible shape contorted itself upward to their level. Lava boiled and long whips of fleshy pulp rippled as the volcano god moved. The central mass bulged in a rounded tumescence across which a deep red slit opened like a maw: it surged towards them avidly. Jakodark swore lustily as he realised that the revolting mouth was preparing to suck them into it. It was lined with cartilaginous projections. Steam and breath commingled to roil over the watchers in a fetid, nauseating cloud. The Voidal thrust his sword into the reiver's free hand. "Use this! Thrust both weapons up into the roof of the mouth and hold them there for as long as you can. Time warps here. A few seconds for you will mean far longer for me. But each second is priceless."

"Yes, but in all the hells, *what are you going to do*?"

"Watch."

Krogarth was almost upon them, his glistening skin slick with lava rivulets that ran like scarlet sweat from his monstrous body. Boiling magma slopped at the ledge on which the men stood. Heat incessantly washed over them, singeing their hair, their throats scorching. The Voidal waited until that gaping slit was about to close over them.

"Now!" he shouted.

At once Jakodark darted forward and rammed the two blades upward. They hissed as they sank into the roof of Krogarth's mouth and a rumble like thunder shook from deep within the thing. To Jakodark's amazement, the Voidal ducked down and jumped forward into the very maw, his body blurring. The teeth-like projections looked capable of grinding stone. Jakodark was forced to use all his strength and guile to keep the mouth open by manipulating the swords, but he almost lost his grip on the hafts when he realised what the dark man was doing. For the Voidal had entered the lower maw and, armed with nothing more than one of Jakodark's dirks, was beginning an insane *descent*.

Krogarth began to thrash about, his awesome bulk throwing up fountains of sizzling lava. Hot juices slopped over Jakodark from above, his skin blistering where fluid dripped over it. But he held on as the floor writhed beneath his feet, worse than any vessel in a storm. The Voidal was gone from sight, and it seemed unlikely that he could survive such a lunatic adventure. But Jakodark recalled his words. *Time warps here.* He must keep the mouth open for as long as he could. He could scarcely breath and the swords were wrenched this way and that by the manic squirming of the thick flesh of Krogarth, but for now they held. The Voidal must have imbued them with magic of some kind. Behind him, Jakodark could faintly hear the sounds of battle, far off and dampened by Krogarth's stentorian bellows.

The Voidal wriggled his way into the narrow, suffocating tunnel that led to the very innards of the volcano beast. The stench was foul, the atmosphere almost impossible to breathe, but using the knife viciously, the dark man worried at the fleshy walls and forced them back, slightly facilitating his descent into darkness. He did not know what powers coursed through the steel, or the swords of Jakodark, but there was unquestionably dire sorcery at work. This quest was madness, but for once he was able to use the craft of the Dark Gods against them: they had made him immortal, so that he could not perish. He did not pause to think of being stranded here in this undulating pit forever, merely of triumph. He must secure his hand. Crawling now, he slipped further downward.

After what seemed an age of wriggling down that mucous-thickened tunnel, he reached a pulp obstruction that he took to be a valve leading to the stomach itself. He lifted his right hand, but it was limp from the wrist on, as if withered. So the Dark Gods had let him come this far, but would not help him. He had to use the dirk in his left hand, hacking and chopping now at the pulp. Exhaustion and the cramped space combined to thrust despair upon him, but he made greater efforts. Jakodark, he knew, could not hold back Krogarth for long. If the beast sank back down into its fiery magma retreat, doubtless swallowing a river of lava, the Voidal would, after all, be entombed here. Was that the fate that the Dark Gods intended? Was this a trap, a reward for all his attempts to defy them?

The thought enraged him, and though nausea threatened to black him out, he fought on, knowing the goal was essential. Suddenly he burst through the last strands of filaments and toppled forward into utter darkness, falling into a thick, steaming secretion. It bound his legs and he could not stand, clutching about him blindly, his weapon thrust into his belt. But he had arrived in the stomach of Krogarth. For an age he groped about in this appalling place, his strength sagging. The walls of the stomach began to roll in on him slowly, covering him in a thick film of juices. Krogarth meant to digest him. Several times the Voidal's head slipped under that foul surface, and he thought he heard the wild laughter of his tormenters. It drove him on and at last his fingers found something solid.

His left hand closed on it - moving fingers, wriggling like worms, closed on his. He pulled furiously and something tore loose in the dark. The locked grip held. Then he was groping for the damaged valve, seeking a way back up into the remote promise of light. The stomach fought him like a living thing, seeking to slow him and draw him back into it and crush him to jelly. By inches he tugged himself through the punctured opening he had made.

Jakodark's strength was also ebbing fast, though he had been here no more than a few minutes. But the muscles that worked the jaws of Krogarth were also tiring, having sunk the two swords deeper into themselves by their own strivings. Yet Krogarth's pain forced him on and soon he would crush the intruder. Jakodark sensed this and decided that he would have to abandon the Voidal and escape while he still could. To win the prize now was impossible. He would have to return with better weaponry. The skies were filling with lava wights, blotting out the Warrior Stars so high above, and the reivers would be lucky to escape at all.

Just as Jakodark was about to relinquish his grip on the swords, something clawed its way up from the throat beyond him. In utter amazement, he saw the dark man wriggling toward him across the floor of the sucking mouth. Somehow the Voidal had returned! The dark man could not stand in the closing mouth, and even Jakodark was now on his knees, striving to hold the lips apart for a few last seconds.

"Let us leave. I have the hand!" gasped the Voidal.

"Get clear!" Jakodark cried in disbelief, but he could see a dismembered hand *clutching* that of the Voidal. The dark man slithered and rolled out of the mouth and straightened up on the rock ledge beyond. Jakodark got to his feet and leapt back, the mouth slamming shut immediately, like a sprung trap. The reiver let out a scream of pain as he toppled on to the ledge, only just rolling clear of the lake of lava. Krogarth did not rush forward upon the two men. Instead, evidently afire with excruciating pain, he began to subside; the lava drained down into the well slowly with him. Krogarth's agony shook the walls of the crater and started thick slabs of rock collapsing down on top of him.

The Voidal glanced briefly at the sprawled reiver to see that he was alive. Satisfied, he held his limp right hand, the Oblivion Hand that belonged to some grim god of the shadows, and held it over the lava pit. He took the dirk from his belt and in one swift arc, sliced the hand from him at the wrist. He felt no pain, no blood flowed. "Take this, Krogarth, in payment for what I have taken from you." Contemptuously he kicked the fallen member out over the pit and watched it fall after the receding volcano god, whose mouth opened a last time to receive the grisly offering. Thus the black hand was gone.

With his left hand, the Voidal reached down to help Jakodark to his feet. The man's face was streaked with tears of pain.

"It is over," said the Voidal.

But Jakodark let out a gasp of horror and held up his arms. "Over? Not for me! Never for me. Do you see?" Blood oozed thickly from the twin stumps of wrists where his own hands should have been. Krogarth's closing mouth had shut down on them and sliced his hands cleanly away.

The Voidal cursed. "Then the Dark Gods have had their fee," he snarled, looking impotently about him. Hurriedly, controlling his fury and bitterness at the perfidy of the Dark Gods, he forced Jakodark up the still shaking slope to where the battle yet waged incessantly. Shielding the reiver, the Voidal added weight to the affray, though his strength was waning rapidly. He called out to the invisible Elfloq, whom he knew would be near, shielded on the astral.

"Elfloq! Tell them on the ship that we are ready! Get the gliderorchid as low as it dare come and drop the vines."

He was answered and at once the anxious rescue began. Getting the men to swarm up the vines was difficult, for the lava wights attacked from the air. Few of the reivers were still alive, and those that had manned the gliderorchid were under severe attack themselves. The Voidal cursed anew: was he to be the only survivor of this lunatic quest?

Elfloq was suddenly by his side, eyes distended with a new fear. "Master! We dare not tarry! See, the vengeance of Krogarth!" he pointed.

Behind the dark man, Krogarth's lava well was spewing up its contents in thick gouts of fire. The mass that was the living god boiled as though its insides were in turmoil. In the earth there appeared cracks; an earthquake stirred itself. Abruptly the demon swarms turned to see to their lord and the offensive abated. The reivers used this merciful respite to clamber up to the ship, and the Voidal was quick to follow, Jakodark now draped like a sack over his shoulder.

"Get under way!" shouted the dark man to the last of the reivers. "Jakodark has won the prize! But Krogarth is dying and it will be a furious death!"

News of the victory was enough to give the survivors great heart and the gliderorchid sensed their delight. It beat its mighty wings and began to slip away from the scene of carnage. Below it, darkness closed in like a fist, but the Voidal could see the shape of Krogarth, enclosed now by the hot fires of his pain. The first detonation rumbled across the heavens as Krogarth exploded. For a brief second, even the Warrior Stars paused to listen to the reverberations.

* * * *

Jakodark's gliderorchid drifted through the murky portal to Intercelestis and emerged in the inner world, coasting above a span to the citadel. Jakodark watched the docking from the prow of his vessel, where he had been sitting, stiff as a statue for the entire journey home. His arms were wrapped in cloth. The Voidal and his familiar sat some distance from him, both also silent.

Suddenly Jakodark jumped up and came to them. The face that had been so full of misery had changed, the features brightening to reveal an old smile.

"I have done with brooding," he announced with more than a little of his old bravado. He held up his bound wrists. "For my part in the quest, I have paid with my hands, that were quicker than most eyes. But after all, we have won! Many of my lads paid with their lives. Thief of Thieves shall be my name from henceforth! A thief without hands I may be, but it is said a man may buy anything his heart desires in Intercelestis. There are some fine armourers here. And besides, there will be other Challenges. Next season *I* shall issue one! Who could hope to name a better challenge than mine - to find me new hands?"

"I would suggest," grunted Elfloq, "that you avoid sending anyone to recover those that Krogarth consumed."

"No need! In all this turbulent omniverse, there must be powers who could forge me new hands, possibly with magical properties."

The Voidal's feelings were mixed. He was pleased to hear Jakodark's optimism, but disturbed by the hint of ambition. "Just beware those gods who would mark you with a worse fate." He thought again of the frightful member he had cast into the volcano. It had not returned. "But enjoy victory, Jakodark. It was well earned. Take this trophy and present it to the Oligarchs. I will verify its genuineness. I want none of the glory."

One of Jakodark's men took the cloth bundle on his captain's behalf.

"When they proclaim me Thief of Thieves, it shall be yours," avowed the reiver.

The Voidal nodded. "Winning back my hand was not easy. It seems that the Dark Gods have again relented a little in their curse upon me, allowing the hand to remain."

Elfloq, who had been preening himself with apparent indifference, coughed gently. "Well, master, let us pray that the Dark Gods will relent even further and allow you to win back what else they have stolen from you."

"Are you then so eager to ignore their warnings?"

Elfloq scowled, thinking of the Sword of Shadows.

Jakodark was about to speak, but the Voidal cut him short as though he had read his words. "We may meet again, Jakodark. But remember this, the Dark Gods mark well any man that calls me friend."

The pirate's face split in the first real grin since the terrible ordeal on Vyzandine. "Well, at least I shall be rich now. Richer than any other man! And all that Intercelestis has to offer will be open to me. She will hide me for as long as it suits me. So, come to the celebrations, friend."

The Voidal shook his head. "Take the familiar. When you have done with the prize, he will bring it to me. All I wish to do now is to sleep, for I feel an unnatural drowsiness upon me. I know what it means." He turned to Elfloq. "I will cross this span. Look for me beyond."

Elfloq nodded. "Well met," he called after the retreating silhouette.

He and the thief caught the soft reply. "Well met in hell."

PART NINE

IN THE PRESENCE OF PAIN

If one possesses power, no matter how small, no matter how co-
lossal, one must spare the time to demonstrate its dimensions. Fail
in this and one would lose one's veracity. Once lesser beings, over
whom one exercises one's power, begin to doubt it, that power will
surely be reduced. And if they have no belief in it whatsoever, it will
not exist.

A being without power lives in a universe with a population not
exceeding a unit of one.

> —**Salecco**, adherent to the faith that knowledge is
> power.

* * * *

Into the utter darkness came a long spear of light. As it struck the
narrow, spiral stairway, it shattered like water on rocks, creating a pale
cataract. In its flow, the stairs wound upwards in a steep curve. Their
silence was complete, as though no sound had ever penetrated the stones
of this place.

Until this moment.

On the stair, the spectral figure of the dark man listened. He could
hear the soft footsteps begin, far below him, coming upward unhurriedly.
Now he could hear the breathing of whoever it was that climbed. It was
a while before he realised that the footsteps were his own.

He moved on up the stairs, his hand - his right hand - reaching out to steady himself on the stone wall, as though he were dizzy, or feverish. The wall was cold to the touch, but as he climbed ever higher, it grew warmer, as if somewhere above him there was a fire.

Eventually he had reached the top of the stairs and stood upon a small, dustless landing. Before him was a door, lit by a solitary jewel that contained its own secret light source. The door itself was hewn from some black metal and looked impassable. It had no handle or lock. The dark man reached for his sword haft, but there was neither sword nor scabbard at his waist. Only momentarily confused, he stretched instead for the door and pressed his fingertips against it. It opened with a sudden abruptness, as though flung by the wind.

Within, all was darkness, deeper than space, deeper than the Abyss. It was the hungry, chilling darkness of dread. The man wanted to reel back, but he was sucked forward as though by a current. It became a torrent. There was no escaping it. He was forced to stagger into the room, and as he did so he heard the shriek and whine of tornado force winds about him.

The door slammed with a sound like the heart of thunder, the echoes rolling away into the distance. There was nothing now but the darkness and the silence, fused into a knot of terror. Dread clutched the dark man like something physical, squeezing its way into his bones, blizzard cold. It was a dread as complete and final as entropy.

Again light parted the darkness and he saw a small fire burning to his left, flames wriggling upward, escaping through a black flue. In the shifting glow he could see before him a table. It was hewn from stone, perfectly circular, no more than a few feet across. Its top was smooth, unmarked as though no dust had ever settled upon it, and it was empty. There was a simple stone seat before it, but opposite this the darkness seemed thickest, a gash in space. It was within this darkness that the man's terrors had their roots. But he could not help but stare directly at it.

He could not move, for there was power here. Colossal power. Its depths were as evident as the compacted hub of a galaxy, its potential far more devastating. It could swallow universes and spew out new ones. Sitting before it, the dark man felt the gravity of a star.

He knew that his surroundings were not a part of it, merely trappings, convenient images for this meeting. For it was to be a meeting.

Looking again at the epicenter of that power, that darkness, he saw that it had adopted a shape. A simple one, that of a flowing robe with a cowl, made solid by something within. The fire did no more than dab a very faint outline on the cloak's edge. Whatever had created this vision remained anonymous. But the dark man knew intuitively from the withering radiation of power who it was.

For the first time that his memory would allow him to recall it, he faced one of the Dark Gods.

This realisation threatened to burst his heart. Again he felt the onset of dread as the throb of power pulsed over him from across the table of stone.

"Sit."

It was a calm voice, lacking in any malice, but rich in command. There was no disobeying it.

The dark man sat groggily at the stone table. No more than a few feet separated him from the invisible Dark God, yet the being seemed unreachable, invulnerable.

The sleeves of the God's robe trembled, then their edges touched the top of the table, but no hands were visible, only dark vents. Slowly, like a serpent slipping cautiously from its lair, a black hand emerged from the left sleeve and rested on the tabletop, spreading and flattening itself against the stone.

Again the dark man felt a stab of terror, but still he could not move, for the alien power roared inside him like a furnace. He watched the right sleeve of the God. Something moved inside it, but no hand appeared.

"Look down at the table."

At once the dark man did so. He was looking not at stone, but into a well. It was a well of stars, as though a portal had opened and naked space beckoned. It made him reel with renewed dizziness as if he must surely fall into that deep place, but he put both hands on the rim of the table to steady himself.

The voice came now as if from far away. "Voidal. You have carried my right hand in place of your own for a little while, a heartbeat in the life of the omniverse. Through you I have worked. Thus the will of the Dark Gods has been done, to a certain extent. You think you have earned release from this burden? You think you have carried the Oblivion Hand for long enough? You think to wrest back from the Dark Gods those things we have removed from you? That decision is not yours to make."

This came like the sounding of a sentence, a rejection of any appeal, and it was like a physical blow. It omened further torment.

"Where is the Oblivion Hand?"

For the first time it was possible for the dark man to speak, though it remained difficult. The words laboured to form themselves, as though he was under water, or in a dream. "Lost on Vyzandine. I cut it from me and gave it to Krogarth."

"Did you think so little of my charge?"

The Voidal tried to force out a curse, but such an action was denied him.

"I see that you did. However, you must find the hand. It was never yours to dispose of."

The Voidal closed his eyes in revulsion. He knew that he could not fight this overwhelming power. Whatever it decreed, he must do. Must he bear that foul member once more? Yet he would never ask for pity, never demand release. They could not take from him his pride.

The Dark God spoke again. "I have observed that you carry your own hand. It grows there as though it had never been taken from you. You went to remarkable lengths to win it back, as we guessed that you would. But, of course, that served a purpose. As you have come to understand, all things serve a purpose."

Suddenly the God leaned forward and the Voidal felt that he would be engulfed by what was to be revealed, but he saw nothing, only starless night. "We are the gods of punishment. Did you think we were without mercy?"

A chord of hope rang within the Voidal, but its pealing quickly subsided as if muffled by a landslide. Mercy? Their mercy would have its price.

"There is something you must do with that returned hand," went on the God, drawing slowly back. "I will decide if you are deserving of its keeping. So, reach down into that well before you. There is something there which must be rendered up to me."

Once more there was no question of disobedience. To obey was the only course of action possible. No matter how odious the task, the dark man must submit. He had no free will while he sat before this omnipotent being.

Slowly he reached out into the space in the well with his right hand. He felt as if by doing so he betrayed himself and all that he had fought for. He moved with the desperation of a beaten gambler, casting down the last doomed card.

His reach seemed to go on forever, lost in time and distance.

"You said Vyzandine?" breathed the God.

The word seemed to sink into the well and introduce a new element into it. *Heat.* It grew in intensity. Molten heat. The Voidal felt his right hand being scorched by sudden blasts of hot air. It sank down into a white cauldron of fire. Magma.

"Continue," said the God.

"Krogarth?" murmured the Voidal through billows of searing agony. "I thought that - "

"His volcano erupted and he was dismembered in the explosion. He was evil. His fate was earned. You served us well there. But the hand you cast away was sucked down into the very core of Vyzandine. Now you must find it. Bring it up to me."

The Voidal was not permitted to collapse or sink into oblivion. He was made to endure the impossible agonies of the magma as his hand clutched ever downward. Its components boiled, made molten themselves by the heat. But he would not allow himself to cry out with the torturing pain. His left hand gripped the stone edge of the table, and the stone splintered where his fingers bit into it.

"Bring me the hand," repeated the God impassively.

Something snatched at the Voidal's fingers down there in the star-hot core of Vyzandine. He tried to shake it loose, but it had fastened on him, its fingers intertwined with his own, immovable. Now he was able to draw back his hand, inexorably slowly.

Up through the fire, then at last air, then space, his arm came, blazing with pain. He felt himself reeling, every nerve screaming, but he shook his head angrily, tears of sweat and anguish trickling from his gaunt face.

The tabletop was once more an expanse of polished stone. The well had closed. Bemusedly the dark man saw that his right hand was grasped across the table in the right hand of the Dark God, as though the well had, after all, never existed. Yet that shrieking pain had, and still did. For a moment he thought of the frightful incident on Intercelestis when he had played Bulgarst at the Grip Game. He stared down at the linked hands with a surge of renewed horror and nausea. Many incidents of this past came back to him like waves breaking over a rock. The destruction of Ugnarg and the Slaughterer, the fall of the Deathmare, the events at Icehaven, Krogarth's doom. The hand that yet clutched him could wipe him away in the blink of an eye.

He could not free himself from its fiery grip. The lava had been less painful, and he began to understand the true nature of the suffering that the hand of the Dark God brought. For what seemed a long time they sat motionlessly. A thin trickle of blood ran from the Voidal's mouth as he clenched it shut, determined not to cry out.

At last the Oblivion Hand released his own and he swayed back. His hand was numb, and he feared that it must be dead, useless. It glowed with angry weals. Was this the price he must pay for regaining it? Even so, it would be better than to carry again the black terror of the Dark God's hand.

Now the tone of the God changed. It became markedly cold, dispassionate, almost cruel. "Do not think you are released from your fate, Voidal. You have made some amends for your sins, and I will take back my hand. You need not bear it for me again. But remember this much, your own hand is not as it was. Something of my power has passed into it. It will never leave you as my hand has done so often, and it can never perform the grim acts of destruction that the Oblivion Hand performs, but it has power. Some men have called you Fatecaster. So shall you remain.

"Remember this meeting. Remember your duty. Perform it well, Voidal, and you may win back for yourself other lost powers. It does not have to be your destiny to serve us for all time. But we guard your destiny jealously. If you desire to recover it, obey us in all things, the quicker to fulfil this desire."

After that, the room was empty, save for the fire. The Voidal got up and went to it. He stooped before it, warming himself, for though his hand still felt like rock, there was a chill in his bones that reached deep into his being, almost to the purloined soul he had yet to find.

He stretched out his right hand before the tiny flames. Shocking life pulsed back into the nerves slowly, but the hand was healed. What powers would it have? None that he wanted, he felt sure. But better this than what had gone before. Thinking over this, his eyes grew tired.

The dreams beckoned him anew. It was not long before he had succumbed. Then for a time, there was an end to pain.

* * * *

Thus a cycle ends.

There are, I ought to explain, many more myths, legends, tales, rumours, hints and exaggerations about the exploits of the dark man (and more specifically his familiar) that relate to this Cycle of the Hand, as one might term it.

There are the Lost Parchments of Khnimniec, Valdor Olosor's Gray Observations and the Technocratic Treatise of Megraphasm, to name but a few, and although thoroughly entertaining in their own rights, I have been moved by the constraints of stringency to omit them here.

In my two-volume history of the Oblivion Hand, I have chosen to select the elements most pertinent to it and have striven to modify the worst excesses of the originals. The veracity of the cycle is, I believe, reasonably sound, though, I admit, colorful.

Furthermore, it would not be difficult to chronicle more of the exploits unique to Elfloq, and it may be that I shall in time attempt this, although it is with these tales that one has to exercise most effectively the prerogative of the editorial role, given the rampant rhetoric that suffuses their original format.

I will content myself with moving on, in due course, to tempt further the wrath of the gods, to record the remarkable events in the

Voidal's history subsequent to those of this Cycle of the Hand. It is they who, after all, have chained me here with little else but the tools of my art and I am forced to cling to the conviction that they must have done so for a purpose!

You, patient follower of these tracts, shall learn of the Weaver of Wars, of Orgoom, of the Dark Destroyer, of bottled universes and of the monstrous Evergreed.

Oh, and so much more.

—**SALECCO,** thrower of light upon matters dark and obscure, that the omniverse might be enriched.

www.ingramcontent.com/pod-product-compliance
Lightning Source LLC
Chambersburg PA
CBHW050739250626
47155CB00005B/1837